DAVID-JACK FLETCHER

INDENTURED

Published by Truborn Press
Edited by Max Booth III
Cover & Interior Design by Truborn Design

ISBN 979-8-9915969-4-7 (Paperback)

FIRST EDITION

10 9 8 7 6 5 4 3 2 1

INDENTURED

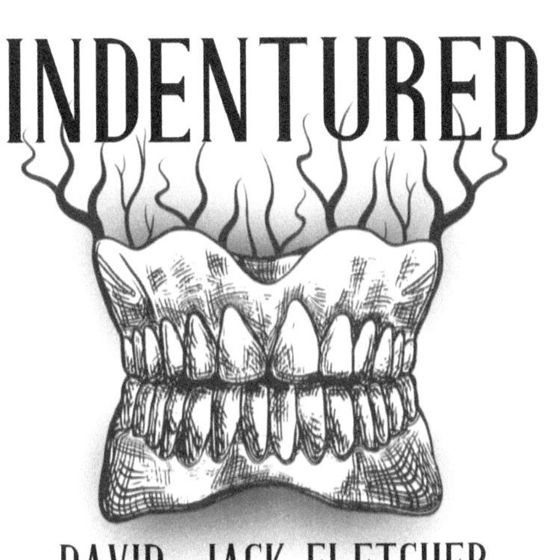

DAVID-JACK FLETCHER

PROLOGUE

Gary

The day's menu consisted of postman leftovers. The ill-fated postman had been kind enough to help an ageing Gary a few days earlier when he'd pretended his package was too heavy. He'd had a lot of appeal: young, lean, not too hairy. A well-kept, hairless frame saved on prep time. The postman—Felix, he'd said—didn't fight too hard. Of course, he'd cried and begged once his future became clear, but they all did that. As Felix had carried the package into the living room, Gary surprised him with a firm whack over the head with a lamp. He wasn't too happy that the lamp smashed against the bone, but at least Felix was down.

Felix tried to crawl away, making a mess all over the ecologically friendly floorboards as he went. Gary grimaced at the blood soaking into the floor. If it was anything like red wine, that was going to absorb right up, leaving a dark stain. Gary's teeth started chattering—like a terrible clamour—anxious for their next meal. The hunger was not his own. The teeth were famished, and it was time to eat. In those first few days with the teeth, Gary had been able to stave off the cravings, but the roots had spread throughout him and now he was a puppet in his own body.

Climbing over Felix's back, Gary squeezed his eyes shut. This was the worst part. His teeth sank into the thin flesh on Felix's neck. The postman cried for help, struggled to fight Gary off. The old man was too strong. The roots in the teeth had been branching throughout his body, gaining control of everything but Gary's thoughts.

As he tore through the postman's neck and shoulders, Gary pleaded for them to stop, to have mercy. To eat something more appropriate, even. The steak and bacon from Day 1 had been a gateway meat to live cows and pigs, which had been the gateway meat to humans. And now, nothing else could sate the teeth's hunger.

The postman had sat in the pantry ever since, attracting flies and stray cats. The internet was divided on what a group of maggots should be called— parliament sounded appropriate—but Gary couldn't think about that now. He just ignored the wrigglers as best he could while devouring the postman. Gnawing at the last remnants of flesh, the sticky blood trickling down his mouth, Gary wiped at it with his elbow. The legs and arms had been picked clean over a few hours and as Gary sniffed at the corpse, sucking in the rot, he screeched like an animal in heat. Tried to push the flesh out of his mouth with his tongue. It was no use. Gary hadn't been able to resist for days, despite his general disapproval of cannibalism. He stretched his jaw, revolted at the taste of days old flesh stuck between the teeth.

Surveying the bones of what had once been Felix, Gary shook with rage. He couldn't go on like this, eating people the way he was. Not least of all because the flooring couldn't withstand much more damage.

As the thought to end his own life crossed his thoughts, the teeth chattered again. A sign of deep dissatisfaction. Gary stood, wiping the flesh from his tongue onto his shirt sleeve and fighting the urge to vomit up Felix's fleshy calves.

The clamouring grew louder.

Gary strained his muscles, tried to move as the teeth sensed his intentions. The kitchen wasn't far. He could make it to the knife block. One strike across the neck and he'd end this once and for all. But his legs were now not his own, concrete stumps that refused to obey. He fell to the floor and crawled.

"I'm going to end this," Gary said through clenched teeth.

His fingers gripped the floorboards, leaving scratches among the bloodstains. They would definitely need to be replaced. The teeth roots had stretched to his hands, but Gary maintained control of his fingers most of the time. He crawled through the kitchen. The knife block was in sight. All he had to do was reach up.

The teeth clamoured louder and louder. His arms became heavy, resisting the orders his brain gave them. Gary tried to reach the knife block, but it was no use. His body was not his own.

The teeth stood him up, moved him to the front door, and into the street. Fighting their host had taken a bit of energy and they were hungry again. Gary's body stumbled down the median strip, his brain screamed, though no sound came out. The teeth had clenched his jaw shut and ordered him down the street. A puppet master intent on destruction.

A semi-trailer careened in Gary's direction, and he knew this was his last chance. He had to gain control, if only for a second. His body stopped, turned towards the semi-trailer, and as his teeth chattered in an attempt to strengthen its puppet strings. The semi-trailer skidded and screeched down the road as it came toward him. Gary shed a tear at the thought that this was truly the end. The teeth chattered, trying to take control. But Gary stood his ground, daring the semi-trailer to hurry up and get it over with.

The container on the back of the semi veered towards Gary, sliding along the tarmac like skates over ice. His knees buckled.

"Fuck you!" he yelled as onlookers gasped and pleaded for him to move.

Nobody was brave enough to help the old man and he was pleased at their cowardice. In the seconds before the metal grille tore Gary's body apart, the teeth managed to raise his arms as shields.

The flesh on his arms and face ripped apart, his chest following, throwing bone and blood and internal organs into the street. Onlookers unlucky to be too close were gifted with a splash of intestines and stomach acid and hurried to wipe away the mess. Gary was gone now, nothing but an empty skin sack and a ruin of entrails staining the tarmac.

The driver jumped out of the cabin, shaky, yelling for someone to call an ambulance. He performed CPR on what appeared to be a chest, despite Gary's head lying several metres away, eyes dangling from their sockets. As the driver realised his life-saving technique was doing nothing, he recoiled and rocked back and forth and watched the dead man's mouth open.

"Hey." The driver ran to Gary's disembodied head, mistaking the movement for life. "Are you okay?"

The man's teeth fell to the road, chattering after landing. Through his shock, the driver was sure he saw black roots, like thin wires, retracting into the teeth. He leaned forward to get a closer look, but it was only an old pair of dentures, unharmed from the crash.

1

MIKE

The human mouth is one of the most disgusting things in existence. People smile with their sparkling teeth and minty breath, but only to hide the fact that this hole in their face hosts thousands of germs. Gum disease, tooth decay, actual fur grows on the teeth that takes a decent amount of pressurised scrubbing to remove. Twice a day. The tongue, well, that's another level of grossness. People smoosh them together in the throes of passion without first inspecting this harbinger of millions of germ spores.

Taste buds, those wonderful little pits smattering the tongue, may be the worst offender. People are so concerned with facial pores, but spare not a moment to consider that the pores in their tongue are as backed up as that guy in the office who hasn't taken a dump in a week. For the more sensitive in the room, he was unable to squeeze his food waste into a precious diamond. I thought his name was Dave and we all avoided him when he came back from the bathroom, panting like a thirsty dog. It's called Metamucil, Dave.

I considered these thoughts as I ran my well-brushed tongue over my clean teeth, the words of my dad's dentist from last week echoing in my grey matter. *He needs dentures. His entire mouth is compromised.*

Compromised. It sounded like his mouth was a presidential security unit and they were really bad at their job. His entire mouth, too. Dad was eighty-five, so the state of affairs in his bog of a mouth wasn't too unexpected, all things considered. The problem for me, though, was that Dad had never been what you might call "good with money". I learned that a long time ago, when he would disappear to the pub every Saturday. And Sunday. I'm pretty sure I didn't see him on Mondays, either. After Mom died, it was different, but he was always distant, and I never understood why.

And now his teeth were my problem.

The bill was due to be well into the thousands, all so Dad could chew on hard candy. It was beyond me why he couldn't just mix up some oats and be happy like everyone else his age. I also wasn't thrilled by the idea of spending my savings on the old man again, not after his back surgery and the knee replacement. At this point, he was a cyborg without any of the cool time travel and no mission to save the world.

I tried to remember why I had paid for all of those things in the first place. He was my dad. I may not have cared much for him, but you only get one father. Well, unless you have gay parents, in which case, you're one lucky son of a bitch. All the studies indicate you're more rounded and psychologically stable being raised in a same-sex home. My parents were straight—I never stood a chance.

I lamented my ordinary upbringing as I drove to his retirement village, where bingo sayings like "legs eleven" and "two fat ladies" were still in vogue. Why they couldn't at least be two fat men, I couldn't fathom.

It was a Sunday, which meant two things. I was about to cop an earful of "Huh" and "Speak up" from the village people, and my dad was going to want to "borrow" money. It was always something: cheap cravings like cigarettes or dark chocolate. But today was the day I would say, "No more". As I parked the car, I studied myself in the rear-view and took a deep breath. Confident, strong.

I thought about the guy—some random I bumped into—from the café earlier that morning. I'd just gotten the news from the dentist and was imagining the drain on my bank account when he'd appeared out of nowhere. He'd sensed my anxieties, and was one of those people who drew out conversations from total strangers. I hated those people. I'd ended telling him all about Dad's teeth.

"I hate to complain," I'd said, "it's just so much money, all the time."

The guy had nodded, understanding my concerns. "You shouldn't have to bear that burden. He should have had the money saved already."

"Exactly!" I'd said. I didn't care that he was probably just telling me what I wanted to hear. He was right. It wasn't my issue that he was shit with money.

Sitting in the car, outside the nursing home, I thought about his words. The way he'd been so casual, but confident about it not being my problem. He'd ended up telling me I should put my foot down on the subject, and that these things had a funny way of working themselves out.

I didn't believe him, exactly, but I also didn't want to spend the money.

Looking in the rear-view mirror once more, I said, "You can't have any more money, Dad." I practiced a few times, gaining confidence with each repeat.

Grabbing the traditional six-pack of whatever beer was cheapest on the day, I headed to see my father. When I made it to Dad's room, he was lying on the bed with the radio blaring right-wing drivel. What was it with these people? They were always against something or someone, and these floods and fires and catastrophes were all because of gay marriage.

"Hi, Dad." I feigned cheeriness as I entered the room.

"Huh?" He cupped his ear and swivelled round to me. "Speak up."

Dad was riddled with age-related issues. Arthritis, dead legs, cataracts, and the only thing his ears were good for was growing tundra. Why his teeth were so important was beyond me.

"It's me, Dad," I said over the radio, sitting at the edge of his bed.

As Dad's glasses settled onto the bridge of his nose, he squinted at me and slumped. "Oh. It's *you*."

The disappointment was like a dagger in my chest. "Yes, Dad. It's Sunday." I sighed.

From his position on the bed, I made out a faint shrugging motion, though it more resembled like a skeleton having a mild seizure. I grimaced a little at his deterioration. A bleaker image of my own future, I had never seen.

I helped him up, careful not to tear his skin apart. It was no easy feat with all the medications he was on, but I was getting pretty good at manoeuvring him into his wheelchair. We made our way to the dining room for the traditional Sunday lunch. Roast…something. I wanted to say chicken, based on the stray feather I almost choked on, but you could never be too certain these days. Another reason the mouth is so disgusting is that you never really know what goes into them.

Halfway through lunch and three beers later, I was starting to get nervous. Dad would wait until he'd finished eating to launch into his stoicism and reach across the table to take my hand. It was always the same, like a B-grade movie. You want it to be different, you can see the potential in the script and the acting, but you're left with a deep and unending disappointment.

It was strange watching him eat with no teeth. He bypassed chewing altogether and kind of just shovelled tiny pieces of food straight down his throat. There was something inhuman about it and I didn't think it was healthy. A low, deep burp came from Dad, and he wiped his mouth with a paper napkin.

Here it comes.

I straightened in my chair and laid my hand on the table in the usual spot, ready for the grabbing. Held my breath.

Dad cleared his throat. "So, son—"

"I'm not giving you any more money." It burst out, leaving a bad taste in my mouth.

Dad was taken aback and let go of my hand. "I don't want your money." He scoffed, offended.

"Well," I said, unsure how to proceed. "Good. That's good, Dad, because I don't have any to give."

The skeleton shrugged again, looking fragile and calcified in the bleak light of the dining hall. I say hall, but it was a bunch of trestle tables in a tiny room arranged in a U-shape.

"That's fine," Dad said, folding his arms and sinking lower into his chair. "I don't need any money."

He stared towards the vending machine, his cataracts not blinding him from the sweet treats held within. The same treats that led him to the dentist in the first place, hollering like he'd been shot in the mouth.

"Well good," I repeated, straightening my back to display a confidence I didn't feel. "Then I guess you don't need me to pay for your dentures!"

"You don't have to," Dad mumbled and turned away from me.

I stuffed some cold roast meat into my mouth and chomped on the wiry bird. Washing it down with some beer, I tried not to smile. Dad might have been upset, but the point had been made. My words had gotten through his deaf ears and sunk into that brain somewhere.

My face dropped after I'd wheeled Dad back to his room and left without saying goodbye. I couldn't get his disappointment out of my mind. Maybe I'd been too harsh on the old bastard. It was just money, after all, and it's not like I had kids to spend it on. And porn was free these days.

Just as I pulled away from the curb, I saw a sign taped to the telephone pole at the traffic lights. "Garage Sale – Deceased Estate". Everyone secretly loves garage sales. *Everyone*. It's like enjoying telenovelas when you don't speak Spanish. The drama is universal, it transcends language. Garage sales are like that, too. The items always seem exotic, like the layers of dust hold secrets. Old clothes that smell like the person who wore them last, maybe even died in them. Books the dead guy didn't finish reading. Plates they'd eaten from, spat on, scraped mouldy leftovers off.

I couldn't resist.

I followed the signs to an old worn-down cottage with browning hedges for a fence, tables of junk strewn across the lawn, and a kid selling lemonade on the front porch. She gave a childish wave and blushed, like she'd never seen another person before. It was weird. I waved back as I got out of my car, and avoided her like the plague. Kids are the fucking worst.

"Looking for anything in particular?" The voice came from behind me. A short, older woman gazed up at me through the thickest glasses I'd ever seen.

"No," I said. "Just browsing."

She pointed out some of the more attractive items scattered through the front yard and I feigned interest, dawdling along beside her.

"My husband just died," she said, taking a deep breath coupled with a yawn. "You aren't one of them Vinnie's bastards, are you? You seem like a churchy type."

"No, ma'am," I replied, furrowing my brows and grimacing. "No God inside this brain."

"I hate that God shit. God this, God that. My husband believed in all that and look where it got him.

Dead, that's where. Dead and buried like a…a…" She scratched her head, revealing a few bald patches.

Frowning, I stepped away, leaving her to her thoughts, frightful that she was a vision of my own future. Looking between old records and pieces of a life already half-forgotten, it was there: the answer to my father-related guilt. Shining at me across the lawn, a pair of dentures. Following my gaze, the old lady swooped in next to me once more, eager for a sale.

"These were my husband's," she said. "They were found next to his body."

"Really," I said, inspecting the dentures. "What happened to him?"

She shrugged and mumbled something about cannibalism and a murder-suicide. "It happens to the best of us," she said weakly.

"How much?" I asked, reaching for my wallet.

"Seventy-five bucks."

"I'll give you fifty." Showing her the cash, her entire body lit up.

She considered for a moment, took the money, and handed me the dentures. I could not believe the twist of fate, like this old guy had died just in time to solve Dad's dental crisis.

Rushing back to the retirement village, I burst into my father's room to see him unmoving on the bed, right-wing talkback radio blaring from his Bentmax FM system, knocking women for wanting to have babies. He seemed so peaceful that I had to check his pulse. It was there. A whisper.

Good enough, I thought.

I left the dentures on his nightstand with a note to say I'd changed my mind and purchased these state-of-the-art, ready-made dentures, brand new. The marks on the teeth were just from taking them out of the box. He was going to be so happy when he woke up. Maybe he'd have some spare money to get those cataracts seen to or drill new holes in his head so he could hear something for a change.

Either way, I left with a sense of deep satisfaction that good things were about to happen between me and Dad.

2

PHIL

The radio blared some kind of misogynistic trash towards women as I stirred awake. I twisted the sound dial counterclockwise until their hyper-masculine voices disappeared from the ether. I loved those right-wing screwballs. All their cock-a-meemy ideas about the world was like watching a gripping fantasy film or experiencing the radio broadcast of *War of the Worlds* for the first time. I often got a good giggle from their ridiculous viewpoints. I'd never really considered how my listening habits appeared to others and was often taken aback at how offended people were when they heard my radio blaring from down the hall.

"How can you listen to that crap?" Harriet Reiner, two doors down, would mutter over a cup of lukewarm coffee.

"It's people like you who've made the world what it is today!" Barry Goldsmith, across the hall, spat at me once. "I'm glad our generation is dying out!"

So was I when I thought about it. My generation had started *and* ended two world wars, not to mention all the miniature ones nobody talked about anymore. I thought about this as I sat up in my bed. I coughed a few times, something I often did these days. I hadn't been to a doctor lately, but I was worried my lungs were heavy with tobacco. Those ads on TV showing the black tar leaking from the lungs had never deterred me from smoking a pack of Camel Lights a day. Now that I'd started coughing up blood, I was starting to think maybe Nicorette might have been helpful.

My cough settled with a few hard slaps on the chest and through my cataract-induced haze, I saw a pair of dentures sitting on the nightstand. The sheen of pearly whites stared at me. I picked them up, holding them in my hands as I inspected the dentures with a grimace. I read the note Mike left me and gave a surprised "Hmm."

Mike, I thought. *He's a good kid.*

I had been the best father I could be in a time of my life when addiction and regret had plagued my every thought. I'd married a good woman, but we'd both known it was a doomed pairing. We'd agreed to tell Mike that a gambling addiction was the reason for the divorce. To this day, the kid still believed that. When my ex-wife had died a few years earlier, I was grateful our secret would be dumped in the soil alongside her. Mike would never know the truth.

I shoved away my regret and focused on the dentures. A little yellow around the gums and they had a strange stench to them. It wasn't altogether off-putting, and somehow familiar. I held them to my nose and sniffed.

What is that smell?

Gazing at the back teeth, I noticed something wedged between the molars and pried at it. Whatever it was, it had a fleshy texture, like days old meat. It was greyish and had that faint aroma of dried blood. I sniffed deep, reminiscing about my youth. There was one person in particular I thought about. So many faces from my past, but this one was memorable, for so many reasons.

Tobias.

I pulled at the piece of whatever it was and placed it on my tongue. Meat of some kind. Old. Sour. Still, my taste buds wet themselves with excitement. I recognised the flavour, even though it was rotting. I surveyed the room to make sure I was alone. No nurses traipsing past. No annoying residents peering in at me as they sometimes did. I swallowed the rotting meat, relishing that familiar taste.

It was clear to me that the dentures were not state-of-the-art or brand new, but Mike had given me a gift. The presence of the meat did raise certain questions. On the other hand, I'd been taught that you never look a gift horse in the mouth. And you *never* bite the hand that feeds.

Running my tongue along my vacant gums, I considered my options. I did need new teeth. I didn't enjoy pummelling food down my throat like an overused laundry chute to my stomach. I couldn't taste anything that way and, as strange as it sounded, I loved the sensation of chewing. The things you miss when you can't partake. The act of chomping on that chicken breast, feeling it tumble around the mouth, its juices sinking right into the taste buds. Or the saltiness of that crispy bacon melting through the entire mouth. I even missed using little bones to pick the remains from my teeth. There was something satisfying about that, like the final struggle of the animal, clinging to the tooth like its life depended on it. Bad news, boys and girls, your life ended long ago in an act of globally industrialised slaughter. I sometimes felt like a slaughterhouse animal, being ushered closer and closer to death.

My options were limited here. Either shove these used dentures in, grin and bear it, or ask Mike for that money. I couldn't bear that option, not after his display earlier in the dining hall. The guilt and regret for how I'd treated my wife was nothing compared to the guilt I experienced when I asked my only son for large sums of money. How Mike's face would drop.

That knowing stare that pierced me to the core. I had always wanted to be a better father, to take care of my son, but the shoe had been on the other foot ever since Mike was a kid.

Eyes closed, breath held, I inserted the dentures.

They were warm as they suckled against my pink gums, shifting into place with ease. As the dentures took their rightful place in my mouth, it was as though they were made just for me. Sculpted to fit the shape of my mouth. I wheeled myself to the bathroom mirror. Though my vision was poor, my new set of teeth sparkled and shined. I tried a smile, gave a wink. This was sure to get me some attention around the village.

Stud, I thought, and laughed.

On my way out of the bathroom, my stomach grumbled, and I found myself chattering like a schoolboy in line at the canteen. My appetite had struck like lightning and with a force I hadn't felt in years. I needed food *now*.

One of the things about retirement villages is that they come with different levels of care. Self-contained living quarters were reserved for people who could take care of themselves. Cook, clean, dress. This did not describe me at all, hadn't for a few years now. With the loss of my legs and vision and hearing—and my ability to get a hard dick—I was designated as a high-care resident, which was just a nice way of saying I was knocking on death's door.

Knock knock knocking on de-eath's doo-oor...

As much as I wanted to go to the fridge and chomp on some meat, I lived according to the facility schedule. Shower at six am, breakfast at seven. Be sure not to miss these allocated time slots, otherwise you ended up sitting in your own filth until the next day, starved and ashamed. I had seen it more than once. I joked to Mike on occasion that Nurse Ratched ran the place like clockwork, but the reference went way over his head, even though he was old enough to know what I was talking about. In truth, it wasn't a joke. The head nurse led the ward like a prison. Ms. Pratchett, her name was. Pronounced as Miz. It rolled off the tongue like a box rolled uphill.

I held my belly as I glanced at the digital clock on my nightstand. I'd have to wait another two hours before the dinner round. I wasn't sure I *could* wait. Rolling into the hallway, I headed to the kitchen. The doors would be locked, but I could always hang around on the off chance that someone would throw me a bone. Or a slice of ham. I wasn't picky.

I peered through the kitchen windows, licking my new teeth. The overweight chef was traditional, wearing an oversized white hat and a filthy apron. I watched as she chopped raw beef for the dinner stew, wiping her hands on the apron. The red streak marks looked more appetising than the beef itself and I sniffed the air, hoping for a whiff of the flesh.

The chef dumped it into a pot and moved onto chopping vegetables. My teeth chattered. I had never in my life chattered at all—except that time my ex-wife had locked me outside in the rain—so this new habit was beginning to unsettle me. My stomach gave an intense grumble at the sight of my meal being prepared.

I gazed upon the chef, watching her wipe sweaty hair from her rosy cheeks. Her aorta pulsed in her neck as she busied herself with the vegetables. I'd never paid attention to this woman before, but for some reason I could not look away. She glanced up at me through the window and gave a short wave. Her full lips curled upwards, and she wandered over to me.

"Hello there," she said. "A bit eager for dinner service?"

I nodded, unable to speak. Now that her full body was in view, I found a new appreciation for her plump, round features. I noticed her neck pulsing again, veins throbbing under the skin.

The chef tilted her head. "Are you okay?"

I cleared my throat and rubbed at my stomach. "Sorry. I'm just so hungry today."

She gestured like she had an idea, stepped back into the kitchen, and searched a few containers for something, lifting lids and rearranging boxes. Finally, with a "Ah ha!", she pulled out an apple—the green kind—and offered it to me with a wink and a finger on her lips.

"I don't think management will miss one apple," she said, and closed the kitchen doors behind her.

The apple smelled rancid and looked like a green ball of shit. I half-expected a worm to poke out at me. I could tell it was fresh, but as I sniffed at the fruit, my body revolted. I snarled and threw the apple down the hallway behind me.

It was unusual behaviour, I reflected, but didn't pause long enough to try understanding what was happening to me. Instead, I peered through the kitchen windows once more, and waited for the chef to disappear. Everyone had to pee eventually.

I had a vision of the chef taking her garments off to reveal the flesh beneath, and caught myself. I wasn't prone to fantasy, and when I was, it was not of this variety—I wasn't attracted to the chef at all. My fantasy was not based on her, though. It was her flesh, those meaty rolls hidden under her apron. Her sweaty armpits. I could tell her skin was salty and I craved to lick her all over. Maybe I could stuff the apple in her mouth and throw her on the spit.

What the hell? I caught myself again. I shook off my thoughts, directing my attention back to the stew. That's what I wanted. Stew. Something to satisfy my hunger.

After what seemed like forever, the chef left the kitchen. I didn't know how long I had, but the dinner service was still a while off and I couldn't wait. My belly grumbled and groaned, an order to consume that I couldn't resist. My teeth chattered as I wheeled into the kitchen. A slight pain in my gums as I drew closer to the stew. My nostrils flared as they filled with the thick aroma of beef and potato and onion.

My mouth ached.

Figuring it was just from adjusting to the dentures, I shrugged off the pain. As I wheeled past the metal kitchen cupboards, I caught a glimpse of my reflection and stopped to admire my new teeth. I lifted my lips as far as they would go, revealing my gums. I squinted and rubbed my eyes, sure that the black roots taking hold across my gums was some kind of illusion. They were rough as I glided a finger along the roots, like the teeth had veins. A life force.

"I must be really hungry." Denial was a powerful thing. I knew that firsthand. So had my ex-wife.

My teeth clamoured before me, their rapid and violent motion separate to my own desires. I recoiled my fingers from my mouth and witnessed the roots throbbed, like they were pumping something through me.

I wheeled to the stew and ladled out a piece of warm beef, dripping in thick broth. The flavoursome beef did nothing for me. Sure, my tastebuds were getting a buzz, but there was no sense of enjoyment.

I spat the meat back into the ladle and returned it to the pot. Someone else could enjoy that tripe. I needed something fresher. That meat had been too…cooked. Spoiled. The blood had all but dried up. Searching the fridge, I found a stack of pork chops wrapped in butcher paper.

That'll do, pig, I thought as I tore into the raw meat.

My teeth clamped down on the bone in the pork chop, gnawing at it like an obstacle to be beaten. I didn't know what I was doing or what was happening. Grinding that bone down and chewing that squishy red meat was the most exhilarating thing I'd done in years. Blood dribbled down my chin as I devoured the pork chops, my heart racing with adrenaline. The chef would be back soon, and my stomach was telling me that my hunger was only just getting started.

3

PHIL

The chef returned with a relieved sigh and a renewed energy. She waddled through the kitchen with a hum vibrating from her lips. I couldn't tell what the tune was intended to be. All I knew for certain was that my stomach did flips at the sight of those pudgy lips pushing oxygen into the air. Small black hairs sprouted from her upper lip, soaking up grease and steam and clutching onto crumbs of whatever she had decided to chew on.

Her gaze fell on me, appearing weak and fragile in my wheelchair. She kneeled in front of me, full of something like affection. Her eyes caught on the dribbles of blood I hadn't managed to wipe away. Affection twisted into concern.

"Are you alright?" she asked, pressing a hand to my forehead. "What happened to you?"

I shrugged, unable to ogle anything but the chef's full cheeks. My stomach rumbled and gurgled and as she pulled away, my teeth chattered.

"Are you cold, sweetie?" The chef stood up, ambled to a phone hanging on the wall. Muttered something about senile old farts.

My deteriorated ears soaked up more than they should have.

"I'm not senile," I said through the pauses in the teeth's clamouring.

My jaw muscles stretched and contracted, excited at the thoughts forming in their owner's brain. I wheeled towards the chef. I could smell her. A sweetness. Rich blood, thick with sugar and salt and fat.

She twisted to me, fingers hovering above the speed dial button for the nurse's station. "Oh, honey,"—she frowned—"they all say that."

The teeth chattered anew, the roots of the dentures taking hold. They were angry. Angry and hungry. Like a hand was reaching out of my mouth, begging for a last meal. I was right in front of her now, assessing my options. Lips, neck, waist. They all looked delicious.

What are you doing? Leave her alone.

My hands squeezed the wheels of my chair, muscles burned with inaction as I tried to spin away. But there was something inside me that needed to taste her. I was hungry and there was only one thing to satisfy it.

The chef was pressed to the wall now, searching for a non-violent solution to the old man. She tried to move around me, but the chair was large and clunky. Blocked her way past.

"You have something I need." I clenched my jaw, the muscles in my neck tensed.

"I'm sorry," she said, "but you really need to wait for dinner like everyone else."

I grabbed the chef's apron. Pulled her down with a strength I didn't realise I had. The chef struggled against me, cussed like a trooper as she fought against me. But it was no use.

The chef's neck was against my mouth now. I fought to keep my lips pressed shut, but the teeth were too strong. There was nothing to be done. What was happening was happening. I could either go with it and enjoy, or fight it and watch as a puppet while devouring the chef, anyway.

I sucked the sugary scent of her fear into my nostrils.

"Please!" she cried. "Somebody, help me!"

"Nobody can help you," I whispered, licking my lips. "We're all senile, remember."

She squealed a stream of cuss words as I sunk my teeth into her neck, letting her warm glucose-filled blood pour into my throat. My teeth were powerful, the roots feeding on the blood, extending through my cheeks and neck. With each millilitre of blood and flesh that I swallowed, the teeth grew stronger.

I grew stronger.

The chef bled out faster than I would have liked. Her struggles and cries ebbed away into nothingness, overtaken by the sound of my own heart beating and the stew boiling over on the stove behind me.

Dropping her body to the tiled flooring, I reached for the chef's apron. Wiped blood from my arms and mouth, licking my fingers clean. My gaze fell to her motionless body, to her rolls of fat under the blood-drenched clothing. From my place in the wheelchair, I had to lean pretty far over to hold onto her. She was so easy to lift into my lap, though, and I marvelled at my strength.

I tore the clothes from her body, examined the carcass. Her thighs, thick with meat and fat. Her stomach, the skin stretched and weighed by years of junk food and beer.

Pushing her down to the floor, I climbed out of my chair, ignoring the sensation in my toes. Phantom movement, I was sure. I clawed my way over the chef's body, licking her flesh, sinking the teeth into the chef's flabby back in a frenzy of hunger and passion. I was well-aware how it would appear should somebody come in and discover what I was doing, gyrating over the corpse of the nursing home chef. The adrenaline and the orgasmic taste of flesh under my tongue prevented me from stopping. Like a teenager thieving a skin magazine, I was going all the way. Consequences be damned.

The flesh was tender, falling away with each grind of the teeth. I delighted in the taste. Familiar, yet strange. Again, I tore at the rolls around the shoulder blades, thick red juices spurting across my face.

As I moved from the chef's body to the pool of blood seeping across the linoleum flooring, my tongue flicking back and forth like a lizard's, I was more alive than I had been in years. The sensation in my toes continued to grow, like pins and needles. In the midst of my feeding, I was sure my big toe moved. A jerk, just one.

I pushed away from the floor and took stock of the situation. The chef was dead, her sweaty armpits and rolls of white meat losing their appeal with each lifeless moment.

"What the fuck have I done?" I said, and wiped blood from my lips.

If you get caught, Phil... The thought wasn't mine. It came as a whispered voice in the back of my mind, scratching at the top of my mouth. *Clean up and return to your room.*

Dragging myself back to my wheelchair, the sensation in my toes vanished. My backside firm in the wheelchair now, I knew what to do. Just as the voice had said, I would clean up and get the fuck back to my room.

Like I was never here.

I found some cleaning products and a mop, and set to work.

4

MIKE

"How's your dad?"

I shrugged.

"Don't be like that, Mike, I'm taking an interest," Kyle said.

I peered at him, his legs draped over me on the couch as I caressed him in slow motions back and forth. We both enjoyed it, but for once it'd have been nice for me to be the one getting pampered. Being a service top was hard fucking work.

"He's…Dad. A cranky old man who listens to right-wing radio and hates his son," I said, and stopped caressing. I rested my hands on Kyle's bent knees and studied my boyfriend's face. The little dimples when he frowned, the emerging crow's feet. "You are so cute when you try to be serious."

Kyle laughed. "I *am* being serious." He paused

36

for a second, attention diverted to the television. For a guy in his twenties, he sure loved *Home and Away*. I remembered when Sally was a kid and had an imaginary friend. The characters now were not even half real. "Did you tell him about us yet?"

There it is, I thought. *That's what he wanted to talk about all along.*

Alf Stewart was yapping on about flaming this and flaming that and the caravan park was his legacy or something. I tried to pay attention to that, to pretend I hadn't heard the question. Kyle was drop dead gorgeous, smart as hell, but also eighteen years younger than me and only just starting to understand what real life was about. He didn't get that my dad had been one of the cops at the first Mardi Gras, arresting people and spitting on them.

"Babe?" Kyle asked.

Babe. Such a straight term. I scratched at a tooth with my tongue. "No, I didn't get the chance."

Kyle shifted his legs away from my lap and twisted into a sitting position. That face of his also twisted, reshaping into something more serious, like the world was ending. Youth came with lots of things, the superego most of all.

Here we go.

Sometimes when Kyle went off like this, his holier than thou attitude, trying to tell me how the world worked and how homophobia operated and blah blah blah, I wanted to shout at him that he was an amoeba when I first started sucking cock. He wasn't even a sperm when I was getting arrested in the 1980s for daring to kiss another man. I tried to listen to him, I really did. But as I watched him—sitting with his arms and legs crossed, back straight, telling me how he felt invisible in this relationship because I hadn't told my dad we were together—I laughed.

"What's so funny?" Kyle asked. Crow's feet, like usual. Still cute.

I sighed. "Kyle, I hate to say this, but none of this shit matters."

He stared at me, perplexed.

"I'm sorry,"—I coaxed one of his hands free—"but whether or not my dying father knows we're together or not just doesn't make a difference."

"You're ashamed of me." Kyle bit his lip the way he always did when he held back tears. Which was too often. Youth and all that.

"You know that's not true," I said. "I love you. Even if you are a drama queen sometimes." *Fuck. I didn't mean to say that out loud.*

Kyle knew it was true, though. He had at least that much self-awareness. In a way, I was glad I said it out loud, because if he blew his top about it, it would just prove my point. This way, he could let it fester inside him for a while and *hopefully* he'd emerge the other side with a bit more perspective.

"You love me?" Kyle replied, relaxing.

"I do," I said. "And I have plans for our anniversary next week. If you can get off work, that is."

Kyle beamed. "I can totally do that."

Totally. Totes. Yeah bro. Tsk. Stop it, Mike. Fuck. "Good."

It was true that I did love him, despite his youthful indignation and his obsession with Nicki Minaj. He was sweet and funny and kind. But he had a lot to learn about life. About love. About everything, really. The same as every other twenty-three-year-old. Still, he saw something in me that I hadn't seen in myself for a long time, and he brought it back to life. My zest. My pep.

Kyle settled back into the lounge cushions, replanted his legs over my lap, and breathed deep as he returned his attention to *Home and Away*. I watched with my head hung low, focusing above the rim of my glasses, begging for a plot twist where Alf was a psycho killer. Everyone in that town could burn for all I cared. I just wanted to go to bed.

Is this what pep feels like?

The thought stirred around my foggy brain. I traced my hands over Kyle's legs—pulling lightly at the hairs around his knees. He loved that for some reason. He'd want sex before bed, so I had to get in a quick power nap while the drama unfolded on the television. Kyle was very energetic, in the best possible ways, and I couldn't always keep up. Youth and all that...

"Babe?"

I jerked and pushed my glasses up to rub away the encroaching desire to sleep.

"Babe, your phone's ringing," Kyle said.

I reached over Kyle's legs—*Thanks for moving*—to grab my phone.

"Oh. It's my dad's home."

Kyle flinched. Always hopeful, like a puppy.

"Hello?" I answered.

"Mr Benson?" the voice asked.

"Speaking." I glanced at Kyle, who was squinting, straining to hear what was being said.

"Hi, Mr Benson. This is Julie, I'm the nursing manager, calling from the Emerald Falls Nursing Home. It's about your dad."

My breath caught. "Is he—"

"He's fine, but… Well, there's been, like, an incident here at the home." Her voice was calm and cold, but underneath the façade was a slight tremble. "I asked the police to let me call you."

"What's happening?" Kyle whispered, concerned.

"Our resident chef has had a, uh, an accident. The police haven't said much. But they told me I could let you know, being the next of kin."

"Let me know what? What happened?"

"Your father was found with the chef's body, he—"

"Julie, was it? Yeah, I'll just come by. Thanks."

"What's happened? What's this about a body?" Kyle asked.

"My dad's been involved in some kind of accident," I said and jumped from the couch, letting Kyle's legs go wherever they fell. "I have to go."

He stood and headed to the bedroom, taking his tank top off. "I'll come with. Just let me get changed."

I shook my head. "No, Kyle, it's okay. I have to go right now." I didn't look back as I grabbed my car keys and headed to the garage. I heard him say he loves me, I think I mumbled something in response, but I was too focused on getting back to the home.

After the exchange earlier in the day, yelling at Dad, telling him I couldn't afford to help him anymore… It weighed on me. We were all either of us had. The last in the family bloodline, and it's not like I could get Kyle pregnant.

Screeching through the streets, running red lights, and ignoring road rules, I made it to the home— all the way across town—in less than five minutes. Granted, it was quiet and there was no traffic. Still, I was pleased. Not pleased enough to tell the cops, still meandering at the scene with Styrofoam coffee cups and tired eyes. I gestured to them as I passed, and raced into the building. The receptionist, a young thing who seemed bored and way overdressed for the industry, motioned to hand me a clipboard. I ignored her and breezed past, straight to Dad's room.

"Woah, hold up there, son," an officer at least half my age said. He held a hand to my chest, his expression daring me to disobey. "This is an active crime scene."

"This is my dad's room,"—I pointed over the officer's shoulder—"is he okay? I heard something about a body and—"

"Woah now," the officer repeated a few more times. "What's all this about a body? I'm going to need to interview you, sir. You could be a key witness."

"What? I just got here."

Another officer, plain clothes and wearing a heavy trench coat, entered the hallway with a heavy sigh. "Reynolds, fuck off, will ya?"

Reynolds, the "woah now" officer, suddenly found something interesting to inspect on the floor and ambled away from the scene.

"Kid's just got here from Goulburn. I think it's his second or third day. Fucking newbies, but we all start somewhere, right?" Plain Clothes said. She flashed a badge and introduced herself as Brooks. "You're Mr Benson's son?"

I nodded. "Also Mr Benson. Mike." I shook her hand and watched her watching me. Searching me. "What happened, Detective?"

Brooks took her hand back, wiped it on the

thigh of her pants, and peered back into the room. I could just see just beyond her, another two officers taking swabs from Dad's mouth. He seemed to be enjoying the attention. "The chef, she, uh… Well, she's dead, Mike. Your father was seen mopping up blood right next to the body."

"Holy fuck," I whispered. "Is he okay?"

Brooks shrugged. "Why wouldn't he be? He ain't dead." She sized me up to gauge my reaction. I ignored her and kept staring past her. "He's fine."

"You don't think he—"

"He was found at the scene, but when we interviewed him he seemed really out of it. Shook up, traumatised. Plus, he's pretty old, not really the strength to feed himself, you know? Well, you'd know, being his son and all. We think maybe he saw something—someone—but he can't remember. Your dad have dementia? Alzheimer's?"

"No."

"Hmmm. Probably in shock. The EMTs checked him out, said he's fine to stay here." Brooks paused, surveying over her shoulder. The other two officers had finished with him, were packing up their gear. "I'll need to speak to him again, to see if he remembers anything later. But at this stage, we just need to know why he was cleaning up."

I gave a short 'Hmm' sound. "I'll talk to him, see if I can get anything out of him. Can I go in now?"

Brooks stepped aside and the two officers considered us as they exited the room. I rushed to my father's side, and he gave a confident stare. Not the traumatised man I'd expected to see. Brooks stood in the doorway, her shadow stretching into the room and across my father's body.

I flashed my teeth in a broad grin. *Go away.* She took the message.

"Dad? Are you okay?" I asked, kneeling next to his wheelchair.

He stared at me for a few seconds, like he was choosing his words carefully. "I'm hungry."

"Of course," I said, and sighed. "You missed dinner, didn't you? Maybe I can take you out for a bit, I'm sure under the circumstances it would be okay. Get you a burger or something."

Dad looked away, pursed his lips. "You don't have any money for me."

Didn't take long to throw that one in my face. "Come on, Dad. You want some food or not?"

He muttered.

"Hey, you've got your dentures in, they fit okay?"

"Where'd you get them?"

"Just a place around town. I can't remember the name of it."

I wheeled Dad out of his room, avoided the gazes of neighbours through cracked doors. Breathing heavy against the wood and drooling at the gossip they'd be sharing in the morning.

"They feel funny," Dad said after a while, after we'd made it to the sign-in counter I'd bypassed earlier.

"You didn't sign in." An older woman pointed at me. Julie, I presumed. Her eyebrows were raised in that *Bitch, don't cross me* kind of way.

"Sorry," I said, and signed in. Julie watched every pen stroke and I took the opportunity to apologise once more. She didn't seem like the type to piss off, especially if I was taking a resident out past curfew.

I kept wheeling Dad out the front door. "What do you feel like?"

As the night air rushed us, and I headed for a down ramp, Dad muttered, "Meat. Get me some meat."

5

MIKE

The steakhouse was busy for a Wednesday night. I never went out during the week, much to Kyle's chagrin, and reserved my well-earned money for more expensive restaurants known for fine dining and imported wines. I'm not a snob or anything, I just really like good food.

At short notice, though, this would do. And Dad had said he wanted meat. So, a steakhouse seemed the perfect option.

Sitting there, though, he squinted at the menu in their low light, and chattered his new teeth. Licked his lips a lot, too. I stared at him, intent on getting a cheesy garlic bread and a Caesar salad. Kyle said he liked my curves and my bearish belly, but I wanted—and sometimes tried—to lose a bit of weight and care for myself more.

46

Maybe avoid the garlic bread, then?

"What you having, boys?" a waiter asked. He'd come out of nowhere. He saw me jump a little and touched my arm. "Sorry to scare you, sir."

There was a twinkle in his eye, the same one lots of young gay guys gave me now. I didn't subscribe to the daddy label, but it sure as hell seemed like that's all the boys wanted these days. Kyle wasn't like that, thank god. We just clicked, age be damned. I remembered he tried calling me daddy once while mid-coital, and I'd gone soft as soon as the word left his mouth. He never tried it again.

"No worries," I replied politely.

"You ready to order?" Notepad and pen at the ready.

"Dad?" I asked. "What are you having?"

His false teeth clanging together were like nails against a chalkboard. I waited a few seconds before probing him again, at which point he glared at me from over the menu.

"I can give you a few more minutes," the waiter said, winking at me. "I'll be just over there."

I followed the end of his pen, which pointed towards the bathroom. He winked once more and trailed off, and I wondered if he wanted me to follow him. Kyle and I were monogamous, so even though I had an itch in my groin for the skinny twink, I stayed where I was.

When the waiter came back, disappointed I hadn't flagged him down or followed him around like a lost puppy, his attitude was far less jovial. He took my order and helped my dad when he asked what a chat potato was. And what chipotle mayo meant.

"How's it different from regular mayo?"

"It's spicy," he replied, giving me a bored expression, as if to say, *Take me away from here, daddy.* He took my dad's order of blue steak with chips— "Regular, none of this 'chat' stuff'"—and waltzed off with a "Won't be long".

There was something different about my father, I couldn't place it. He was smiling, but seemed concerned. His teeth kept clamouring like he was lost in a snowstorm, and he busied his hands with a blunt bread knife. I wondered what he'd seen earlier, why he'd been mopping up blood, and why Kyle was so desperate to meet him.

"Dad?" I broke the silence.

He glanced at me. He'd heard me and I wasn't even speaking loudly. In a crowded restaurant, where children played, music thumped through speakers, and the clanging of cutlery against dishes mixed with a slew of adult conversation, he'd heard me.

Something was definitely not right with him.

"Dad, what happened tonight?"

"I thought the cops told you."

He always did that. Avoided things so we didn't

have to have a real conversation. He picked up the bread knife and stabbed it into the table. It fell flat and clanged against the fork.

"Don't do that to me," he said. "I'm your father, goddammit. Show me some respect."

One thing about being someone's child is that it doesn't matter how old you get. You'll always be their kid. There, at that table, my forty-six-year-old self felt like a five-year-old. I looked down, stared at the pattern in the tablecloth—plaid, like a cowboy shirt—and muttered an apology.

"You have no idea what's going on with me," Dad said. "All you care about is your *fucking* money."

"Dad, that's not fair."

He was filled with rage, and something else I didn't recognise. His mouth moved in weird ways, like his lips were trying to seal shut, but they kept fighting to stay open. Dad gripped the knife tight, his closed fist shaking, and bared his teeth at me.

"Dad, what the hell are you doing?" I asked, pushing my chair back a little.

Does he have dementia? Alzheimer's? Brooks's words rang in my ears as the behaviour unfolded.

"I…" He swallowed hard and slapped his other hand to his mouth. His face, still full of rage, also filled with terror. Whatever had been there before was gone, but I searched for it anyway.

"Should I get you back home?"

"Blue steak and *regular* chips," the waiter said, dropping Dad's plate down. This kid was like a ninja, and I jumped again. "And a Caesar for you, sir." His flirtatious attitude returned, the tug of a smile at his lips.

Kyle and I might've been monogamous, but everyone loved window shopping. "Thanks," I said. "That's twice you've startled me now. I never heard you coming."

My dad stared between us, one hand still clutched over his mouth.

"I'm full of surprises." The waiter smirked, played with a shirt button by his stomach, and lingered for just a second too long. "Well, you let me know if you want dessert."

I thanked him and circled back to Dad. "Friendly guy," I said.

He breathed hard, and I asked him for the second time if he wanted to go home. We could get takeaway containers for the food, no big deal. He shook his head and eased his hand from his mouth, like he was testing something. His jaw no longer trembled through chattering teeth. "Let's eat," he said.

I always forgot Caesar salads come with anchovies. Some places don't serve it that way, but a traditional one has the salty fish in it. I set my fork down, the general flavour destroyed, and sipped my water. Dad pushed his steak around his plate.

"No good?"

"It's overcooked." The sadness in his voice didn't match the situation. It was as though he'd just discovered the moon landing was fake. His entire reality was shattered because his steak was overcooked.

"It's hard to get blue steak right, Dad. Do you want me to take it back?"

"It's no use. It's too late." His tongue kept sucking at his teeth as he spoke, and that small, sharp sound—like teenagers kissing—filled my ears. "It's far too late for that, son."

"It's just a steak, Dad," I said. "It's not really a big deal."

"You don't understand."

"Tell me, then. What's wrong?"

"It's happening again," he whispered, and surveyed the surroundings. His jaw started—up and down, up and down—teeth chattering like a fucking weirdo. "We have to go."

The waiter eyed me from across the room, hope draining from him as I wheeled Dad to the pay counter. An expensive meal, considering neither of us ate it. I couldn't resist a wink to the young man as I headed out the door, and he beamed, sending me a cute wave—one of those spirit finger ones gay men are fond of.

The drive back to Dad's place was awkward as hell. He stared out the window, didn't thank me for lifting him from the wheelchair into the passenger seat. Didn't say a word at all. Just sat there, holding his jaw.

"Dad, please talk to me. What's going on? Are you hurt?" I could feel the pressure in my eyes—tears building. Like all the moisture in my body was being sucked to my eyeballs, ready to explode.

He stared out the window.

"Please, Dad."

Nothing.

I wheeled him back to his room, helped him into bed, and headed to the exit, ready to slam his door shut behind me, when a small voice whispered from the darkness.

"Help me, Mike."

Spinning on my heel, I went to his bedside. "Tell me what to do." My heart raced. My dad needed me. He was opening up. He was—

"I need food."

—hungry?

Fuck's sake.

"Please."

"Dad, you just had a steak you didn't eat."

"Please, don't ask questions. I need you to help me, for Christ's sake." Through the dim room, his eyes were begging me. Despite the forcefulness of his voice—the thinly-veiled anger—he was begging me.

He needed me.

Even if it was just for some food, he needed me.

I sighed. "Sure, Dad. What can I get you?"

His jaw trembled again and he stretched it like he was getting ready for a giant piece of pie. "The kitchen is closed, I know. But I need some raw pork. Has to be pork."

"Dad…"

"Just… *Please*. Don't ask any fucking questions, just get me the fucking pork."

Lying there on his bed, weak and fragile, unable to walk or do much of anything, he was asking me for raw meat. Of all things, pork.

"Please."

Despite the red flags and alarm bells screeching in my head, I nodded once, and headed to the kitchen.

6

MIKE

"**W**hat the fuck am I doing?"

The kitchen was closed, but the door was still open. Active crime scene and all that. The cops had all left. They'd collected samples and whatever else they did, and taken the chef's body. As I stood by the blue-and-white police tape, wondering how my night went from *Home and Away* to break and enter, I spotted the fridges.

Dad needed pork, and he needed it raw. There was no way this was normal, and I intended to ask him about it, but I needed that dead pig as bait. Wave it in front of his face, so to speak, until I got answers.

Pushing the police tape up, I ducked underneath and entered the kitchen, flicking on a light as I did so. It was eerie being there, knowing that a metre away the chef had been killed. The details were still fuzzy, but the faded stains on the linoleum indicated there'd been quite the mess. It could have been anything—grape juice or red wine—had it not been for the little, numbered yellow cards placed around the area.

A shiver ran up my spine as I stepped towards the fridge. Found the meat I needed, and spun fast to get the hell out of there. A young woman, chewing hard on some gum, stood in the doorway, hands at her hips.

"What ya doing?"

Hiding the meat behind my back, I stumbled to find some words.

"Are you, like, a reporter? Checking out the scene?" Her eyebrows were bouncing up and down as she studied me. "Do you want to interview me?"

I shook my head. "Why would I interview you?"

She cleared her throat, tidied her rather frizzy hair, and approached me, a hand held out. "I'm Taylah, I'm, like, a nurse here. I was here when this shit, like, went down."

"Really? You saw it?"

She pursed her lips, somehow still managing to chew the gum. "Well, no, but like I was totally here in the buiiiilding at the time and the cops were all like soooo full on. But you'd know that, since you're writing about it, right?"

The pork was getting cold in my hands, but it sounded like this young woman might know something. Between all the likes and totallys, her words hid a deeper truth. I hoped. "Did you see my Da—Mr Benson? With all the blood?"

Taylah nodded, a hand going back to her hip. She stood on a slight angle, one leg stretched out to the side, and with her free hand she fidgeted with her staff lanyard. "Listen, liiiike, I'm not saying this is what happennnned, and like, you didn't hear this from me, but Mrs Denton from room twenty-one told Mr Mayer in room twenty-two that she, liiiike, saw someone in a wheelchair hanging around the kitcheeen. And, like, that could be anyone, right?" She giggled. "So anyhooow, your dad was, like, mopping up all this bloooood, like gallonnnnns, and the chef—"

"My dad? You mean Mr Benson?"

"Dude, it's okay. I saw you here earlier, like… I see you here all the time, drinking your beers and whatever. Anyway, the thing waaaas, Mr Mayer said your dad had blood, like, all over his mouth. And he was talking to someone, but, like, he was alone. Anyway, I just thought you might be a reporter, which would have been totally aaaawesomeee because like, my friend Darby has this cousin in Perth who's like—"

"Taylah, I have to go." Talking to her was insufferable, and the pork was growing heavy in my hands. Plus, Dad was waiting.

"No worries, boo," she said and patted me on the arm. "I won't tell anyone about the pork, it's all good."

Fuck. "Thanks. Nice to meet you." I stepped around her and exhaled hard, thinking there was a strong possibility that she and Kyle would get along really well. I did love the guy, but was the age gap too much?

Dad was holding his jaw when I got back. He grabbed for the pork in my hands, but I moved it just out of reach.

"Give it to me," Dad said, his teeth chattering with desire.

"Dad, I heard that you had blood on your mouth when you were found with the chef." Dangling the pork in front of him, his stare was unmoving from the meat.

"CPR," he said fast. "I tried to give her CPR."

I laughed. "Really? Tell me, Dad, what actually happened to the chef? I heard there was gallons of it. Why so much blood?"

His gaze settled on me. "Give. Me. The. Meat."

I held it closer to him, still just out of reach. He snatched at it like a wild animal.

"Why so much blood? And why try CPR when it's pretty clear the chef'd be dead with that much blood loss?"

Dad huffed. "It's none of your business. Now, please, I'm hungry."

"And why the raw meat?"

"I like it that way, now please just give it to me."

This was going nowhere. He didn't want to talk, he just needed me to do his bidding for him. And I'd done it. Throwing the meat in his lap, I stormed off, and muttered, "Get yourself into bed, I'm not helping you anymore."

The last thing I saw as I shot a glance back to him was his new teeth tearing into the raw pork.

. . .

I took the long way home, which still only lasted about ten minutes. As I pulled into the garage, a strip of light flicked on from under the interior garage door. Kyle must have been waiting for me. When I got into the main house, he was leaning against the wall opposite the garage door, wearing nothing but his tight little boxers.

God damn, I thought, and bit a lip.

"How is he?" Kyle said through a stretch.

"Same old, really." I kissed him on the cheek and pulled him close into a hug.

Kyle's arms wrapped around me and his warmth sank through my whole body. I sighed hard and squeezed him tighter, realising just how much I needed him. How much I needed his warmth, his arms around me. Despite the problems that came with dating a younger man, he understood that in this moment, I needed silence. I needed him to do nothing but be with me.

We stayed that way for a few minutes until Kyle pulled away just enough so that our lips were an inch apart. He kissed me, a gentle one, and gazed into me. I gave a sad smile in response and stepped out of the hug. Led him through the house to the bedroom, where I kicked off my shoes, and plunged myself onto the bed.

Kyle crawled next to me, above the covers, and held my hand. "Do you want to talk about it?"

I really did. But as I gazed over at him, those puppy dog eyes wide and naïve, I couldn't. I couldn't do that to him, burden him with the realities of adulthood. He was just finishing up university and starting his career in hospitality. He'd never had a dying parent or even a sick one. I had to let him be young.

"I just need to sleep," I whispered.

Without a word, Kyle rolled over, shimmied underneath the blankets, and went to sleep. I could almost feel the anger seeping off him, but he'd be grateful in the morning. Ignorance was bliss, and naivety was a gift. I wished I could go back to that.

After I took my clothes off and crawled back into bed, I tried cuddling Kyle. Pulling his body into mine and wrapping my arms around him, he felt like home. But his body was tense, rigid, full of anger. I nuzzled into his neck, whispered, "I love you," and waited in the darkness for a response.

None came.

Rolling over, I stared at the digital display of

my bedside clock. Kyle thought it was cute that I still had one of those, what he called 'old school alarm clocks'. I just never found a reason to replace it. The green numbers ticked by, one minute after the next, and I watched time disappear until I couldn't bear to stare at the numbers anymore.

What is happening to Dad?

The pork, the anger… He'd never been a happy man, but I'd never known him to be so full of rage. The way he studied me, like he could have actually killed me if I didn't throw the pork to him. Like feeding a lion at the zoo.

I didn't feel sleep come, but the next thing I heard was the shrill *beep beep beep* of my alarm clock. Slapping the top of it, I rolled back over to give Kyle a hug.

He was gone.

7

PHIL

I hated treating Mike that way, I hated being so standoffish and angry with him. He was a good kid, he didn't deserve it. I couldn't talk to him yet, though. Not until I was sure what was going on. The pork was wet and soppy on my lap as he wandered out the door, and I'd not been able to wait. I had to taste it, had to devour it.

I'd gotten in two bites before I had to throw it to the ground. Watched it splat on the carpet, the juices leaking into the fabric like piss.

Overcooked. Raw meat and it was fucking overcooked. *How is that possible?*

That's not the problem.

Cracking my neck, I stared down at the meat, hating myself for knowing what the problem was.

Hating that stupid voice in my head, the one I was sure I'd gotten rid of years earlier.

You know the problem.

That fucking voice again.

I switched on my radio, turned up the volume. House rules be damned. As the talkback filled the room, I realised the voice had only come back after putting those dentures in.

Rolling my tongue over them, they were bumpy. I wheeled myself to the bathroom, flicked on the light, and stared at myself in the mirror. My paper-thin skin from all the medications, my white hair and wrinkles. I was a fucking mess.

But my teeth.

White, pearly, fresh.

Baring them into the mirror now, I stared at the falsies. At the black veins growing from them. I'd seen them earlier, just before I ate the chef—*That poor woman, what have I done?*—but I'd thought it was a trick of the light. Even if I could feel them pushing through my flesh.

That ain't no trick of the light.

I brought a frail hand to the teeth, traced the edges and the top of the bottom row. Pulled away as I cut myself on the left incisor. The blood dripping down my finger was so red, so full of life, that I didn't mind the pain. It reminded me I was still alive.

Unlike the chef, who was still working her way through my digestive system.

I pushed the memory away, tried to focus. On the blood. On my arthritic finger.

On my teeth.

"None of this happened until I decided to wear you," I said, still baring the teeth in the mirror. *Or are they wearing you?*

Reaching deep into my mouth, I pulled at the dentures. They didn't budge. I tried a second time, more forceful, but it was like they were glued in place.

"Fucking things."

The black veins pulsed in my mouth, pushing past my gums and into my cheeks. Down into my jawline and underneath my tongue. My stomach clenched and knotted at the thought of these things inside me.

I used both hands to pull at the teeth, ignored the scratching at my fingers to get a better grip. The veins surged with energy and I pulled harder.

They moved. Just a little, but they moved. I pulled as hard as I could, until the dentures began to peel away from my gums. They were stuck, though, I couldn't move them past my lips. Looking into the mirror again, I saw the veins, like thread or wire, attached to the dentures.

You can't get rid of me that easily.

The voice taunted me as I strained with all my might to pull at the teeth. I gripped tighter, my fingers pulsing with agony as I cut myself over and over. The dentures came past the lips, the veins taut now, stretching. They were inside me now, gripping onto my skin, digging into me, and I screamed. One of the veins snapped and recoiled back inside my body. It only made the other veins grip tighter.

A new one grew from the dentures, shot into my mouth and down my throat. I coughed and wheezed, choked as another black vein shot down there, affixed itself to me somewhere in my chest.

I kept pulling.

Felt weaker.

My reflection had changed; my skin paler and sagging, the wrinkles deeper. My hair had started to fall out.

I kept pulling. *Fuck you!* And pulled and pulled, but the veins grew stronger, drawing their strength from me. My fingers ached, my nails reddened with my blood from scraping against the dentures. The dentures grew another wiry vein, like a web of black tendrils attached to my mouth and throat. As more blood ran down my hands, the energy began to leave my body, and my grip loosened.

Yes, old man. That's it.

One hand dropped to my lap and I pulled again with the other.

No use.

The second hand dropped, and all I could do was stare at my weak body in the mirror as the dentures were slowly sucked back into my mouth. The tendrils sunk deeper into my body—forcing their way through my neck and shoulders now—and as the dentures re-glued themselves to my gums, I had no choice but to let it happen.

When they were back in place, I sighed with a deep shame that I hadn't been able to stop it. It. The hunger. More than that, though, my body perked up. I watched the change in the mirror—my skin growing a few shades deeper, the wrinkles fading a little, my hair regrowing.

The tingle in my toes.

You want to walk again?

"I do," I said, and hated myself for it.

You can do that, and more.

"What do I have to do?"

Eat.

. . .

I slept the best I had in years, despite the radio blaring through the room. The nurse didn't bother knocking as she stormed in to switch off the racket. Blinking awake, I heard her yelling how the other residents were complaining of the noise.

"I'm not deaf, you know," I said, and realised it was true.

"Well, then why is this bloody thing so loud, Phil?" the nurse asked. Her expression was pleading, and I could tell she'd had a long day, even though it was only 8:03 am.

"Sorry, luv." I frowned.

She sort of nodded, but it was more of a *Don't do it again* kind of gesture. Walking to the door, rolling up the sleeves of a cardigan, she stopped and leaned against the door frame. "Oh, you have a visitor."

I perked up. "Mike?"

"Nah," she said through a sigh. "Some young guy. Ah, here he is now."

Sitting up a little in my bed, I spied the fresh meat—the young guy—as he entered the room. Looked to be about in his twenties, a thick head of brown hair styled with a quiff at the front like those old-fashioned movie stars. His polo shirt was creased, unironed, and his jeans were a little too tight around the groin.

"Hi there, Mr Benson." He waved from the doorway as the nurse left us to it. She did a quick double-take, her gaze resting on the young man's arse. She winked at me and headed off.

"Uh,"—I sized him up—"hi?"

He seemed reluctant to enter the room, dawdling at the door and peering back out to the hall. I encouraged him in with a short pat on the duvet. "What's up, young man?"

Taking a spot at the edge of the bed, he cleared

his throat. "My name's Kyle. I wanted to introduce myself to you."

I focused on him, searching for a reason for this kid to be here.

"Look," he said, rolling a hand through his hair. "This isn't how I wanted to do this, but Mike doesn't know how to talk to you. Your son and I are…"—he cleared his throat, more confident this time—"in a relationship."

"Oh," I said, digesting the news. I gripped a hand on my stomach, remembering the chef was still in there.

"That's it?" he asked, surprised. "Oh?"

I shrugged, feeling the denture veins pushing up past my nose now. I'd known for years that Mike was gay, it wasn't really a big deal. The age gap here was a bit of a quandary, but at that moment, with the dentures forcing themselves deeper into my body, all I wanted to do was find out how long it would take to eat this kid.

"It's lovely to meet you," I said with a small wave. "How, uh, how old are you?"

Kyle frowned and rolled his eyes. The urge to gouge those fuckers out and swallow them whole was almost too much. "I'm twenty-three. I know there's a bit of a gap there, but we love each other. And isn't that the most important thing?"

The veins in his neck were throbbing and for the first time in years—the veins in my dick did the same. The dentures hadn't reached that far, but fuck they were powerful. My toes moved, too, and as Kyle scratched at his upper arm, I noticed the bulge of his muscles. He'd be stringy, whereas I liked a lot more meat.

Beggars can't be choosers.

I breathed slow and steady to silence the voice. To silence this kid, whose heart was beating so fast I could hear it. God, the taste of the chef's heart when I bit into it. The way the dentures had tingled in my mouth. The fleshy muscle sliding down my throat—

"Don't you think?" Kyle brought my thoughts back, and I let his sweet smell linger in my nose.

Stretching my jaw, I felt the dentures. Their desire. They were hungry again. *God he smells good.* I could smell his organs, though I wasn't sure how. The scent of raw liver from the butcher was all over this kid, and I fucking wanted it. "You have to go." My teeth clamoured a little, and I clenched my jaw shut.

"I'm sorry, I—"

"Kid, get the hell out of here." I breathed through my nose. The chattering was starting anew, the wiry veins pushing deeper down my neck. Giving my muscles more strength for ripping and tearing. "GET OUT! GET OUT!"

Kyle almost fell off the bed in shock as I yelled at him. It wasn't the way I wanted to handle the first meeting of my potential son-in-law, but my dentures wanted him. They wanted to eat him so bad, stringy or not. His liver would be healthy.

I licked my lips and screamed at him one more time. It was all I could do to not climb out of the bed and bite into his perfectly defined chest.

The kid scrambled to the door, tripping over himself a few times as he stared back at me, wide-eyed and terrified. "Help!" he cried, calling for a nurse to come. "He needs help!"

You need help, kid.

A nurse tore into the room to see my teeth bared and my eyes crazed. She ushered Kyle away and raced to my side, asking me what happened, what was wrong. I reached up to her, grabbed her by the lanyard, and pulled her close.

"GET OUT!" I screamed, as the teeth forced me closer to her neck.

She fought me off, rushed out of the room.

I started to climb out of bed, noticed Kyle was back in the doorway, his phone held up with a little light beaming at me. Throwing my covers back, I fell into my wheelchair. The veins had taken hold, pumping through me, pushing their way farther down. Through my shoulders, into the top of my spine.

I wheeled forward, screaming at him to fuck off and never come back. I wanted to tell him, to tell *Mike*, that I wanted to know this guy. I wanted Mike to bring him to me and introduce me, tell me how they met. I wanted to spend time getting to know both of them. But all I could do was scream, because I hated that I would devour every inch of him, inside and out, if he didn't run away and never return.

"Never, ever come back here!" I screamed.

Kyle was pushed aside by the nurse, who rushed at me with a syringe. She forced herself through my waving arms, tried to get into position to stab me in the arm. I held back as long as I could, but the veins surged through me, the teeth chattering, biting at the nurse.

I leaned forward in my chair, my arms wrapped around her waist, and I drew her in, teeth bared.

"Fuck!" she screamed, and whacked the side of my head.

Dazed, I fell back, tasting blood and fabric, and studied the damage. She recoiled, her hand covering the bite mark, blood oozing through the wound.

"You fucking bit me!" the nurse wailed.

Another nurse came to her aid, a young thing whose pace was slower than a mule. "You good in here?" she asked.

"Help me!" the first nurse said, readying the syringe again. "He's having some kind of fit."

"GET THE FUCK AWAY FROM ME!" It was all I could muster between my jaw trembling. The nurse's blood drained down my throat. I needed more.

Eat the bitch.

Both nurses stormed at me, one grabbing each arm.

Yes, I thought.

I tried to bite at them, but the first nurse had lodged her forearm under my chin, pressed hard to keep my head in place. The needle went into my arm and I was thankful. Nobody got hurt—not *seriously* hurt—and the tranquilliser in the syringe was already working its way through me.

As I stopped fighting them, and the teeth relented, Kyle was still at the door with his phone. The way he stood, his whole body tense, it was clear. He was full of fear. It was also clear that I'd fucked up. I always fucked up.

"I'm sorry," I said, over and over. "Tell Mike I'm sorry."

The nurses let go of me as my breathing became shallow. The first nurse staggered from the room, holding her wound, while the other nurse stood by and watched the sedative do its work.

"Fucking oooold people, like, seriously," she said with a grimace. Looking at me like I was vermin in her toilet.

I tried to tell her to get fucked and die, but the sedative was already working. Instead, I succumbed to sleep and prayed I didn't wake up.

8

MIKE

I knew Kyle wasn't happy about how things had gone down the previous night, but I didn't expect him to just up and leave without a word—and before I even woke up. The norm for us was, at a minimum, a kiss goodbye.

The three texts I'd sent him had gone unanswered—typical for one of his moods—and I was left wondering if we were compatible, after all. The things that mattered to him were just not important to me, like meeting my ailing father. What was the point of that? So Dad could grimace and say I was fucking someone young enough to *actually* be my son? I wondered what the right-wing radio DJs would say about it.

As I pulled up to the office car park, I saw Dave waving at me. His shirt was untucked and his buttons had been stuffed through the wrong holes. I waved back with the biggest *Fuck you* smile I could manage, and he beamed. Social cues weren't his thing and because I'd engaged, he'd wait for me to park the car so we could be seen entering the office together.

"Morning, Mr Benson," Dave said as I shut my car door.

I replied with a friendly yet dismissive wave. Then, "Dave, you can just call me Mike."

He beamed once more, adjusted his wide-framed black glasses and combed his hair with his fingers. It was still a mess. We strolled—together—into the office, and I avoided the awkward glances from my colleagues. I didn't hear the whispers so much as sensed them, and I suspected poor Dave thought this was the best thing to have happened to him in some time. Being seen with another person.

As we headed to our separate desks, Dave waving goodbye to me, Zac—the nineteen-year-old intern—smirked. Like he knew shit about shit. Like he belonged there. With a gentle elbow rib to another young colleague I didn't recognise, they both watched Dave plod around cubicles searching for the desk he'd been seated at for the last three years. What was worse, the big boss, Trish, stood by the water cooler grimacing at him.

It hit me like a blast of radiation. A hot flush of anger. At Zac and Trish and all the others staring at

Dave with disapproval. At myself for having joined them in that for as long as he'd been employed here. My memory flashed back to my dad, how he was always so disappointed in me, always so disapproving.

As the rage washed through me, my hands tight in a ball, I breathed hard, relaxed as much as I could, and cleared my throat. "Hey Dave," I called. He spun, almost tripping over his own momentum. "Let's do lunch today, pal." *Fuck all of you.*

For the third time that morning, he beamed.

Zac and his mate grimaced at me, like I'd just flashed my cock or something. I didn't see what Trish did because my back was to her now. I sensed her staring down my neck, though.

It felt good.

Dumping into my chair, I pressed the power button on the computer monitor and the corporate logo faded into existence. I used to be proud to work for a bank, but then people like Zac showed up, getting promoted well before me, well before they could even shave. Trish was always issuing Monday morning emails to inspire us; gifs with dogs skateboarding, or gifs with a baby dressed as a goat or some shit. I deleted them all, only to realise later the IT department could track the view rate and open rate and all sorts of data, streaming right from my computer.

And they all thought Dave was the problem.

My phone buzzed. *Kyle.*

"Good morning, sexy man," I answered.

"Babe… BABE!" Kyle stuttered. His voice was raw and strained.

"Kyle? What's wrong?" I spun my chair to the grey cubicle wall, to focus on nothing but him. "What's happened?"

"I… I…um…" His weak sobs echoed down the phone. "I went to visit your dad."

My heart stopped. "You *what?*"

More sobbing and the distinct sound of a hand wiping up runny snot. "I'm sorry, babe, I'm sorry." Weep weep weep. Whatever. He continued: "He tried to attack me. He attacked the nurses… They had to sedate him. You didn't tell me he was like that."

That perked me up. "What do you mean he *attacked* you?"

"He bit one of the nurses. I filmed it all."

"Are you okay?" My heart was pounding. My poor Kyle. My poor *dad*. What the fuck was happening?

Kyle sniffed. "I'm okay. I just… I thought you were embarrassed of me. But you're embarrassed of *him*."

He still wants to make this about him?

I breathed heavy, digesting everything Kyle had said. My dad had never been sedated before, not for violence. I remembered when I was a kid, my mum used to tell me he was sleeping all the time, but when I peeked through the doorway, he was staring at the ceiling. I hadn't thought about that in years, but now, with Kyle weeping in my ear, that memory popped right back up. My mum grinning at me with dead eyes, shoving…something…behind her back. It was a flash, incomplete, and as quickly as it had started it was over.

"Kyle," I said, "where are you now?"

"I went home." He sniffed a second time. "I watched the recording and, Mike, his eyes…"

"What about them?"

"They were so…wild. Inhuman."

"But you're okay?"

He mumbled a yes and I told him I had to go. Kyle could drink some water and calm down. But my dad? It was time for answers.

Just as the login screen demanded my username and password, I stood and peered over the sea of cubicles. Trish was *still* by the water cooler, downing another cup of H_2O and getting in some 'mingling time' where she could pretend to care about her staff, but where she actually just spied on us, taking mental notes for future layoffs.

Practicing my excuses to leave, I headed to her, hands by my side—*Not in your pockets, she hates that*—and gave a polite, "Hello."

"Morning." Trish shook my hand, returning the pleasant smile. "Uh… James, is it?"

"Mike."

She nodded, very enthusiastic, doing the whole *Of course, of course* body language.

"So, look, uh, I'm really sorry, but I need to step out. I know I just got here, but my father is really sick. The home just called and said they've had to sedate him."

Trish downed another cup of water, swallowing in loud, greedy gulps, and wiped a hand over her mouth. Very 'management'. "I'm so sorry, Mark,"—a heavy hand rubbing my arm—"my own father is suffering in a similar way. It's just so—"

"Yeah, it's hard. So, is it okay if I step out for a bit?" I motioned towards the front exit expectantly.

"Of course, Mark," Trish said with a deep breath. "Of course."

Mike. Mike. Mike. It's not hard. "Thanks, Trish. I'll be back as soon as I can."

. . .

I had seen more of this place in the past twenty-four hours than I had in the last month. Racing to and fro like a headless chicken, and I was sick of it. Dad needed to give me answers and I wasn't leaving this time until I had them.

Sitting by his bed, I was met with his dead stare up at the ceiling. Just like when I was a kid. I wished I'd been able to ask my mum about all this, find out what happened back then so I had a plan for what to do now. Watching him drool from the corners of his mouth while he stared blank at the spots of mould on the ceiling was just a bit too much for me.

I reached for his hand, wrapped my fingers around it, and held him. "Dad, I'm sorry." My voice came as a low, regretful whisper. A day earlier I'd been so spiteful that I grabbed used dentures and gifted them to him, just to save some money. Now, he was lying there like a fucking corpse, and all I wanted was to tell him how much I loved him.

I caressed the back of his hand and noticed his skin wasn't as thin as it should be. It didn't feel like thumbing crepe paper and the fear of tearing his skin open didn't feel as imminent. I glanced up from his hand to the skin on his arms. The spots and scars were all but gone, marks of old age vanishing. His face, too, was younger than the night before.

"M-Mike?" Dad's voice came as a rasp.

"Dad, you're awake." I smiled at him and was surprised when he returned the gesture.

Clearing his throat, Dad said, "What are you doing here?"

"I got a call saying you'd been…violent."

He trembled at the word. "I lost control of it, Mike. I'm so embarrassed."

My heart stopped at his honesty. There was no yelling, no avoiding eye contact, no secrecy. Just his emotions, served on a platter. I could have cried, but I didn't want to spoil the moment.

"What's going on with you? Talk to me." He clammed up a little, but his focus stayed trained on me. "The raw meat, the anger, the violence. Something's wrong... Is it dementia?"

Dad gave a croaky laugh. "I wish that's all it was."

"Then what?"

"I met your boyfriend," Dad said, reverting to his old tricks.

Trying to read the subtext of his comment, I failed. There was no scathing tone, no hint of disappointment. Just a comment. An observation. Like hearing his son is gay for the first time wasn't a world-crushing moment.

I swallowed hard. "Is... I mean, uh, you're not upset?"

A smirk pulled at the corner of Dad's lips, but he didn't say anything.

"Tell me what's going on, Dad. Kyle said you bit one of the nurses," I said, trying to steer the conversation back to him.

He considered for a moment, his jaw starting to tremble again, the way it had over dinner the night before. His eyes flickered with something—anger, I was sure—and he moved his hand away from me. His tongue rolled over his teeth a few more times as he avoided my gaze.

"Dad? I'm not leaving without answers," I said, forceful.

"Where did you get these teeth?"

"Don't change the subject."

"I'm not," he replied. "It's these teeth…" He paused, then said, "The cravings are back."

"What cravings?" I asked.

He scrutinised me for a few seconds, unable to find the right words while I waited—impatiently—and finally sighed. "I need to tell you something."

9

PHIL

1960

There was something special about the scent of a man. I didn't *want* there to be—by God, I wanted to think about anything else, but it was like an addiction. When a man passed me by, his cologne wafting over me, I felt an itch in places society said were forbidden. I wanted to notice women, but I just didn't. I liked how they looked, I could chat to women and be friendly, but when I smelled them it just did nothing for me. Something was different.

On the train to work every day, the same group of businessmen would sit across the aisle from me and talk about clients and whatever else. That's when I first saw him. And I do mean 'saw' him. I had been smelling men for a long time, letting the sweat and musk seep into me for years. I'd never glimpsed, though, never dared. Until one day on the train—on my 21st birthday,

81

actually—when our gazes locked. He was one of the businessmen, but he wasn't the same as the others. I could tell.

It was how he smelled.

Not the same masculine stench, thinly veiled by Brut. This was different. Sweeter, rich with something I had smelled before, but couldn't place.

When he gazed at me, a lazy smile pulling at his lips, a compulsion rose—I needed to meet him. He and his group always disembarked three stops before me. He motioned to me as the train came to his stop, and I found myself following him at a distance.

The street was thick with coal dust, a corner milk bar keeping a steady flow of foot traffic. I didn't know the area, but a sign at the train station read "Central". My first time in the city itself, and I was spending it following a mysterious man through the streets.

I followed him to a newspaper building, the headquarters of *The Sydney Morning Herald*, where I got all my news. Well, that and talkback, but some of their views were…not for me. Standing by the road, staring at the building with its obnoxious gold lettering and understated entrance of revolving doors, I searched for the man. His group was there, heading into the building, but they were just three now, instead of four.

"Why are you following me?"

I spun round to the voice, saw the mystery man

gazing into me. His cheeks were flushed, and he held a bowler hat in one hand, a suitcase in the other. His jacket was hung at the crook of his left elbow.

"I saw you on the train, and I…" There was no way to finish the sentence without sounding deviant. With the McCarthy administration in the US hunting deviants and commies, I had to be careful.

"You…what?" His eyebrows were raised, expectant.

I swallowed hard, and began to trudge away, my hands trembling.

"Don't go," he said.

Turning to him, a crowd of people swooping in and around him on their way to their own offices, I saw something in his eyes. He was one of me. I'd met a couple before—never acted on anything, but I'd met them. And I wasn't the only one. Something in his expression told me he wanted to tell me, but the street wasn't the right place. Too many ears.

"Coffee?" I asked.

He nodded, his whole energy suddenly darkened, and he pointed past me, up the street. "I know a safe place."

I let him lead, checking my watch, knowing I'd be late to work. Probably fired. I had been considering a career change since I'd started working in retail, maybe now was the perfect chance.

Thinking it over as this man led me to

wherever he was taking me, I said, "Sorry for being quiet. I get lost in my thoughts sometimes."

"No worries, mate," he replied, and stopped. "We're here."

The building was just a brick veneer with a hanging sign out the front, 'Chip's Coffee'. The large, grimy window revealed a few tables and chairs inside, and an older man with a pencil behind his ear working at a counter. Shuffling about with condiments and coffee beans and fresh bread.

The stench of bacon and eggs hit my nose as we strode in.

"Take a seat." Mystery Man ushered me to sit, pulled the chair out for me. It scraped against the wooden floor and shivers went up my spine. Like the chair was telling me to get the hell out of there. Telling me I didn't belong, that I was doing something wrong.

I sat, though. I sat and waited for him to order the coffees, watched the way he walked and moved. I didn't think about him the way I did other men. He smelled different and I wanted something from him that I hadn't had from anyone else before.

Taking the seat opposite me, he sized me up and leaned his forearms on the table, his watch clanging against the wood. "I'm Tobias," he said.

"Phil," I replied, meek and soft.

"Good to meet you, Phil."

We stared at each other for a moment, unsure

what to say next. I didn't know how to do this—whatever *this* was. We stayed that way until the older guy brought our coffees over, and dropped a plate of raw bacon between us.

"Here you go," he said. "Just the way you like it, Toby."

I stared at the meat, then at Tobias, who was gauging my reaction. The older guy stepped away, muttering something about good bacon being wasted.

"It's raw," I said.

Tobias nodded.

"Is that… Shouldn't he cook it?"

"Ever tried it raw?" Tobias asked, smirking.

I shook my head.

He gestured at the plate of bacon. "Try it."

As the words hit my ears, I inhaled. I didn't know how I'd missed this before, in all my years of living. The smell of raw bacon, the way the meat seemed to call me. Fresh, tender, untainted. Looking at the strips of flesh, I noticed the streaks of white, the fat. Salty, sweating in the summer morning.

"I shouldn't," I said, and pushed the plate away.

"We both know this is what you want," Tobias replied, and pushed it back to me. "Eat it. Then we can talk."

With shaky hands, I picked up a strip of bacon, my lips almost trembling with anticipation. It wasn't like I'd never tasted bacon before, but it had always been cooked and always came with egg or sauce, or something.

It hit my tongue, the bacon squishing under my teeth as I chewed. Slow, slow. I relished the flavour. It was like eating a smell, and I let the chomped-up bacon sit on my tongue for a few moments before swallowing it down with an "Mmmm."

"Do you know pork meat is the closest to human flesh?" Tobias interrupted my food-inspired orgasm. "Taste, texture, all of it. But…it can't replace the *real* thing."

He fingered a bit of bacon, then licked the end of his pointer finger.

"I knew when I saw you," he said. "It was your eyes. So full of lust for something you didn't even know you were lusting for."

I took another strip of bacon. Felt the meat between my fingers before stuffing it into my mouth.

"Let's be real. You don't want that"—he fingered the bacon with a firm finger—"you want to eat something else."

"I don't know what you mean," I said, eyeing the exit. *He knows.* Thrusting my chair back, I headed for the door.

"It's okay, Phil." He held up a reassuring hand, grabbed me by the elbow. "I've got the urge, too."

"I don't know what the hell you're talking

about!" I seethed, though the crack in my voice gave me away.

He led me back to my chair, insisting that it was okay. There was nothing to worry about and I should have some more coffee. "I wish I'd had someone to help me the way I'm going to help you," he said, then sipped his coffee.

"Help me? With what?" I sat on the edge of the seat, ready to bolt.

"To be a cannibal."

. . .

I should have run when he'd said it, but the word held so much weight, like I was wearing steel boots. He'd spent the next hour getting inside my head, telling me about how special we were. Chosen by some higher power to have this gift, to be the arbiters of life and death. He talked about it like we were in some special club, and I had to admit that the idea struck a chord. Everything he was saying made sense, the way he described his own urges matched mine perfectly, and for the first time in my entire life, I didn't feel alone.

That's why I'd agreed to it. That's why I was there, on the outskirts of Sydney, with this man.

Tobias.

My new friend.

I stared out through his windscreen, the summer moon glaring down on us with a blue tinge.

The yellow of his headlights faded as the car stopped, and I took in our surroundings.

"Where are we?" I asked, frowning. I'd never felt so lost and yet… so found.

The moon cast an eerie glow across the world, but it was dim enough that I could still see. A lot of trees, some housing development, and a lot of dirt. When he'd said earlier in the coffee shop that he had a surprise for me, I didn't think he meant taking me to a pile of dirt.

"Do you know what the council is doing out here?" Tobias stared through the windscreen. "Raping the land so they can build more houses." He spat the words like venom, droplets of saliva at the edges of his lips.

Smelled him.

Tried to stay focused.

"Well, people have to live somewhere," I replied.

He gave a soft *hmph* through his nose and shook his head. "It's all part of a scheme to get more people to have babies."

I frowned. "What do you mean?"

Tobias searched my face through the dim glow of the moonlight. A moment later, he gave a sad half-smile. "Nothing, don't worry about it, mate."

The silence that followed reminded me of the ones I had at home with my parents. When I'd come home from work and greet them, only to be met with vacant stares and the uninterested "How was your day?" from my mother. I never answered her, and I never established if she even noticed.

"Tobias," I said, "what are we doing here?"

"I work for the paper, you know that, right?" he asked me, narrowing his eyes just a little. "Well, I'm writing a story right now about land rights, development, baby booming, all of that shit. The government wants people to have babies so they need bigger houses, and the councils are in their back pocket, doing whatever they want. The land developers are…" He exhaled, slow and steady, in and out, and his gaze fell away, back to the piles of dirt outside.

"I don't understand," I said.

"Look in the boot."

I spun toward him, my expression asking the question—*What for?*

"Go have a look."

Getting out of the car, my heart thumping, my head spinning about land rights and babies and housing developments and bacon and how sweet the smell from the boot was, I clicked it open. Pulled it up.

"Fuck," I whispered, stepping back.

It was the eyes I noticed first. How they stared at me like a deer in the headlights—shocked, confused, fucking terrified. They begged me, the intensity of the stare, the sweat rolling down his forehead into the corners of his green orbs. The tiny red veins, bulging, bulging, crying for help.

He smells so good.

His hands and feet were tied, his mouth gagged with a pair of blue socks and some rope. The weak whimpers coming from him made him seem less human, and as the smell of his fear hit me, I leaned into the boot to chase more. To let it fill my whole body.

The fuck am I doing? He's a person.

"I'm going to get you out of here," I whispered, and peered around the boot to check on Tobias. Still sitting in the driver's seat, one elbow leaning against the window, holding the side of his head. "I don't know where we are, but when I get your feet free, run. You hear me? RUN."

The man's head jerked up and down in small bursts, his muffled whimpers resembling a "Thank you thank you thank you."

I worked on the knots at his feet—Tobias had tied them well and it was hard to see in the deepening shadow of the night. I kept working, ignoring the smell and my growing desire to taste him. I wasn't used to being in such close proximity to people, especially not at night in the middle of nowhere. Tobias's words kept echoing in my mind, how he'd told me I was special. We were the same.

I don't want to be the same. I don't want to do this.

The man was as patient as he could be, his body tense, his mouth trembling.

The knot started to loosen.

Thank god.

I could feel the rope unwinding as I pulled, and the man started shuffling his feet to help it along. The rope fell to the floor of the boot and the man kicked, kicked hard. He whacked me in the side of the head and I stumbled back, surprised, holding my cheekbone. A flicker of rage rippled through me and I fought the urge to tackle him to the ground.

"Run, for fuck's sake," I said through a grimace, and pointed somewhere in the distance. "Get the fuck out of here!"

He launched himself out of the boot, hit the ground hard, and got to his feet.

"Before he sees you!" I whispered.

He ran.

I watched him get smaller and smaller in the distance, consumed by shadows.

Thank god.

Peering around the construction site, I considered my own options. Tobias couldn't be trusted, and I needed to get to a police station. Thinking it over, I started in the direction the man had run, but stopped at a hand grabbing my arm.

"Block your ears," Tobias said.

Just as I glanced at him, saw his arm raise, a

loud bang rang through me. My ears throbbed with a high-pitched ring and I brought my hands up. Another bang and I saw what he was aiming at.

"No!" I cried.

Yes.

The thought came like a bullet, just as Tobias shot a third time and the man went down with a dull thump in the dirt.

"What did you do?" I screamed at him, my words muffled by the high-pitched ringing in my ears.

Tobias lowered the gun, pulled at my arm, and dragged me through the dirt until we stood by the man's writhing body.

"Oh, fuck, Tobias, what the fuck?"

He kneeled. "Can you smell it?"

I can. Oh fuck, I can.

The musk ebbing from the bullet hole, a vapour. *His* vapour. His life eking out in a trail of smoke, the blood soaking into his suit jacket.

Tobias studied my face, the micro-expressions indicating how fucking turned on I was. "Ah, you do smell it. I knew you would. The thing is, Phil… Well, what we have here is an opportunity. The guy is just about dead, what do you want to do?"

I stared at him, fighting off tears, fighting the urge to scream and tell him he was a fucking psycho and to run the hell away. He was right, though. The guy had already been shot, was already on his way out. We were kilometres from a hospital. There was nothing to be done about it.

Nothing, except…

"I did this for you," Tobias said, his eyes sparkling under the moon. Something in those sky blues called to me. Like they mirrored my own except that he was proud of his urges rather than scared.

"I can't…" I said, but the words were just for the sake of it. I understood what I wanted, and so did Tobias.

"We'll do it together." He encouraged me to kneel next to him.

My hands trembled, my breath was stuck inside my body, and my tongue rolled along my teeth almost of its own volition. The urge was real now, not just something I fantasised. The guy in front of me, his life ebbing away, was like…

A deer in the headlights.

A deer. That's all. Just a deer. People ate deer all the time without even thinking about it.

Tobias stripped the man down, shuffling the jack off first, then turning the man to his back. Ripped the shirt open, buttons flinging into the dirt around me.

His exposed flesh drew me in. The belly button, round and shallow, the entry point. I wanted to taste him. To lick the sweat from his body, to feel the scrape of skin against tongue.

"How do we…" I said, short of breath and licking my lips.

"I'll show you," Tobias replied, and positioned himself so his mouth was over the man's neck. "I start here and work my way down."

His teeth sunk into the man's neck, blood spurting from the veins and pooling in the dirt. The way Tobias acted—how he lurched forward to catch the spillage, lapping it up like water from a tap, and then tore the thin skin of the neck away with rabid teeth—excited me, terrified me.

I can't do this.

But my body was already moving, my nose caressing the tender flesh of the man's belly. The closer I got, the more I smelled his insides. Like buried treasure. I heard the chewing and moaning of Tobias at the neckline and I wanted my own section to try. Even though my thoughts screamed at me to go home, to get away and never even think about doing this again, I bit down into the belly.

It was surprising how easy the skin came apart. Trying to take a chunk at a time wasn't going to work, but when I tried smaller bites to break the skin, to burrow into the fleshy meat beneath, it was like tenderised lamb. It came straight out.

My cock grew hard and I didn't stop to think about why. Didn't care. My hands, my whole body was tingling, the tip of my dick was wet, and the blood and flesh in my mouth were like coming home. Coming to a place I had yearned for so long and had finally made it.

Heaven.

As I dug deeper, separating skin and flesh and ripping out muscles, the smell of the organs grew stronger. They each had a different scent; the kidneys—I don't know how I knew it was the kidneys—were a rich aroma, as though the organs had been marinating in calcium and potassium and whatever else. The liver and the pancreas also differed from each other, and I grabbed at something, pulled it free with a juicy, succulent *snap*, and brought it to my lips.

I moaned hard as I bit into it, the grainy texture of the kidney like a thick crumbed kiev, the liquid middle seeping out as a blob of goo. I swallowed down the first bite, feeling the electric itch in my groin as my cock leaked with excitement. I took another bite, forgetting Tobias was there at all, and then another.

The body was naked and empty by the time we'd finished, Tobias having wrestled his clothes off—thrown to the construction site—and feasted on the arms, legs, and picked his teeth with torn-off parts of the spine. My stomach was full, my hands and neck and arms covered in blood and muck and strips of flesh and bone. The man was a shell, devoured in the dark with nothing left to show for his existence.

I needed more. I *wanted* more. The smells were gone, though, and I was left feeling empty, hollowed out like the corpse in front of me. As the excitement wavered and waned, Tobias reached across the body, grabbed the back of my head, and kissed me.

He tasted like death.

I kissed him back, not knowing why or even realising he was another man in that moment. I just kissed, tasted, searched his mouth for the flavours I might have missed out on. He was on top of me, his hand thrust down my pants, working at the zipper, a new scent filling the air.

In the moment, it wasn't about sex. It wasn't about getting off. It was far more primal than that. The urge to devour was so deep inside us and the meal wasn't enough. His tongue found its way to my groin, tasting me; it was nothing more than the final vestiges of our need to feed.

So I let him do what he needed to do, and I did the same.

Lying naked next to each other in the dirt, resting our heads on the carcass and staring into the night sky, I beamed with a happiness I'd never had before.

"How was that?" Tobias asked, rolling to his side and gazing at me.

For a moment I was speechless. I needed to digest what I'd done, process a range of conflicting emotions and thoughts and feelings. There were no words to describe the ecstasy of eating another human being.

"I know," Tobias said, sensing my thoughts. "It's impossible to describe. That's why I brought you here. So you could experience it for yourself."

I rolled to my side, met his eyes, and they twinkled. "Thank you."

We stayed like that for a while, until the night was so deep we couldn't see much of anything, and Tobias buried the bones in some dirt where a house was due to be built. Before he'd taken the clothes to dump along with the bones, I searched the pockets. Took the guy's wallet.

Damien Smith.

Having a name changed things somehow, and despite the joy of eating every inch of him, I felt sick. Holding a hand to my stomach, where Damien Smith would live until I shit him into a toilet bowl, I realised what I had done.

Damien Smith.

I had his address too, right there on his driver's licence.

Tobias came back, easing into his clothes and throwing mine at me. We drove back to his place, where I could clean up and wash Damien Smith's bodily juices down the drain. I picked out some of his pubic hair and chest hair from my teeth, and watched that sink away, too.

What have I done?

When I'd finished washing and joined Tobias in his living room, rubbing a wet towel against my hair, he was sipping at a steaming coffee. A second mug sat on the table waiting for me.

"It always helps bring me back to 'normal,'" he said, emphasising the word *normal*.

"I can't do that again," I said. "We killed a human being."

Tobias sipped once more. "You will. Many, many times."

"No, I—"

"You will, Phil. You absolutely will. Trust me. There's no going back now."

"I can't go around killing people." I approached him, cautious and a little unsteady, my head reeling from the ecstasy and the orgasms and the sheer knowledge that I'd ripped a man apart. I sipped the coffee, letting the liquid warm me.

Tobias sighed. "I only take people who won't be missed."

"Damien Smith won't be missed?"

"No," he said. "And you shouldn't have looked at his ID."

I frowned and took another sip of coffee. He was right, it was bringing me back to 'normal'.

"Don't worry, Phil. I'll take care of you," Tobias said. "We're going to have so much fun together."

As my stomach rumbled, I knew he was right.

10

PHIL

I probably shouldn't have told him *everything*, but I was in trouble. The only way out of this was to get my son's help, even if it meant exposing the deepest secret of my life. It was happening again, the urges, and they weren't coming from me this time. It was those fucking teeth.

"You have to tell me where you got the dentures from," I begged.

Mike stared, jaw dropped at what I'd told him. He blinked a few times, stood across the room, and gazed out the window. Into the real world, where cannibals didn't exist, where his father hadn't eaten an actual human being.

"You're telling me that you're a…a…"

"I *was*," I said. "A long time ago. And I'm deeply ashamed."

99

Mike scoffed, his head shaking non-stop. "This is–I–I don't understand."

"I never killed anyone, Mike, I want to make that really clear."

"What about the chef…"

"That's different," I said. "It's these"—I pulled at the dentures, the black veins covering my gums now—"fucking teeth. Look at what they're doing to me."

My son was smart, he was observant. He'd seen the changes in me. And I needed him to understand that this wasn't just an old man searching for attention, it wasn't me losing my marbles.

Mike came over, and I lifted my top lip so he could see. He stepped back at the sight of the black veins, thick and viscous, pumping into me. "What the hell is that?"

Shrugging, I dropped my lip. "I don't know. I tried to take them out, but they won't budge. It's like…they're a part of me now."

"I have to go," he said, throwing his hands in the air. "I'll go find out about these dentures. You stay here, and for Christ's sake, try not to eat anyone." He stormed out before I could say anything.

11

MIKE

Dad had gone insane, that's all there was to it. Cannibalism, having weird animalistic sex with some random dude in the dirt. There was no way. I remembered all those times Dad had grimaced at gay people on TV, how he'd been working at the first Mardi Gras, bashing gays because that's what happened in the 1980s. Now he was telling me he was the world's longest closet case.

And a cannibal. That's what matters here.

I stormed off after his story, ignoring his pleas for help. He had killed the chef, the cops were all over his back, and now he wanted me to get him out of it? How was that even possible? At the same time, I did want to help him. His voice, his expression, the glow of his eyes when he'd told me that story… He was serious about all of it.

Any normal person wouldn't believe a word of it, but the last few days—especially since I gave him those stupid dentures—had been so strange. The death of the chef, Dad cleaning up the scene, his anger and the raw meat. All of it. I didn't want to believe him, even if I could tell he believed it, but something told me it was true. A deeper memory, buried somewhere in the cold corners of my brain, was slowly coming to life. It was a whisper at the moment, but it was enough to tell me to believe him.

The black veins in his gums, too. They didn't look right. I'd seen them pulsing, like they were pumping something into my dad. It was a surprise when he'd shown them to me, a surprise he'd told me anything at all. In all my life, he had never been so honest with me, I couldn't turn my back on him now. It was like seeing him for the first time, and even though it scared the shit out of me, it was also a relief. Maybe he'd stop hiding things, now that the worst was out of the way. Maybe we could have an actual relationship.

So I would help him, in any way I could.

Even if that meant going back to the address of the garage sale and finding the old woman. She'd said something at the time that I'd ignored, about a murder-suicide. Maybe she suspected something. In any case, that's where the dentures came from, so that's where the answers would be.

Pulling up to the house, the front yard was

empty now, cleared of all the junk. The grass had brown patches where the tables had been, and the little girl and her lemonade stand were thankfully gone. I got out of the car, sussing out the house. I hadn't really paid any attention to it earlier, I'd just wanted to take my mind off things. Now, as I walked up the concrete path in the middle of the front lawn, I took in the two-storey Federation-style home, the white façade stained with time and neglect. The windows had grime growing from the corners and there were dull green vines crawling up from the garden, as though the earth was trying to swallow it.

I jogged up the four steps at the entryway and hovered for a second before knocking on the front door. I had no idea what to say, how to approach it.

Hey, so I bought teeth here the other day…

Not sure if you remember me, but you sold me some used dentures and my dad thinks they're cursed or something…

The same old lady from the garage sale answered the door. She stared at me, sleepy, suspicious.

"Hi, um, I'm not… I don't know if you remember me?"

She shrugged. "I ain't buying nothing." Went to close the door.

I smacked a hand against the wood and laughed. "Sorry," I said, realising I seemed a bit eccentric. Maybe even threatening. "I bought something at the garage sale the other day."

"No refunds," she said, and tried closing the

door on me. I pressed hard against it, surprised at her strength.

"I'm really sorry,"—I removed my hand and stepped back a little, deciding to change tact—"I just have a few questions about your husband. You said it was a murder-suicide? I'm so sorry for your loss… Can you tell me what happened?"

She relented a little, and sadness filled her expression. "Gary was a wonderful man."

"I'd like to hear about him."

Stepping aside, the woman bowed her head. "Won't you come in?"

Got ya! "Thank you," I said, "I'd love to."

She invited me in with a pointy finger, directed at the lounge room just off the main hallway. I obliged and took a seat at the Chesterfield lounge. Some dust rose from the cushion at my weight, and my nose tickled.

"Tea, luv?" the woman asked from the entranceway.

Tea and biscuits were the easiest way to have a conversation with a stranger. Once both people had settled in with a hot cuppa and some Scotch Fingers, the words seemed to just flow. Just what I needed.

"That would be lovely, thank you so much," I said.

While I waited, listening to her potter around the kitchen in the next room, I checked my phone. A few texts from Kyle. I had been hard on him earlier. Since hearing about my dad's foray into cannibalism, Kyle's being upset somehow seemed very appropriate. Dad had bitten a nurse right in front of him, I'd have been scared, too.

The nurse… I hadn't seen her there, and hadn't received a call from the home about that yet. I didn't think anyone had seen me going inside, I was invisible. Even so, someone should have spoken to me about Dad's episode and his violence.

Maybe they went straight to the police. Regardless, someone should have called.

Too many things weren't adding up, like why Kyle went to visit my dad in the first place. He should have known I wasn't ready for that. Wasn't ready for Kyle to see my dad like that, so frail and homophobic.

Except he fucked a man back in the '60s.

My head started reeling and I pocketed my phone—I'd reply to Kyle later. The kettle boiled in the other room, The old woman clattered around with some plates. The crackle of plastic wrapping. I wasn't sure I could eat anything after hearing about my dad ripping out someone's kidney.

I almost vomited, but managed to keep it down, and focused on my surroundings.

The room was quite dull, dusty, unkept. The usual furniture one would expect in a living room, minus a TV. A single painting hung on the wall, a portrait of a man in a tuxedo and a tall top hat, holding a cane. He was thin, gaunt in the cheeks, with thin lips around pearly white teeth.

Fucking teeth.

A bronzed nameplate sat at the bottom of the painting, reading 'Sir Brentwood, 1824'. I'd never heard of him, though I wasn't a history buff. Or any kind of buff, really.

Standing up, I moved closer to the painting, studied the staunch frame of the man. His thin fingers wrapped around the cane's handle were long and slender, almost ending in sharp points.

The woman returned, carrying two cups and saucers of tea, Scotch Fingers resting precariously on the edges of the saucers. The ceramic shook in her hands, the tea sloshing back and forth near the rim of the cups, and I rushed to take one of the hot drinks from her. She smiled at me in appreciation and sat down.

"You said you wanted to know about my husband?" she asked, and picked up a Scotch Finger.

I nodded, sitting, and blew on my tea to cool it down. "There were so many interesting things at the garage sale," I said. "It gave me the great sense that he lived quite an adventurous life."

She struggled with the Scotch Finger, chewing on the biscuit like it was made of iron. The biscuit squelched against her wet lips and gums and tongue as the sweet, buttery thing rolled around her mouth. She seemed to be considering my comment, and dipped her biscuit into the tea to soften it.

"My dad is using the dentures," I said.

She swallowed down a mouthful of Scotch Finger. "You don't care about my husband at all, do you?"

I looked away and then back to her, sighing. "I'm sorry. It's just that—"

"He was a brave man," she said. "My Gary."

More silence. I blew on my tea.

"He was a fireman for fifty years. Saved a lot of lives." Through a mouthful of Scotch Finger, she continued. "I can't understand why he did it."

"What did he do, exactly?"

Taking a long, sad breath, she set her tea down on the coffee table. "He…ate…the mailman. Then killed himself." She stared at me, gauged my reaction. "Threw himself in front of a truck."

He was also a cannibal?

"The funny thing was, Gary had been a vegetarian for years. Now that I think about it, he only started eating meat again once he got his dentures."

"Where did he get them from?" I asked, leaning forward.

She considered me, creased her brow. "You know… I'm not sure."

"A local dentist, maybe?"

Shaking her head, she motioned towards the staircase, to the second floor. "He just sort of…had them one day." Another sip. "He was rummaging around in the attic. I remember because I was worried he'd hurt himself, being on the later side of seventy and all."

"Of course," I said.

"And he came down with these teeth."

"You just let him put them in?" I asked. "Is that sanitary?"

She shrugged and sniffed.

"After he put them in, did he start acting strange?" I asked.

She shot me a cold stare. "Yes. He ate the fucking mailman."

"I'm sorry," I said, leaning back on the lounge. "I didn't mean to offend you." I avoided her gaze, instead lingering on the painting behind her. Sir Brentwood.

"Why are you so interested, anyway?" she asked, repeatedly dabbing at her tears. "Why are you here, drinking my tea and asking about dentures?"

Standing, I mumbled an apology, and moved to leave. "I'm so sorry I bothered you. I really am. I'm sorry about your husband." She watched me stumble around furniture, dipping her biscuit a few more times before deciding it was wet enough, and I stopped at the doorway. "Can I ask, sorry, just one more thing? The man in that painting… Who is he?"

"My husband's great-grandfather. They were almost identical."

"Thanks," I said, and moved to the front door.

She hadn't told me much, but my gut told me that she'd given me exactly what I needed to know. Little granules of information, like Scotch Finger sinking into the tea, swirling around my brain just waiting to form something solid.

He already had the dentures. Up in the attic. In storage.

That piece of information stuck at the forefront of my thoughts during the drive back to work.

Why would he already have had them? Where did they come from?

They might have been a family heirloom. There was a long line of Brentwood's in Sydney, stretching back to the 1800s, but dentures weren't exactly a hand-me-down. Unless you were a cheapskate like me, and bought them at a fucking garage sale.

As I parked the car at work, daring myself to endure Trish and Zac and whoever else was in there, I decided to sit for a moment, and called Dad.

The phone rang out, and my heart stopped.

What if he's done it again? What if he's eating—

I tried one more time and he picked up on the first ring.

"Dad, thank god," I said. "When you didn't answer I got worried."

It took a second for him to reply and I almost asked if he could hear me. "I'm okay…for now. Did you find out anything?"

"Not yet," I replied. "But I'm working on something. Hey, maybe ask the nurses for some sleeping pills tonight? That way if you have another…episode…you might be asleep for it?"

He agreed, but his voice was low and soft. A mutter that faded into nothingness.

"I…"—I wanted to tell him I loved him, but choked on the words. It was such a hard thing to say to him—"I'll check in later, okay?"

"Okay, son," he said, sounding fragile.

The rest of the day was a blur, going through spreadsheets and attending meetings and dodging Trish by hanging out at Dave's desk. We'd agreed to do lunch the next day and he'd pinched himself—not even figuratively—to make sure it wasn't a prank. I wasn't sure I'd ever treated him less than human, but I couldn't be sure I hadn't, either. That was a problem I was going to fix. I squeezed his shoulder as I left his cubicle, and he gave me an expression of pure joy.

The difference one action can make, I thought.

By the time 5 pm came, I was tired and cranky and still mentally stuck at that old woman's house. Even during the drive home, weaving through traffic, I couldn't stop thinking about the fact that Gary—her dead, cannibalistic husband—already had the dentures somewhere in his attic.

Gary wasn't the start of this, and it had been foolish of me to think he might have been. Something much deeper was at play here, and I had no idea how to find out what it was.

I was so deep in my thoughts that I almost rear-ended a blue Volkswagen, and swerved into another lane. I ignored the guy giving me the finger as I overtook him, and sped the rest of the way home. Mobile speed cameras and police be damned.

In the garage, I watched the automatic door slide down and descend me into darkness. I turned the engine off and sat in the car for a moment, thoughts still churning in my grey matter. Pulling out my phone, I googled Sir Brentwood. He was some millionaire from the 1820s, owned half of the businesses in Sydney. The records themselves were a little dodgy, some articles saying he was a philanthropist, others saying he was a greedy despot. I found one article from *The Sydney Herald* about a policeman going missing in 1831 only to turn up dead, with Brentwood suspected of foul play. It was a scanned copy of a real article, so it was grainy and hard to read. From what I could tell, it seemed Brentwood was found at the scene.

What's that word?

The word was smudged. I decoded it one letter at a time.

Crying.

He was found at the scene, crying. The

journalist had written that "Sir Brentwood was inconsolable at the scene, crying and shouting incomprehensible words, even as the police carted him away. The blood on his clothes and hands appear to have come from the victim, 23-year-old Constable Parkes."

Brentwood was never formally charged, and returned to his status as Sydney's greatest philanthropist only a few short weeks later when the next article appeared. I scrolled through article after article, even as Kyle stood at the internal garage door asking me if I was okay.

I gestured at him, waved him away with a "I'll be there in a second," and kept searching. I was on the verge of something, I was sure of it. Somehow, all of this connected back to Brentwood.

Finally, I rested on a photo of Brentwood. He had the same stance as in the portrait—straight back, and cold, powerful eyes, his cane with a wolf head this time. There were photos of him everywhere, always alone, and always in that same suit and top hat. He had a bit of scruff at his chin, wisps of hair around his jawline, but never a full beard.

"Babe, what are you doing?" Kyle asked, still standing at the door. His expression held such pain, such concern, and it was for me. He'd had time to think about things, and he always ended up on the side of empathy. It wasn't about him, he would understand that now.

Realising how odd it was to sit in the car with the engine off in a dark garage, I unfastened my belt and opened the door. Kyle rushed to me and I hugged him tight, letting his warm breath and body give me strength. The stress of the day began to melt away, and my body relaxed.

"I'm sorry about everything," Kyle whispered into my chest.

"Me too," I replied, and kissed his forehead. "I love you, Kyle."

He glanced up at me and I kissed his thick lips. He kissed me back with so much passion I could taste the love oozing out of him.

I pulled away, took a breath. "I'm sorry I didn't introduce you to Dad. It's just so hard for me. Dad and I have never been close, I barely know him. I never meant to upset you, it was more about my issues with Dad than anything to do with you. You understand that, right?"

Kyle frowned. "I know, and I shouldn't have gone there. I don't know why I did it."

"Never mind that now," I said. "Come on, let's go inside."

We retreated to the living room, and Kyle passed me a plate of food. He'd spent the day cooking—his love language, I was learning. He was quite talented in the kitchen, mixing things around until they tasted good. I was more of a takeout kind of guy, hence the ever-growing belly that he liked so much.

Chewing on chicken breast marinated in a lemon butter, and roasted vegetables with the aromatic scents of herbs and spices, I thought about Dad biting the nurse.

Dad eating the chef, pulling at her skin, tearing her veins and nerves with his teeth.

Dad licking at the blood on the kitchen floor.

Dad gripping a kidney and biting at the crunchy organ.

Dad fucking another man on top of a corpse.

"This is delicious, Kyle," I said, setting my food on the coffee table after a few bites. "I just can't eat right now."

He was captivated by *Home and Away* again, but peered at me, melancholic. "I understand," he said. "Just save it for later if you feel up to eating then. Can I do anything for you?"

This is why I love you. I shook my head and invited him to cuddle me.

Kyle shifted into his usual position with his legs across my lap. I stretched my arms across his body, feeling up towards his midsection and his tight butt. He let out a soft "Mmmmm" and held my hand for a moment before returning his attention to the TV.

I took out my phone. Safari opened up and I was met with Brentwood's face. I tapped the photo and Google gave me more images of Brentwood. The date ranges for the photos seemed to stretch a lengthy span of time, but I was more interested in the images themselves.

In every single one of them, he was flashing the same grin, wide eyes sparkling. His stare was commanding and cold, like he wanted the viewer to die for him, to do anything he demanded.

It wasn't his eyes I was seeing, though.

It was his thin lips, curved upwards like a serpent tail. Behind his smile, I saw what I'd seen at the old woman's house.

What had bothered me at the time, though I didn't realise it. Staring right at me, in every single photo of the man.

His teeth.

12

PHIL

Earlier That Day

The nurses didn't know what to do with me. Their shadows stretched and twisted by the doorway in the hall, followed by their muffled whispers filtering into my room. The one I'd bitten, she was there, peering over the threshold. I'd mostly gotten a mouthful of fabric, but there was blood at the end of my teeth and my jaw was trembling like a junkie on crack.

It had been years since I'd given in to the hunger, years since I'd actually felt it. It had to be those dentures, and their goddamned black veins forcing something into me like a fucked up IV line.

"I don't know," the nurse whispered to the second shadow, just out of my line of sight. "Should we call the cops or something?"

"I mean, liiike, he is a suspeeect, right? Like, with the chef and all?"

Taylah.

"He's just an old man," the other nurse said. "He's normally okay, I just think maybe he had some kind of seizure?"

"No waaay," Taylah said. I heard the *tsk tsk tsk* rolling around her tongue, too. "I saw him, he was, like, totally raging. An animal. He, like, assaulted you."

Where are you, Mike?

He'd know what to do, he always did. I remembered when I was younger, his age. I was so weak, fighting with my ex-wife, getting thrown out of the house. Poor Mike, he hadn't a clue what was going on—Darla and I agreed to tell him I was a problem gambler. In a way, I was. I was gambling with my life, with other people's lives.

Don't get sucked into the past.

Anxiety poured through me as I heard words like *crazy*, *violent*, and my foot tapped at the bed frame.

Wait.

I peeked down. My foot was tapping. My foot was *moving*. I hadn't had feeling in my feet for years, not since the major stroke. Then there was the chef and the short-lived sensation down there. Now, there it was, tap tap tapping away with anxiety and nervousness.

Smiling, I almost laughed with excitement. The

nerves in my legs started pulsing, a spark of life in my dead limbs. Somewhere inside me I understood that the movement came from the teeth. It was my body, but it was also *theirs*.

I can do more for you...

The smile vanished and my ears perked up to the nurse saying, "I'm going to call them. It just doesn't feel right after what happened to the chef."

I was up. Out of bed. Before I realised I'd even moved. My feet were unsteady, toes gripping at the carpet. It was abrasive, like sandpaper, but it was beautiful. Glorious. My upper body swayed at being so high—I hadn't stood to my full height in so many years, I'd forgotten what it was like.

Wishing Mike was here to see this, I spun around, getting used to my newfound strength. My legs jerked a little, wobbled with the first step. I took another, heading towards the door, my gums aching.

My jaw grew heavy.

It was time. Either of them would be fine, so long as the dentures got what they needed. So long as nobody called the cops or reported what I'd done.

What you will do...

The voice came as a throb in my jaw, stinging at my teeth, their black veins wiggling through my chest like worms searching for healthy soil. Coiling and rolling and tasting the inside of my body, getting to know their new home.

I took another step, steadier this time, and noticed the shadows moving down the hall. My heart stopped for a moment at the thought of them heading to reception, picking up the phone, and calling Detective Brooks to tell her I had a taste for blood.

"Help," I called. "Help me." I moved to the ground, arranged myself as though I'd fallen from the bed. "Please... Help me!"

There was no nurse on the planet who would refuse an elderly man struggling on the floor.

She rushed in—not Taylah, the other one, the tasty one—and saw me clutching at my hip. She stepped towards me, hesitant, sizing me up. Watching me.

"Please..." I begged, and grimaced as best I could.

"What happened?" she asked, glancing between me and the door. Her hand rested on her midsection, right at the wound I'd given her.

"I... I fell. Where am I?" I said, scanning the area. "Help me..."

Her expression turned from suspicion to pity in a heartbeat. Eyebrows drew in, lips pouting a little in a *Oh you poor dear* kind of way.

Yes. Get her close...

I could smell her now. The cheap perfume disguising the sweet scent of her body. It wasn't the same as a man, never would be. If it were my choice,

I'd have let her go, waited for the guy on the next shift—Rob—who always smelled like gym towels and body spray.

This wasn't my choice, though. Even though I wasn't fighting it, even though part of me was enjoying it… It wasn't my choice.

"How did you fall?" the nurse asked, coming closer. Too close. Strands of hair fell around her face as she kneeled next to me. Reached her arms under my armpits to help lift me up. "I'm going to get you back to bed, okay?"

I nodded, breathing in hard through my nose.

Eat.

The word gave me pause. I wasn't fighting. Like I'd never fought when I was younger, when Mike was a kid. Like I didn't fight when I'd eaten that guy at the construction site all those years earlier.

Eat.

That's all I'd ever done. Eat. Feed my urges— food and otherwise. Maybe it was time to not give in for once. Maybe it was time to fight.

"Leave me be," I said to the nurse. "I… I can do it."

"Don't be silly, come on. One, two…" She tried to hoist me up, but I resisted, dead weight. The pain in her face as her wound stretched and tore was intense. "You've got to help me, Phil."

Eat.

My jaw started to tremble again.

Eat.

"Get away from me," I yelled, and pushed the nurse away.

She searched my eyes for logic. When she didn't find what she was looking for, she stood and sighed. "I'll have to get someone to help you."

She'll call them… She'll call the police…

"Wait," I said, holding a hand up and beckoning her back to me. "I'm sorry… can you please help me?" *What am I doing?*

You're saving yourself…

Giving a loud, deep sigh, the nurse approached me.

The teeth chattered, tasting her before she had even kneeled before me.

"You be gentle, okay? If you get rough, I'll have to call security or someone, okay?"

I agreed as she leaned in, the company lanyard dangling in front of me. Her neck right there. So close I could lick it.

And I did.

"What the fuck, Phil?" She slapped me hard and moved back. "Oh my god, I'm so sorry." Drawing her hands to her mouth, she shook her head, repeating the apology.

I wasn't listening. The droplet of sweat I'd tongued from her neck was salivating on the tip of my pink muscle. My tongue wasn't my own anymore, either, and as the nurse stepped away again, I knew she'd seen it. The black vein growing spreading across my taste buds like wire.

Eat her. Eat her. Eat her.

The voice was relentless, yelling at me, screaming for blood. Her blood.

She ran to the door.

I was up. Fast. She was halfway out of the room. I grabbed at the lanyard swinging behind her. It pulled at her neck and she made a brief choking sound. I yanked hard, pulled her to the ground. Dragging her back into the room, I swung my door shut.

"I'm so sorry," I said through clamouring teeth. "This isn't me."

"The fuck, Phil? What's gotten into you?" She struggled against my grip—so strong now, with the veins giving me power—and fought to get away from me.

Eat her.

Launching myself on top of her, my mouth stretching wider than I thought possible. The skin across her jugular tore. Her scream ebbed away into a gurgle.

I tasted the blood.

Yes, Phil. Eat.

She struggled for a few more seconds as blood continued to spill to the carpet. A second or so later, she was near catatonic.

"I'm sorry," I whispered, and caressed her pale cheeks. Combed some hair back behind her ear.

The thing was, I wasn't really sorry. If I had been sorry, I wouldn't have done it in the first place. The teeth—the dentures—had seen something in me that I'd buried a long time ago. They'd awoken the desire, the desire for human flesh that Tobias had seen in me.

The truth was, I was starving. Chicken, beef, even pork, none of it was enough.

None of it could replace human meat.

The teeth knew it. I knew it.

Now the nurse did too.

She stopped moving.

I was drenched in blood and guilt and my stomach was purring with anticipation. I licked at her neck. There was a healthiness to sweet blood, but the nurse's was sickly, thick with acetone and diabetes. Her organs wouldn't be as supple and juicy as others, they'd be dehydrated like jerky. The teeth didn't care, though. They were starved, and my stomach purred.

Tearing her clothes off, I started at her belly, the way I had with Tobias that first time. It was a ritual now, one not performed for a long time. I'd dig past the layers of muscle and fumble around until I could pull out the intestines as spools of thick spaghetti.

As my hands burrowed into the nurse, the end of her lower intestines between my teeth like a dog's chew toy, I heard the creak of my door, and spun around.

"What the fuuuuuck?" Taylah's jaw dropped and she spewed a line of green puke to the floor.

Get her!

My legs, like springs now, raced across the room before Taylah had a chance to bolt. I grabbed her by the hair, saw a flicker of Mrs Denton, the Peeping Tom, through a crack in her door, and shoved Taylah back into my room.

Just the slightest presence of blood and guts in my system, my body was on fire. Alive. More alive than I'd ever been. The chef had been the start of something incredible, awakening the power of the dentures. Now, it was time to find out how far that power went.

I threw Taylah across the room and she crashed headfirst into my wardrobe. The dull thud was followed by a sharp cry, and the young woman spun fast. Fists up, she blew hair from her face and narrowed her gaze.

"Come get meee, you prick," she sneered.

She was going to taste good.

Taylah was on her toes now, bouncing around like a kangaroo, throwing air punches at me while I stood by the door sizing her up.

"Come on," she said, "I've studied Kraaav Magaaa. So come on, try me, ya fuckwit."

Moving towards her, she anticipated by steps, came in close. She swung a punch. I tried to dodge, but she connected with my ribs and I doubled over. My body might have been healing and growing stronger, but a gut punch was still a gut punch.

Good, I thought. *Hit me as much as you can. Stop me.*

"Ha!" Taylah celebrated.

Still doubled over, I lunged at her, taking her by surprise, and tackled her to the floor. I ignored the "Fuck you, cunt" as she went down, and scrambled to grab her wrists—those punches were deadly. She kneed me in the spine and managed to get one leg around the front of my torso. In one swift motion, she took me down, and my cheek scraped against the carpet.

Yes, Taylah. Stop me!

Taylah was on top of me now, her fists pummelling my nose and mouth and cheeks. Between punches, she was smirking, like this was the best day she'd had in ages. I lost count at six punches, bruises already forming under my skin.

It's for the best, I thought. In that moment, I meant it. If Taylah beat me to a pulp, I couldn't hurt anyone else. Even if the urge to suck down those intestines and chew on a cervix for hours was making my eyeballs tingle. My face was ravaged, blood pulsing from cuts and split lips, but I still wanted to eat.

Eat.

The teeth were ordering me again, and as Taylah punched one more time, my mouth opened. When teeth would normally shatter, mine did not. Taylah's fist landed between my upper and lower teeth, and I clamped down hard, tearing at skin and knuckles and veins. The little hairs on the back of her hand came off as she removed her fist from the death-trap of my mouth.

She tried with the other fist, aiming for my nose, but I grabbed her by the chin and thrust her back. We both scrambled to our feet, and she was up before me—my body wasn't as young as hers— heading for the door.

Grabbing her, she elbowed me in the nose, a squirt of red flinging through the air. My head went back, and as I brought it back up, she held a lamp in her hand.

"No, wait," I said, but it was too late. She smashed it against my head, and I fell to the floor.

"I'm going to tellll everyone what youuu did!" Taylah shrieked and threw the door open, bolting into the hallway.

Lying there on the carpet, drenched in sweat and blood, I thought my life was over. Taylah would be at the phone now, alerting the authorities. Detective Brooks would show up, I was sure of it. Lock me up with murderers and rapists, throw away the key.

You can't do that…

"Fuck off," I said to the dentures, surprised I could still talk.

I need food…

Just like that, I was up, stumbling down the hallway, searching for Taylah. Mrs Denton's door was still ajar, but the old bitty was gone. It didn't matter, I just needed to find Taylah. I could smell her and her bloody fists, they weren't far.

The desk was vacant, but as I approached, I saw the phone was off the hook, the black cable coiling under the desk.

And whispers.

"Who are you calling?" I asked, coming around the desk.

Taylah was curled underneath, knees drawn to her chest, the phone held by her ear.

"Get awaaay from meee," Taylah sobbed.

The phone rang on the other end. She hadn't connected to anyone yet. It wasn't too late. I reached down, pried the phone from her hands—even as she kicked at me—and slammed it back in the cradle.

"That better not have been the police," I said.

Taylah shook her head, but she was lying. The phone rang at the desk, and a quick inspection of the digital display indicated 000.

"Wait here one sec." I picked up the phone. "Hello, this is Taylah."

"Uh, Taylah, is it? This is Constable Jameson from the Sydney Police. We just had a missed call and we're phoning back to make sure everything is okay. Do you need assistance?"

I sneered down at Taylah, balled up and crying. "Nooo," I said, doing my best impression, "it's allll gooood. I was, like, totally freaking out because one of our residents was like, you know, like choking on some soouuup. Sooo sorry."

The line was silent.

"Thanks so much, though," I continued.

"Sir… ma'am… if this is a prank, that's an offence—"

I slammed the phone down again and turned back to Taylah. "It's going to be easier if you just come with me."

She shook her head, wiped at tears. "Don't even fucking tryyy it!"

With a heavy sigh, I reached under the desk and yanked her out. She punched at me once more, but I didn't feel a thing.

"Oh, Taylah," I whispered. "You're going to make a fine meal." I slipped my hand under her chin once more.

Crack.

I swivelled her head fast to the right, and she fell limp. Krav Maga or not, a neck was a neck, and necks were easy to break. The security camera system ran from reception, which I thought odd, but took it as a blessing. I fumbled around with the computer for a bit until I found the 'Record' option and switched it off. The camera feeds went dead, just like Taylah.

Carrying her dead body back to my room, I was so excited I missed the shadow of Mrs Denton at her door. Something registered as a gentle click in my periphery, but I was too busy to care. I didn't notice Taylah's lanyard fall to the ground as I half-walked half-jogged away.

The dentures were hungry, and today was a two-for-one special.

. . .

I'd barricaded the door with my nightstand, on the off chance that someone else came by. I ate as quietly as I could, but my anxiety made the squelching of organs and bodily juices sound like an opera. Still, I ate, and the dentures clamped down on whatever I shovelled into my mouth.

As I picked off the last of Taylah's meat from the bones on her ankles and burped, I realised I had enjoyed every second of it. As always, I craved man meat, as dirty as that sounded. My third woman in two days, though, and I had enjoyed it. As much as I wanted to blame the dentures for everything, as much as I didn't want to admit that my addiction to cannibalism was reawakening, the truth was plain for all to see.

The nurses had seen it firsthand. The chef, too.

Even as the last of the cartilage and flesh was swollen down, I understood the teeth weren't satisfied. *I* wasn't satisfied. I'd learned from Tobias years earlier that our darkest urges were always just below the surface, and that the smallest push would set them free.

He was right.

Sitting in my room, I rested against the wall beneath a small window—blinds drawn, thank god—with a pile of bones on either side of me. On the left, the diabetic nurse, whose insides had been like having dessert before dinner—it was naughty and delicious and just a bit too sweet. Taylah, on my right, had been a fresh cut of meat. She was a healthy one, but not stringy or gamey the way kangaroo can be. She'd been just what the dentures needed.

I examined the wake of my desires, the walls and floors—even my bed—covered in human remains. On the far side of the room, a spleen I hadn't remembered throwing away. It would have been from the diabetic nurse, though, perhaps storing too many damaged red blood cells. Nobody wanted that, not even from animal meat.

The room needed a deep clean, but my belly was bloated and my energy depleted. Eating and ripping and gnawing was exhausting. It was like I had lockjaw, like I wouldn't be able to move it for weeks. Bringing a hand to my injuries, I winced at the bruises where Taylah had punched me. I felt the cuts getting smaller, my split lip stitching itself back together.

More…

The teeth were greedy, and as I managed to get off the floor, groaning with the pain in my bloated stomach, I knew I was too.

I couldn't stop now. I didn't want to. The same thing that had seen me lose my family, created an abyss of distance between me and my son, it had come back. And I loved it.

Wiping at my mouth and burping, I scrambled to figure out how I was going to hide this. From the staff. From the police, who were sure to send a patrol car after my stupid, stupid stunt earlier. From Mike.

Oh god, Mike, I thought. How could I face my son after what I'd done?

With the teeth silent for the time being, sated and sleeping, I had time to think about something other than food.

Humans, I reminded myself.

It was intense how easy it was to slip back to old habits. Thinking of people as sheep or livestock had been Tobias's way, and he'd taught me to think like that, too. It wasn't until Darla that I'd glimpsed humanity again, but that didn't last.

I collected bones and stuffed them under my bed. It was a rudimentary solution, unsustainable, but it would have to do for now. Until I could figure out my next move.

Halfway through my clean up, it occurred to me that my back wasn't sore. My hips weren't aching from overuse, my fingers weren't pruned and stained yellow with age. And I was strutting around as though I'd never lost the ability to begin with.

While having a renewed sense of youth, and physically de-ageing, filled me with a great sense of joy, I was also aware that my wrinkles were gone and I appeared to be around Mike's age.

I checked the clock on the nightstand. Mike would be finished with his dinner by now, probably lazing around with his boyfriend, Kyle. Just the thought of that kid made my stomach ache, and I groaned at the familiar itch in my groin. The same kind I'd given into with Tobias. It wasn't sexual, despite the many times we'd fucked. It was a primal instinct to breed after a hunt. Kyle felt that way. Like the hunter's prey. I thought about calling Mike, but my hand paused at the phone.

Mike never wanted to hear from me. He always thought I only wanted his money, and as my hand drew away from the phone, I wondered how much of that was true. We had nothing in common, not really. We didn't talk. He hated me for leaving him as a kid, and only bothered with me now out of pity.

Just as I decided to walk away from the phone, it rang.

"Hello?" My voice was a rasp, flecks of innards stuck to the back of my throat.

"Hey Dad." Mike sounded kind. I hadn't heard him like that in years. "I just wanted to check in."

I gulped back a tear and stuttered for a moment.

"You know, I was worried today. After everything you told me…" The words hung in the air between us, and I sensed his concern. He'd said he was worried countless times, but his voice always betrayed him—betrayed the fact that he was reciting social scripts and nothing more. This time, he meant it.

"You were?" I asked.

"Of course," he replied. "In fact, I want to see you, we have some things to discuss. Can I come around?"

I scanned the room, noting all the bloodstains and body parts I hadn't yet shoved under the bed. "It's not really… I mean… I…"

"You did it again, didn't you?" A heavy sigh. "I knew I shouldn't have left you."

"No, I just—"

"I'm coming over."

I wasn't going to win this one, and it wasn't like Mike couldn't push past my shitty attempt at a barricade. "Bring some gloves and bleach."

13

MIKE

I hadn't known what to expect when I arrived, not really. Images had surged through my mind: Dad gulping blood out of one of the nurses' necks, squeezing every last drop; Dad gorging on a plateful of livers and hearts. I'm imagined him glancing up at me as I entered the room, an awkward, shy smile on his lips like a kid caught breaking the rules.

The reality was so much worse.

I knocked on the door and waited. "It's me," I hissed. The enviro bag of cleaning supplies weighed down my left arm.

Dad was shuffling around inside, and I heard the sound of something heavy being dragged across carpet. He opened the door a few seconds later. I was right about one thing—his stupid, sheepish grin.

Everything else sent my head spinning and my gut retching.

"Hi," Dad said, and moved aside to let me in.

"You're walking now?" I asked. "How…"

"I don't know how it works, but I feel younger." Dad studied his body up and down, and then waved me in. "We don't want anyone else to see."

"Bit late for that," I said. "I'll be on the security cameras."

"I turned them off."

I moved and heard the squelch of wet carpet beneath my feet, and doubled over just as Dad shut the door. The stench of rot and guts and blood crashed into me and I gagged so hard I thought my own guts would land on the floor. It was like the smell had settled into my clothes, burrowing into my skin, and as I heaved again and again, whatever I'd eaten of Kyle's dinner slithered up my throat.

"Breathe, son." Dad patted my back and I shrugged him off me, shoved the bag of cleaning supplies at him.

Dad did appear younger by several years. He was about sixty now, instead of mid-eighties. And he was walking, *strutting* around his death camp before unpacking the cleaning supplies at the edge of the bed.

"Dad," I said through a heavy breath, "what the fuck have you done?"

He paused and looked at me, stretched his jaw. "You aren't going to tell on me, are you?"

"*Tell on you?*" I raised a hand to my mouth, breathed through the fabric. "This isn't grade school, Dad. There's no slap on the wrist for shit like this, it's life in prison."

Dad just stared at me with that familiar coldness I'd grown accustomed to as a kid.

"No, I'm not going to *tell on you.*"

"Good," he replied, "because I really need you, Mike."

He needs me.

Walking to his side, I did my best to ignore the carpet soaked in blood, and stumbled on something hard and sharp on the ground. I rolled my ankle and cursed. Bent down to pick it up.

"Is that a… Fuck, Dad, it's a—"

"Shhh." Dad held a finger to his lips. "I know this is a lot, but just keep it down, okay?"

I held someone's rib in my hand, and Dad just needed peace and quiet. Something in my memory stirred, but was thrust aside as Dad handed me some gloves and a scrubbing brush. He pointed to a bucket of soapy water, like it would solve all our problems.

Being no stranger to cleaning, I pretended the blood was something else—anything else. Red wine, I decided. Dad got down on his hands and knees and started scrubbing, the water and bubbles from the bucket scratching away at the death underneath.

Following suit, I kneeled next to the bed. As I started to scrub, a new smell hit me, buried underneath the soap and detergent.

"Oh, fuck," I mumbled, my eyes burning with anger and tears.

I was staring at bones.

A pile of human. Fucking. Bones.

"Oh yeah," Dad said, a little too casual for the context, "we'll need to find a way to get rid of those."

All I could do was nod sporadically, knowing if I even tried to speak that I'd end up howling and blubbering. I wanted to go back to the couch, I wanted Kyle's legs draped over me. I wanted to fall asleep to the TV, and then cuddle in the warmth of our bed. I wanted so many things in that moment, and the realisation struck me that all my wants and needs revolved around Kyle.

Staring at the pile of bones—strips of fabric and a lanyard tucked in there too—I somehow saw my future. Or, at least, what I wanted my future to be. It was all Kyle. He could be naïve and impulsive and jealous, but he was also kind and generous and funny and he made me happy.

I realised I'd been staring at the bones for a while, letting Dad do all the cleaning. He had moved to the other side of the room, scrubbing at walls and inspecting minute parts of the paint for remnants of blood.

It wasn't just blood, though. Blood I could handle. It was the other juices from the body that sent my stomach reeling every few seconds. And the bits of discarded skin and flesh, flecks of intestine that had been catapulted across the room as Dad tore away at it like a wild animal.

As I continued to clean, frequently refreshing the scrubber, I found myself adjusting. Despite myself, despite the fact that I was in the most disgusting situation of my life, I was adjusting. I let out a hollow laugh, mumbling to myself about how insane this wall was, when Dad stood and stretched.

"That'll just about do it. When you've finished that patch over there, we can get some garbage bags for the bones," he said, resting his gloved hands at his hips.

"Sure, Dad," I said, and kept scrubbing.

"Next time I'll do a Dexter." He laughed.

I studied him, confused.

"You know, lay down some plastic sheets and all that."

"Next time? You're going to keep doing this?"

Dad hung his head. "Mike… I don't think I have a choice."

"It's the dentures, isn't it?" I cursed under my

breath, knowing the blood of the chef and the two nurses were on my hands.

Nodding, Dad stepped towards me. The carpet was still wet, but the red stains had all but been scrubbed away. Sitting at the edge of the bed, Dad sighed. "It is, but it isn't."

"What does that mean?"

"You know I've done this before," he said. "A long time ago. The desire… It's always there. It's like an addiction. I think the teeth have awoken it in me."

I joined him on the bed, wiped at sweat on my forehead. "We have to get the teeth out of you."

Dad made a sound somewhere between a laugh and a choke. "Good luck. I already tried. They're attached to me."

"Come on," I said, standing and ripping my gloves off. "Let's try one more time."

He followed me to the bathroom, insisting it wouldn't work.

"Sit on the toilet," I instructed.

Lowering the lid, he sat on the toilet, and regarded me, expectant.

"Okay, I'm going to pull those fuckers out. Open up."

Bracing myself with one leg in front of the other, I reached into Dad's mouth, felt around the dentures to get a sense of them. To find something I could grip onto, pull at. They seemed like regular teeth, and the deeper I went, the less convinced I was that I could do this. His mouth was large, larger than it should be. His jaw stretched wider than I thought possible, so wide I could see just what I was looking at.

His throat was black.

The little dangly thing at the back of his mouth—the uvula—was black.

I examined more closely and realised the skin of his cheeks, his tongue, the dangly thing, were covered in hundreds of veins, throbbing and pumping and pulsing. They grew from the teeth themselves, from each individual tooth.

Something at the back of the teeth, near the last of the rear molars, stuck out. It looked like an extra tooth, jutting from the side in the wrong direction. It was sharp and pristine white. I couldn't be sure, but it appeared to be growing, or as though it was being pushed from his skin.

"D'ya sheee eny tiing?" Dad asked.

Shaking my head, I leaned in closer. Felt around at the veins, tried to grab one. It was thick and solid, but also fleshy. I thought I might be able to cut it.

"Do you have any scissors?" I asked. Dad pointed to a drawer in the bathroom vanity and I searched through until I found them. "This might hurt."

I brought the scissors in, angled them towards

a tooth on the side— one with the thinnest vein—and slid the blades underneath the vein.

"Ready?" I asked.

Dad mumbled something through his open jaw and I clamped down on the scissors' handle. The vein snapped, black goo spurting into Dad's mouth, flooding him as he screamed.

"Shit, Dad, what is it?"

He pushed me away, held the side of his face and screamed, snapping his jaw shut. His cheek went black under his fingers, like a deep bruise, and Dad fell to the floor. The black liquid oozed from his lips, gushing out as he spasmed. A few hairs fell to the floor, the skin on his hands and fingers lost some colour, grew more wrinkled.

"It's working, Dad!" I kneeled beside him, scissors in hand, and tried to open his mouth. "I have to keep going."

"No, no!" Dad fought against me, slapped me hard, but I forced my way through his waving arms until I was positioned on top of him. I grabbed his left arm, forced it under my leg at his side. Then his right. He squirmed and wriggled and begged, and when I moved the scissors to his mouth, he cursed and tried to push me away.

"I have to do this, Dad. You know I have to," I said, and pried his jaw open.

He snapped his teeth at me, growled like a

trapped beast, and he flashed that horrible scowl again. The one I had always told myself I'd imagined. Another memory stirred, but I was too busy with his jaw to pay attention to it.

Finally, his mouth was open, the scissors inside him once more. The black goo, like a thick oil, pooled at the back of his throat, and Dad groaned as he swallowed. Fear laced his expression now, and I ignored him, snapping the scissors wildly in his mouth.

"Pleeease," he begged. "It 'urts…"

"I have to!" I yelled at him, pulling his jaw apart with one hand and snapping scissors with the other.

The veins squirmed around in his mouth, trying to avoid the blades, but I managed to grab one. It was thick and hard, like it had been there for a while. It pulsed, sensing danger. I tightened the scissors around it. Dad's eyes squeezed shut, knowing I was trying to help but struggling against my weight on top of him.

I snapped the scissors handle hard.

The blade snapped in half, the shard of metal landing in Dad's mouth.

"Holy shit," I mumbled, wide-eyed.

Picking out the ruined scissor blade, I rested it on the tiled floor next to me, Dad still squirming. The black goo had begun to coagulate, sinking back into the dentures. His cheek, too, wasn't as bruised now. The goo was healing him. Restoring him.

Hurting the teeth was hurting Dad, but as I watched his youth return, his strength along with it, I couldn't let that happen. Grabbing the scissor blade, I pried open Dad's jaw once more. It took everything I had to pull his lower teeth down, as his strength returned in powerful surges.

"Let…me…do…this!"

I got his jaw down, his teeth clamouring, biting at me. Before I would pull my hand away, his teeth clamped down on my fingers, blood oozing as I cried for him to stop. He bit harder and I plunged the scissors into the gap left by my bleeding fingers.

Stabbing and stabbing at his teeth, at the veins, the blade hit something. Dad unlocked his jaw and screamed again. His mouth open now, I stabbed a few times at anything I could see. His tongue, his uvula—all of it—until his mouth was filled with black goo.

"Fuck. You!" I yelled, and I wasn't sure if I was talking to the teeth or to Dad.

As I stabbed, the skin around his mouth and eyes blackened and bruised. His hair started to wilt again, the skin drying out and thinning.

I'm killing him.

I stopped stabbing. My flurry of stabbing had exhausted me, my shoulders aching, my chest heavy. The teeth healed my dad, the veins repairing themselves, growing new branches to further their grip on my dad's body.

He lay on the tiles as the teeth restored him. All I could do was watch, scared and afraid that something like this could exist. He gurgled and spat like a drowning victim at the beach, and I turned his mouth to the side.

"Are you okay, Dad?"

He nodded through his coughing and spluttering, staring at me with wild eyes.

"I'm sorry, Dad," I said, and got off him.

"No," he replied, forward, his arms behind him, holding himself up. "You had to try."

"I can't get them out without killing you."

Dad gestured again, coughing the last of the black goo onto his fingers. We both watched as it sunk inside him, new veins growing under the skin there.

I kicked the scissors away and paced through the bathroom while Dad watched on—his strength was returning, but he was still too weak to use his legs.

"Mike, I'm sorry about all this."

I ignored him and kept pacing.

"Why are you helping me?" he asked.

"What do you mean?"

He shrugged and wiped away a stray tear. Just one. "We're not close, Mike. Let's not kid ourselves."

I sat on the toilet with a heavy sigh.

"I abandoned you as a kid after..." He paused

and looked away. "We've never really been close. But you're always here, every few days, visiting me. Taking care of me."

He seemed like he was on the verge of really losing it, something I wasn't sure was even possible.

"Even after all this"—he waved around, gesturing back to the bedroom, to the murder scene— "you're here helping me."

There was a long silence as the words echoed off the bathroom walls. I didn't know what to say. He was right. I was here and it was fucking insane, but he needed me. He needed help and I was the only one who could provide that for him. Part of me wanted to run—a very large part—but I sat there, no intention of actually moving at all.

Instead, my mind was ticking over, the gears turning. How to get rid of the bones. My first thought was to boil them down as a broth, soften them enough for Dad to eat. When I realised how crazy that was, even for the situation, I thought harder. Burying them seemed like a decent option, and it reminded me of his story from 1960, with Tobias.

"Mike?" Dad asked.

I stood and bit my lower lip. "Yeah, Dad?"

"Why *are* you helping me?"

I shrugged. "Because you're my dad."

The words hung in the air. I leaned against the bathroom wall, opposite the vanity mirror. I was dishevelled—exhaustion bags under my eyes, and dry, cracked lips—and my own skin was starting to crease in places that shouldn't. What Kyle saw in me, I'd never know.

"Dad, if we can't get the dentures out, and you have to keep doing…this…then we need to be much more coordinated."

"What are you saying?"

"I want to help you. I have a plan."

Dad started to move his legs now, and I helped him up. "A plan?"

I bobbed my head. "You can't just go around killing whoever you want. I don't care how the teeth work right now, if they force you into it or whatever. You need to take more control."

"I know, Mike, I'm so—"

"No more apologies, just do this right for me," I said, heading back into the bedroom. "You can't stay here anymore, unsupervised. You're coming home with me."

Dad scoffed. "I can't just leave. They'll notice."

"Yeah, they will also notice that you look more like my brother now, instead of my ailing father." I stared him down on that one, and Dad agreed. "Now," I continued, "if we are going to do this, I can help you. Pack some stuff, and let's go."

Dad grabbed the enviro bag of cleaning supplies and passed it to me. Then headed to his wardrobe and took out an old, dusty suitcase. Blowing the dust off the top, and wiping it down, he flipped it open on the bed and started throwing in clothes.

"I'll come back in the morning to get the bones, but for now, we're going home." I was invigorated, giving orders and seeing him obey without a word. Watching him pack, I kept talking. "We have to be careful about who you eat."

"What do you mean?"

"You've done this before, Dad," I said. "Surely you and Tobias had rules. Don't take anyone who will be missed, don't eat the neighbour, that sort of thing?"

He agreed. "That's true."

"So we'll do the same. No more eating from the nursing home. People are already suspicious of you, that detective is on the case and she'll no doubt be coming back. You can't be here when she does. We have to make up a list of people you can eat. A way to minimise the damage you do."

Dad closed his suitcase and held it firm in one hand. "Who do you suggest?"

We headed to the door, my thoughts in overdrive.

"No kids, that's for sure. No famous people, nobody you know." I thought some more as we traipsed down the hallway to the exit—not too fast, not too slow. Casual, so nobody suspected foul play.

Neither of us saw Mrs Denton's door ajar, her watchful gaze following us as we went.

Neither of us saw Taylah's missing lanyard lying in the hall, pushed against the skirting board.

Neither of us saw the flecks of blood on the ceiling of Dad's room.

14

PHIL

Mike drove in silence most of the way, only muttering a few more bits and pieces of his still-forming plan. He was a smart kid, always had been. I just never realised how methodical he could be, especially about something like murder. Part of me was proud, like he'd inherited it from his old man. Another part was petrified.

He was talking about Kyle, how he didn't want to start any fights, and he didn't need me scaring the guy after what happened earlier. I agreed that I would do my best, and Mike eyed me sideways.

"Okay," I said, more forceful than I'd intended. "I will play nice with the kid."

"He's not a kid, Dad. He's in his twenties. He's an adult."

I choked back a laugh. "And you're in your forties."

Mike shot me a scowl. "*You* want to talk about moral grey zones? Really?" He shook his head. "We're consenting adults, and that's the main thing. I don't know why a gorgeous guy like him, with his whole life ahead of him, wants to be with me. I don't know what he sees in me—a chubby mid-forties man with high cholesterol and blood pressure. But he loves me."

"Mike, I—"

"And I *love* him." I let the words hang for a minute. "So when we arrive, just be nice. Apologise to him for earlier."

I bowed my head. "Okay, Mike. I will."

This side of him came out every now and then, but it had always felt forced and a little fake. Tonight, he meant it. He'd found some kind of strength inside himself, and it was busting at the seams. I peered out the window, watched the street lamps blur past as we headed to Mike's place.

"Dad?"

"Mm."

"You've always been a cannibal, haven't you?" His voice was hoarse now, the weight of his words crushing us both.

"I... Yes."

"How? How is that even possible?"

"I always felt different," I told him. "And not

the way you did when you were a kid. I guess it's similar, but I had this…desire. It was an urge. Neither of my parents had it, I was the only one. I don't know where it comes from."

"How come I don't have it?"

I shrugged. "Like I said, I don't know where it comes from. I just… It's hard to control it. Even back then. It took a long time to master it, rather than letting it master me."

The glow of the moon and the yellow blur of the lamplights cast a shadow over Mike. His eyes were red, welling up fast. He wanted to help me, wanted to do whatever needed to be done to save me from this.

You don't need saving.

The voice rattled in my head and I fought the urge to stretch my jaw again. Battled to avoid the chatter chatter chatter of the dentures.

"Tobias helped me a lot," I said, trying to silence the voice.

"He did?"

"More than anyone can possibly know." My words were low, mumbled, to save myself the energy I needed to revisit the memory.

. . .

1961

It was almost like a routine. Every few days, we met at the milk bar, had a warm cup of coffee, and then headed out.

To hunt.

Tobias had established the rules. He'd been living by them for some time, he'd said. I sometimes got the impression that he was older than he appeared—more worldly, at the very least. Once he'd talked about an old love, Elizabeth, who he'd helped with her urges.

"Bathed in blood," he'd said through a smirk. "Let the desire ebb away as the blood filled her pores. Does nothing for me, but it worked for her."

Elizabeth had passed years earlier, though he never said how. When he spoke of her, he always started with a wide grin and it would fade as the seconds went on. I could almost feel the pain in his expression as though it were my own, so I would change the subject. That's how I'd heard of the rules.

"The first rule is probably the most important," Tobias said. "Although, realistically, they are all *extremely* important to observe. Never, and I mean *never*, hunt someone you know. They are off limits. They can offer alibis, they can be of use to us."

"And we love them," I added.

Tobias eyed me with a smirk. "Sure, Philby, sure. We love everyone."

"I mean, family, friends. Even our co-workers. We have to love them, right, to keep the urge at bay?"

He narrowed his brow and thought about it. "If that helps you, then absolutely. Strangers are the key. Out of towners, people on vacation, foreigners… people that won't be easily missed."

I nodded, taking it in. The rule made sense.

"Rule two: never in public. Remember your first time? And all the times after? We always do it in the dark. We never risk being seen. Even when we hunt, you've noticed how we meet at the same spot, but then always take a different trajectory from there?"

I gave a quiet, "Yes."

"That's because it's harder for the cops to trace our movements. We can establish a pattern of behaviour that blends in with the rest of the population. We are two friends meeting for coffee. Witnesses can say they see us routinely, they can vouch for us without having to know us."

"Clever," I said, though I wondered about being seen at all.

"From there, we are invisible. Once we leave the bar, we are ghosts. Understand?"

"Understood."

He'd been teaching me the rules from the beginning, but hadn't ever verbalised them. I found myself going back in time, remembering each of our hunts, each of the animals—*People*, I thought—we killed and ate. He was right, we were always ghosts. We had established a presence in the community without really making ourselves known. We were two harmless men having coffee and then vanishing into the night.

"She's about to leave," Tobias said, watching a woman from his periphery. "She's the one."

"Why her?" I asked.

"Rule number one, nobody who will be missed. Check her fingers—no wedding band. She's single, at a milk bar at night, at night, *by herself.* Nobody's going to miss her." Tobias smirked, pushed his empty coffee mug away. "Now, we go before she does, that way nobody will say we followed her."

"Right," I said, and got to my feet.

As I pushed my chair back, the woman moved behind me, and I bumped into her. Tobias glanced up and flashed those perfect teeth.

"Sorry, ma'am." He tipped his top hat—a souvenir from some guy we'd devoured a few weeks earlier—and winked.

The woman apologised for not paying attention to where she was going, and I spun around, saying, "Oh no, it was absolutely my fault." I should have been thinking about witnesses, people saying we'd spoken, people remembering the awkward encounter. As I stared into her, though, all I saw were giant green irises staring back at me.

"I am always bumping into things," she said, and curled a finger through her hazelnut hair. It smelled of strawberries.

"I'm Phil." I didn't mean to, it just happened. My hand was in hers, my thumb caressing the back of her palm. My lips pressed against her soft fingers as I introduced myself.

"Darla," she replied. "You are such a gentleman, Phil."

"Oh yeah," Tobias added. "Phil here is a regular Marlon Brando."

Darla giggled and I found my urge to eat something fading. Her touch, her hair, her skin—they were what I desired now, but not in the usual way. I found myself lost in her presence, the way she spoke with such passion and sparked life into every word she uttered.

"Are you here alone, Darla?" Tobias asked from behind me, adjusting his top hat.

She tilted her head, barely hiding her suspicion of him. "I like to get some air at night. I know it's dangerous for a lady to be alone in the streets after sundown, but I find it helps my mind."

"We're just about to go for a stroll ourselves," Tobias said. "If you care to join us."

Gazing between me and Tobias, Darla agreed.

"Well let's go, then." Tobias grabbed his coat and patted me on the back, instructing me to do the same. "Darla, we have some really nice parts of town to show you. Isn't that right, Brando?"

I motioned and followed them out of the milk bar, unable to smell anything but strawberries.

. . .

We'd taken the tram from Central Station towards Circular Quay. The carriages were empty, save for some teens here and there, and couples out for date night. We headed towards the quay, Tobias and I keeping a few paces behind Darla.

"I don't think we should do this," I muttered to Tobias.

"I figured as much," Tobias replied, kicking at the tar beneath us like a spoiled child.

Smiling, I hurried up next to Darla, who was admiring the water—at night, the harbour resembled a beautiful sheet of glass, and I was convinced one hair on its surface would smash the whole thing. I was conscious of Tobias staring at the back of my head. Whether it was jealousy or rage, I couldn't be sure. Either way, we were in an open area with lots of passersby, and there were rules about that. As much as he wanted to devour Darla, now wasn't the right moment.

There would never be a right moment.

"It's beautiful, isn't it?" I said to Darla, and wrapped my arm through the crook of her elbow.

"It reminds me of glass," she replied, stepping closer to me so our arms were locked tight, "the water."

She's perfect.

We talked and laughed and it was so…ordinary.

I smelled her hair every now and then as an ocean breeze crept over us, and the scent of her hair filled me like it was all I could breathe with. It wasn't the best smell I'd ever encountered—I thought back to the men I'd eaten, the parts of them I'd torn apart with just my teeth—but it was still doing something to me. Desire, lust, all of it. I found myself knowing what she'd say before she'd said it, my palms sweaty and my mouth running dry. Her mere presence next to me, near me, around me, was changing me. It was hard to describe, impossible to know what was happening, but she had a presence about her. Mixed between the white glow of the full moon, the sheet of glass-water in the harbour, and the salty air of the ocean, was something I'd only ever felt with Tobias.

Looking over my shoulder, Tobias stared back at me. I smiled, and it was full of sadness, though I didn't know why. Tobias gave me a slight tilt of the head—his "We need to talk" movement—and I gestured my understanding.

"Darla," I said softly, "would you care terribly if my friend and I chatted in private?"

Darla looked back to Tobias, who gave a small wave, and she sat by the water on a wooden bench. Every movement she made was angelic, graceful, as though she commanded the entire universe.

"Stop staring," Tobias said, shaking me from my stupor.

"Sorry," I replied, and glowered at him.

His expression was cold, calculating, and I could almost see the gears spinning in his mind. It wasn't anger or jealousy. Sometimes I didn't know if he could feel at all. No, he was weighing options. For a second, I thought he was still planning out how to take Darla away, how to get her alone and vulnerable, tucked in a corner somewhere knowing she was about to die.

"You need to marry her," he said.

I laughed and gazed at him with a lazy smile. "What are you talking about?"

"She's the perfect cover," he told me, "and you obviously like her."

"Yeah, but—"

"Rule three. Hide in plain sight." There was a sadness to his words, and he brought his hand up to my upper arm, squeezed tight. "You and I are... We are so many things, Phil. We share something beyond what anyone else in this world can understand."

Darla watched us with, curious, and I wondered why she didn't leave. What kept her sitting on that bench?

"Hey, look at me." Tobias rested a finger under my chin and spun my head back to him. "Nothing can change what we have, but you need to find a life."

In that moment, I heard the words he wasn't speaking. *What we have.* He didn't mean the cannibalism. He didn't mean the animalistic sex, or the way we pined for each other during the hours we were apart. He meant something else.

He was in love with me.

"Go and have a good time with Darla," he said, his voice low, hoarse, choked.

Somehow, I didn't want to do that at all. I wanted to grab him right then and there, pull him close to me and bite his lips. I wanted to taste him and feel him and *know* him. Instead, I just stood there, watching him turn to leave.

"One more thing." He paused. "I think you should become a policeman."

I creased my forehead.

"Hide in plain sight. The police and journalists work together all the time." Tobias smirked, tipped his top hat, and sauntered away.

He is in love with me.

It was odd to think I was in love with another man. I'd never given that sort of thing much thought. As his figure faded into the night, my heart clenching in my chest, Darla came back to my side.

"He seems nice," she said.

"He is," I replied. "The nicest."

Darla gave a soft chuckle and leaned against me. "I don't know what it is about you," she said, "but I feel so safe. Is that strange?"

"Not at all." I wrapped my arms around her upper back. "I feel like I've known you a lifetime."

. . .

Now

Mike just drove and listened as I told the story. There wasn't much else to do. I stopped talking and we sat in silence for a while, listening to the hum of the engine until Mike switched on the radio. I peered over at him—his brooding eyes, downturned mouth—and let him be. It was a lot to process, the fact that I'd chosen my career because Tobias told me to. The fact that I'd chosen to be with his mother out of a sense of loyalty to a man. A man I was in love with, had *made* love to, no less.

Rule three. Hide in plain sight.

As jazz filtered from the car speakers into the silence between us, I began to think back on my life. The mistakes I'd made.

"Dad," Mike mumbled, "I think Tobias had the right idea."

"What do you mean?"

"About his rules. Were there more?"

"You're not angry at me?"

Mike choked back a hollow laugh. "I don't have time to be angry. This is getting worse, and we have to seriously come up with a plan before it's too late."

"Too late?"

He didn't respond to that one. Didn't need to. The dentures were quiet at the moment, having eaten two people in one day, but they would wake up at some point. It was just a matter of time. I could feel them pulsing in me, the veins working their way around my guts now. It was almost like they were mapping my body, building something inside me, taking me over to create something new. The worst part was, I didn't know if I was happy about that or not.

I just wanted to eat.

15

MIKE

Dad's stories were hard to listen to, but at the same time, they made him make more sense as a person. The man I thought I'd known for all these years, the man I'd grown to despise and think of as nothing more than a right-wing, homophobic bully, was not who I thought.

I'd seen footage of him at the first Gay and Lesbian Mardi Gras in 1978, spitting on people and beating them. That was real. That was *true*. And while it was sad and disgusting and deplorable, it also made sense. Rule three. Hide in plain sight. He'd devoted himself to Tobias's rules, and they'd had unforeseen consequences, made Dad act in fucked up ways.

Even as I thought about it, I shook my head for making excuses for him. His cannibalism was fucked up, yet that part of him was easier to accept than him beating up gay men at a pride parade. The stuff about how he met Mum didn't really surprise me at all. The fact that Tobias pushed Dad to be in a relationship with her only an hour or so after they'd met was a testament to how much he cared about my dad, how much Tobias wanted for him to have a normal life.

As pretend as it might have been, it had worked for a while.

We arrived back at my house, the lights off, the rest of the street dead.

Not actually dead. I laughed at the thought, despite myself.

Dad was quiet when we got inside, and it occurred to me he'd never been to my house. I'd never invited him and he'd never asked. So much wasted time, so much animosity, and for what?

"Do you want some dinner?" I asked, and then *tsked*. "Sorry, just a reflex."

Dad laughed and it was hearty and full and the joy washed over me, too. Despite the circumstances, we stood there together in my living room, laughing. I didn't remember the last time we'd done that.

"What's so funny?" Kyle appeared by a far wall, near the bedroom, wiping away sleep and yawning.

"Oh, Kyle," I said, "I'm sorry. I didn't mean to wake you."

He ushered me in for a cuddle. I could never

resist, and went to him, wrapping him in a bear hug. He sighed into my chest and the familiar warmth in my heart blossomed when he touched me. The jolt in my groin was nice, too.

"Go back to bed," I said. "I'll be in soon."

Pushing out of my arms, Kyle studied Dad. There was a faint sense of recognition, but Dad had aged backwards a little since the afternoon. Eating people seemed to have that effect on him.

"Who's your...friend?" he asked.

Dad and I exchanged glances. I hadn't even considered what I'd tell Kyle. I'd been too focused on getting Dad out of the nursing home. Away from the crime scene.

"I'm Robert," Dad said. "Mike's cousin. I'm so sorry for the intrusion, and for waking you. I'm in town unexpectedly, and Mike said I could stay here for a few days."

Kyle's face changed into a bright smile, and he moved to Dad with his arms open for a loose hug. Dad accepted, and I saw him sniff at Kyle's neck. Only for a second, but I hadn't imagined it.

"It's so nice to meet you," Kyle said.

Dad bowed his head a little and told Kyle it was nice to meet him, too. "Well, I hate to be *that guy*, but it is a bit late. Old men need their rest."

"I'll show you your room," I said, and ushered Dad down the hall. I swivelled round, back to Kyle, and mouthed, "I love you." He mouthed it back and my heart skipped a beat.

Dad's room was near the front door—I always made the spare room towards the front of the house, away from the main bedroom. Leading him there, I closed the door behind us.

"That was a close one," he said.

"Good save, though," I replied.

Dad surveyed the room. "Nice place, Mike. I realised that I, uh, I haven't ever been here before."

"Yeah, I'm sorry—"

"No, I'm sorry." Dad touched his chin, and I wondered if his teeth were waking up already. "You're still my kid, no matter how old you are. I should have been more interested. I'm really sorry, Mike."

In that moment, I was dumbfounded. With all that I'd learned about my dad in the last two days, with all I'd seen, none of it compared to him apologising. Not like this, anyway. Owning everything, taking full accountability.

"It's okay, Dad. Get some rest."

He sighed and started unbuttoning his shirt, so I motioned to leave.

"Oh, and Dad?"

He watched me, still apologetic, searching for signs that I'd betray him the way he'd done to me.

"Rule one. Kyle's off limits."

. . .

I thought about calling in sick, not going to work for the rest of the week. I'd often had that thought, but never as seriously as I was considering it that morning. Spending a night tossing and turning, wondering if your father—who was ageing backwards and eating people—would sneak into your room and split your stomach open was a pretty good reason to call in sick.

The shower was already on, though, and could hear Kyle humming a tune as the water splashed over him. The throbbing in my groin came again, and I rushed to join him. He greeted me with a wave and I sized him up and down before entering the steamy shower. Every inch of him made me want to stay in that shower forever, just exploring him.

"Good morning," I growled, and pulled his wet body against me.

He gripped my arse as he kissed me. I felt him grow hard against my belly and growled in his ear. Growling drove him wild, and this morning was no exception. He pulled me closer, leaning against the shower wall so the water cascaded over us, and we let our mouths, fingers, cocks do the rest of the talking.

By the time we finished, the water was running cold. I had Kyle's taste in the depths of my mouth, he had me inside him in other places, and we guessed the neighbours—and my "cousin"—were either plugging their ears from the loud, intense moaning, or making a go of it themselves. Either way, it was a great start to the morning.

Kyle dressed, still humming a tune I hadn't heard, and I watched him from the edge of the bed as I buttoned my shirt. It was nice, both of us getting ready for work. On occasion, I would catch him glancing at me, and then blush as he swivelled his head away, which I chose to ignore. This was something that drove me wild, but not in a sexual way, and I reminded myself that youth sometimes resulted in very strange behaviours.

In the kitchen, the strong scent of coffee beckoned me, and I kissed Kyle on the neck as I passed him. Dad—Robert—was making toast and coffee, and had placed a bottle of orange juice on the counter.

"Morning," I said.

"A *very* good morning, by the sounds of it," Dad said, buttering some toast.

I blushed a little, and sat on a stool by the kitchen island.

"Morning, Robert," Kyle said, joining us. He wore a suit shirt and pants, a red necktie swinging loose around his neck, not yet tightened.

Dad poured a glass of orange juice, handed it to Kyle. He and I exchanged an awkward glance, half-expecting the Cocoa Pops or Corn Flakes to come out next. This was something people often did to Kyle, and we found it both funny and frustrating. Going to a café, I would order a milkshake, Kyle a coffee. Invariably, when our orders were brought to the table, the milkshake would be placed in front of Kyle. I didn't think Dad meant Kyle was a child, I didn't even think the café staff thought that. It was just something that happened when an older man and a visibly younger man went out together. Long-held social scripts are embedded into us so deep that it becomes second nature.

Kyle drank the juice and winked at me.

In the corner of my eye, I noticed Dad studying him, sizing him up. He licked his lips, jaw straining. Teeth clamouring inside his closed mouth. He saw me watching him, and went back to his toast.

"You still like peanut butter?" he asked me.

I indicated yes and sipped my coffee, thinking back to Dad's story of the first time he met Tobias. The way the coffee had cleansed his palette after the raw bacon. As a plate of peanut butter toast was slid across the counter to me, the brownish gunk melting into the butter, I suddenly didn't feel like eating.

"Thanks," I said, fighting the urge to add "Dad".

"So, how are you related to Mike?" Kyle asked, sitting next to me and taking one of my slices of toast.

"Cousins," Dad said.

Chewing on globs of peanut butter, Kyle said, "Which side?"

I sipped more coffee, looking between them.

"His mother's side."

Kyle indicated yes. "I never met Mike's mum," he said, solemn. After a pause, he added: "She was an only child, though. Both of Mike's parents are."

Silence.

I stared daggers at Dad, compelling him to stay quiet. I picked up the second piece of toast and took a small bite from a corner. Casual. Natural. Nothing to see here.

"We're not blood relatives," I said, munching away. "Our families grew up together. His parents were like my aunt and uncle, so we've always just thought of each other as cousins."

Seemingly satisfied with the response, Kyle sipped at my coffee and checked the time. "We're both off to work," he said to Dad. "What are you going to do today?"

"I might go shopping," Dad said, eyeing me. "Find some things I've been looking for."

I couldn't let Dad go "shopping" on his own, he'd end up eating the cashier or some unsuspecting waiter. With his impulsive eating of the chef and the two nurses, the truth was that he couldn't be trusted. Even as he spoke, he had flicked his head back to Kyle, and the nostrils were flaring. Drinking in his scent.

"Actually," I said, "Robert is coming with me today."

Kyle raised an eyebrow. "To work?"

"Yeah, he, uh… Well, Robert works in the

Melbourne office and he's up here for work. So he'll be coming to some meetings with me today."

Turning back to Dad, Kyle said, "Why did you say you were going shopping?"

Dad shrugged, his eyes full of lust and hunger. Licking his lips, just once, corner to corner, he said, "A man can dream, can't he?"

16

MIKE

His face was changing. I noticed it as we pulled up to my office, the sun peeling away any doubts I had. It wasn't just that he was getting younger, less wrinkled, more tanned. The shape of his bone structure was changing, too. Dad had always had a roundish chin, but now it was drawn, more pointed. His hairline had changed and even the shape of his eyes were shifting. I wondered if the veins spreading through him were doing that, or if I'd never really looked at him, never really *seen* him. If I'd spent my life ignoring my father, the way children can sometimes do.

There was something familiar about the new shape of his jaw, but I couldn't put my finger on it. He seemed like someone I'd seen, maybe someone I knew.

"Your name is Robert Smith, okay?" I said, as we headed to the entrance.

"Smith, really?" Dad smirked.

I shrugged, and went to give an alternative when Dave popped out of his own car. "Good morning, Mike," he said. "Still doing lunch today?"

As much as I did not feel like eating anything, let alone sharing a meal with Dave, it might have been a good distraction for Dad. So I said, "Sure", and he came to walk with us.

"Who do we have here?" Dave asked.

"Robert *Smith*," Dad said, shaking the man's hand. "I'm an independent contractor, just here for the week to check some things out."

Dave adjusted his necktie and nodded a few times, considering the meaning behind Dad's words. I suspected Dad was causing trouble, that this was a bad idea. It wasn't too late, I could have turned around and locked him in the car all day. Dad was enjoying being here, out of the nursing home. He was in his element, sniffing at Dave as we entered the building, rolling his tongue across his teeth.

I nudged him in the ribs and he cleared his throat. "Sorry," he mumbled. "He smells fucking amazing."

"*You can't eat Dave*," I whispered, and Dad agreed with a frown.

"Did you guys say something?" Dave asked.

We shook our heads, but Dave was still waiting for an answer.

"Just that it'll be good for Robert to be here," I said, trying to not hold my breath. My chest was heavy, though, and I must have appeared anxious, sweaty. "There are some systems issues, you know it is."

Dave checked his watch, uninterested now, and tapped the glass casing. "Twelve, then? For lunch?"

We agreed.

"See you then. Lovely to meet you, Mr. Smith."

I let out my breath and nudged Dad once more. "Come on, just come sit with me."

Dad was distracted, staring after Dave with a slight lick of his lips. He snapped his head to me and then searched again, finding a new smell. And again.

This was a bad idea.

As I led him to my desk and sat him in the chair, hoping the three-walled cubicle would block his senses from searching the office, I scanned the area. Nobody had taken notice Dad was even here, it seemed.

I grabbed a chair from a nearby meeting room and wheeled it back to my cubicle. Dad shuffled out of the way, and we sat in silence while I worked. So immersed in my emails and programs and phone calls, I didn't see him get up to stretch, or leave the cubicle.

It was the laughter I heard first. His raucous, "I'm so funny and charming" laugh. I glanced above the edge of my cubicle. Dad was leaning by the water cooler, chatting to Zac and Trish and some other guy I'd seen around but never spoken to. Dave was lingering, as usual.

Dad couldn't help himself, calling attention and patting arms and rubbing shoulders. Trish's hands were at her hips, unimpressed, but the guys… They loved him. And Dad loved that. He was lapping up their interest, leaning against the wall by the water cooler, one arm raised above his head. Mr Cool. Mr fucking Sleaze.

A clock above their heads read 11:55, which meant Dave was hanging around Dad for lunch. I watched him wave at Zac and the other guy. Watched Trish check her watch and make some excuse to leave, checking him out one last time with distrust. Watched as Dad ushered Dave away from the water cooler, down a hallway, with a spring in his step.

Rushing over, heart hammering, I couldn't breathe. Dad was farther away now, Dave chatting like he'd found his soul mate. I went around a corner at the edge of a bay of cubicles, my stomach dropping as Dad led Dave into a quiet room at the end of the hall.

The server room?

All the company data was kept on local servers, but the room was off limits, always locked. I didn't know how, but Dad had opened it. He'd been up to no good for a while.

How long had I zoned out for?

"Ah, Mike," a voice called from behind.

Trish, not now.

I kept following Dad, the pit of my stomach dropping. Something was happening. I could almost smell the blood already, the anger boiling away at me. Rule one: nobody we know. Yet, there he was, leading Dave into an empty room.

"Mike, a word?" Trish asked in her forceful, commanding, managerial tone.

"Uh, Trish, I, uh, I have to go see to something. I'll be back soon?" I said. "Sorry."

I could only imagine her expression as I ignored her, rushing to the server room. Dad and Dave were already inside, the door swinging shut behind them.

Fuck.

Running up the hall, I reached for the door before it clicked shut, and made it just in time. My feet crunched on plastic. Sheets of fucking plastic, lining the rows of servers. I couldn't see either of them. Dad must have lured him away, to a corner somewhere. I breathed deep, listening to the hum of the servers. Feeling their heat wash over me, the red lights blinking as data was captured and stored.

"…doing in here…"

The voice was low, mumbled, but was laced with excitement. Dave's voice, it had to be. I followed it as more mumbles carried on.

"I don't think we're allowed in here," Dave said.

I rounded a corner, saw Dad pressed against Dave, arms either side of his head. Leaning in, Dad kissed him. Dave's body shuddered and his knees weakened.

"What's going on here?" I asked, clearing my throat. "*Robert?*"

Dad didn't look back, didn't move. Just pressed harder against Dave, who squirmed in embarrassment.

"Mike, I… Please do-don't tell an-anyone," Dave stuttered.

"Mike…" Dad sighed. "I didn't want you to see this."

"Don't do it, Dad," I begged. "Please."

Dave frowned, puzzled at the word "dad" and Dad's hand came across his mouth in an instant. I ran to my dad's side, tried to pull his arm away, but his teeth sank into Dave's neck, tearing at the veins and the flesh.

A squirt of blood gushed across the room, splattering servers and walls, and spilling down Dave's body.

"No!" I screamed.

Dad moved to me, his voice hard and dead. "It's too late now, Mike. You have to help me, or we'll both get caught." He stepped away from Dave, who clutched at his neck, choking out a "Help me", and falling to his knees on the plastic sheeting.

"Shhhh." Dad raised a finger to his lips, his jaw like a deep cave, echoing with that awful tooth-on-tooth sound.

The teeth had awoken, had overtaken him, feeding their needs and desires through him. Even so, when Dad fell to his knees and lapped at the blood leaking from Dave's neck, I wanted to hurl.

No. I wanted to kill him.

"Help me, Mike," Dad said, unbuttoning his shirt.

I glanced back to the door. We were a few rows away, out of sight. If Dave stopped thrashing and just died, we'd be fine.

What the hell am I thinking?

"I wanted to help you, Dad." I held back tears, tried not to yell at him, punch him. "But not like this. Not if you're going to break the rules."

Dave struggled, jerking and kicking as the life left him. I wanted to go to him, to help, to apply pressure on the wound like they do in the movies. But Dad was getting naked, the plastic was drenched in blood already, and he was telling me he needed my help.

Again.

Fuck. "What do I do?"

"Get undressed. We don't want blood on our clothes." Dad shuffled out of his pants and whipped his underwear down. I looked away, but he called me over to Dave's writhing body. "He'll be dead soon."

Bile burned the back of my throat, my stomach aching from the sight of blood and from

Dad's naked body. Yet, I started to undress, too, unsure what he was expecting me to do.

"The first time is always a bit…intense." Dad reassured me with a small frown.

The first time.

He wanted me to do it, too. He wanted me to eat Dave. I kneeled next to him, covering my naked body with my arms, feeling Dave's blood pool at my knees. I retched, more bile spilling into my mouth. I swallowed it back down—it was better than the alternative.

"Just start with whatever smells good to you," Dad said, patting my back.

I watched as he dove in, hurled at how easily Dave's stomach came apart in Dad's hands. How the noodles and meatballs inside him stunk like nothing I'd ever experienced before. I backed away, hands over my mouth to stop the vomit, and rested against a warm server, humming away as if the most vile, disgusting thing wasn't happening around it.

Squeezing my eyes shut so tight they ached, I could hear the sucking and the chewing and the biting. The tearing of flesh. The digging.

The vomit came fast, spilling through the gaps in my fingers, and I let it splat onto my naked belly and groin—chunks of whatever I'd eaten tangling in my body hair and my pubes. Wiping at it with trembling fingers, I opened my teary eyes. Dad was covered in Dave's insides, he'd laid organs in a neat row by the body, and was pulling at Dave's spine through a trench he'd dug up and down my dead colleague's back.

He pulled hard and the top of the spine cracked, snapping away from the skull. It came up and out so easily, globules of blood dripping back into the body. Dad laid it down next to the heart and liver, some kind of ritual he'd established long ago.

I begged him to stop. He couldn't hear me through the sound of bones grinding in the dentures and the squishing of organs in his hands.

The chewing was loud.

So loud.

I fought the urge to keep vomiting, and covered my ears like a child. My whole body shook, I had no control, and all I could think as I tried to block out the noise and the chaos and the stench was that Dad had broken the rules. Nobody we know. Rule one. And he'd *planned* this one. The plastic sheeting, he'd somehow found it, laid it with the intention of eating Dave since we arrived that morning.

Swirling around my brain—as Dad dislodged Dave's head and drank from the neck hole—was a truth I'd known for so long. A truth I had started to forget, started to replace with a much more wonderful lie.

Dad cannot be trusted.

As though reading my thoughts, Dad focused on me, Dave's head gripped in his hands. "It's the teeth, Mike. I don't have the same control as I used to."

There was nothing to say. Nothing to do but turn away so I didn't have to watch Dad tongue Dave's neck hole over and over before shoving his whole hand in there to reach…whatever he was reaching for.

"I swear, Mike," he said. "I didn't want to do this. Not like *this*, anyway."

I burst into tears.

"Mike, please don't cry," Dad said through a mouth full of Dave.

His words grated on me, I couldn't breathe through the stench of raw meat—*Organs, not meat*—and I couldn't believe I'd bought into his bullshit. His begging me for help. And I'd eaten it up like a bowl of fucking Corn Flakes.

"F-f-f-fuck y-y-y-you," I stammered, and sobbed into my vomit-covered hands.

Dad didn't reply.

He didn't stop eating, either.

I waited and waited for the sounds to stop, unsure how I would look him in the eye ever again. It occurred to me that even though I'd wanted to help him, had seen the aftermath of the nurses, I'd never seen the process itself. Sitting there—naked and covered in vomit and flecks of Dave's blood and bone gristle—I didn't want to be part of any of it.

He is my dad.

The thought came from nowhere. It was the same thought that made me pay for his surgeries and medicine and whatever else he wanted. Except those *fucking* teeth. Why had I drawn the line at his teeth? To keep the wet, sloppy, sucking sounds from my focus, I tried to think back.

I remembered that morning, a few days prior, when I'd sat in my car practicing what I was going to say to Dad. I remembered getting into the car before that, the drive to the nursing home. What had happened before that?

The café.

Every time I went to visit Dad during the day, I stopped at a café for a takeaway coffee. The waitress, Maree, had been alone that day, with other staff members calling in sick. The wait was longer than usual, and someone—a man—had bumped into me. In my mind, I conjured the image of the man. He was so familiar now, but at the time I had never seen him before.

An older guy, gaunt in the cheeks with a sharp chin. That chin… I had seen it since, but it was different. As Dad slurped on something, growling and groaning as he did so, I thought harder. Dad was changing, his chin was getting pointier. His eyes were changing, too. The face of the man in the café and Dad's revising face were similar.

He'd said something, too, when he bumped into me.

What was it? Why can't I remember?

The memory played like a silent movie, the man talking to me about…something…and touching my arm. His hands had been soft and comfortable, and I'd shrugged it away with a civil "How ya doin'?" I didn't notice at the time, but they stood out in my memory.

His teeth.

The man in the café had something to do with this. His teeth were the same, with black veins. I'd put it down to bad hygiene at the time, like a fucking idiot. From there, I'd gone straight to Dad's place to tell him I wouldn't pay for his new teeth.

Who was he, though?

As Dad burped and wiped at his mouth, licked his fingers, and burped again, it came to me. The chin. I'd seen that chin at the dead guy's place. The garage sale. The widow had said the teeth came from the attic in her house.

"Fuck." I muttered.

Turning to me, a portrait of blood and bone and guts, Dad frowned. "I'm sorry, Mike. I'm sorry you saw me do that."

I shook my head. "Forget that, Dad. I have to tell you something." I breathed heavily as the puzzle pieces started to fit. "Someone did this to you."

Explaining everything to Dad—from the café to the garage—we wiped ourselves down with towels Dad had stolen from the janitor's closet. He was way too prepared for this, he even had bottles of water from a vending machine so we could wash ourselves. And a mop and bucket, just in case. The stench had made its way inside me now and it seemed…normal. The new normal, like this was my life now. I peeked down at Dave's bones every now and then and found I'd adjusted to that sight, too. It was the adrenaline, it had to be. The anger was still there, the distrust and the knowledge Dad had betrayed me, but in that moment it was waiting on the sidelines, waiting for another time to be dealt with. I was talking fast, telling Dad all about the woman and her husband—Gary—and how she'd told me he'd committed a murder-suicide.

"Who did he murder?" Dad asked as he pulled his pants back on.

I shrugged, doing the same, and reaching for my socks. "I have no idea. Just some mailman. But, Dad, there was a picture in the house. A portrait of some guy, a Sir Brentwood."

"Brentwood?" Dad stopped. "Is this a joke?"

Shaking my head, I tied my laces.

"Brentwood was Tobias's last name."

17

MIKE

I watched the door while Dad shoved Dave's bones into heavy duty garbage bags. It was incredible what could be found in the janitor's closet. My hands were shaking as I held the door handle, scanning the hall and the office beyond. Life continued as it had a half hour earlier, before Dad had eaten Dave.

Hurling the garbage bags over his shoulders, Dad waited for my signal. We were going to get caught. Even if we got away with it now, there were cameras all through the building. They'd spot us entering the server room, then exiting without Dave.

A worry for another time.

I gave the signal and we marched down the hall, taking purposeful, steady steps. Minding my pace—not too fast to draw attention. I wiped at sweat, and tried to breathe as calmly as I could. My head and chest rattled with anxiety and nerves and the all-too-real memory of Dad chewing on Dave's severed cock like it was succulent candy. Drawing the testes out and sucking as though they were everlasting gobstoppers.

We passed the janitor's closet towards the end of the hall, and in one simple motion, Dad flung the door open and dropped the bags inside.

"Mike," Trish called, waving me over. "Where have you been?"

"Uh, we, uh, I, uh—"

"Mike here was showing me the servers. I had some questions about data collection and storage, that sort of thing," Dad said with a smooth, cool grin.

Trish shook her head. "Mike doesn't work in that area, though. He doesn't know anything about servers or data. He's a client consultant."

Dad shrugged. "Well, perhaps you've got him in the wrong area, Trish. Mike knows a lot about it, in fact. When is the last time you asked him about his knowledge base? Gave him a challenge?"

My cheeks, and Trish's, went bright red. He was lying out his arse, I had no idea about servers or any of that stuff. His strategy was solid, though—realign the focus back to her, make her feel guilty, make her question herself. Gaslighting 101. He'd been doing that to my mum since I was a kid, and now I understood why.

Did Mum ever know about this?

"Yes, well…" Trish gestured and faced away

from Dad. "Mike, if I can have a moment? It's about your father."

I straightened, frowned. "My dad?"

Trish ushered me away with a hand on my elbow, spinning me away from Dad, who finished at the closet. Out of my periphery, I saw him kick at the bags of bones, and mouth to me, "I'll move them later."

He was a risk. He was dangerous. Confident and cocky.

"Now, this isn't going to be good news," Trish said, guiding me to a chair by her desk. Closing her office door, she took a seat on the other side. "Your father appears to be…missing." Her eyes were narrow, full of worry, genuine concern.

"Missing?"

"Along with two of the nursing staff from the home."

"Wait, what?" I tried to sound surprised, upset. "What do you mean? Has anyone called the police?"

"They're actually on their way here," she said. "They tried to call you a few times, but when you didn't answer, they phoned me. I asked them if I could break the news, as a friend. These things are easier to hear from someone you know."

This was a side I hadn't seen from Trish before. I'd never considered her a friend, but then, I didn't really have any friends. Just Kyle. And now Dad. Except Dad was insane, and every second those teeth stayed in his mouth, he got worse and worse. I checked back, scanning out the clear sheet of glass that made up Trish's office wall. Dad wasn't there. He'd vanished again.

He can't still be hungry?

"Mike?" Trish's voice was soft. "The police are going to want to talk to you."

I met her gaze and nodded.

"Oh, here they are now." Trish stood and waved out her window, beckoning the police over. As they knocked on the door, she invited them in. "I'll give you some privacy," she said, and moved to leave. Stopping just at the door, she added: "I'm sorry about your father, Mike."

Looking up at her, I gave a weak smile, and then noticed the cops standing in the doorway. A uniformed officer was grinning at me. Next to him, Detective Brooks was grimacing.

"Mr Benson," she said, "I'm sorry to be here."

It was a strange way of phrasing it, but I gestured my thanks. "Nobody from the home called me. Where is my father?"

"That's what we're trying to ascertain," she said. "It seems that, at some point last night, your father exited the nursing home, along with two of the nursing staff who never signed out."

"You think they kidnapped him?" I asked.

Brooks cocked her head. "Why do you suggest that?"

I shrugged. "I'm not, I just... Where is he?"

"Where do you think he'd go?" Brooks asked, pen and notepad in hand.

I shrugged once more.

"Can you tell me why his room smelled of bleach? And why there was blood on the ceiling?" Brooks's voice was flat, emotionless.

We didn't clean the ceiling. FUCK.

"Blood? Bleach? I don't know what you're talking about. Isn't there security footage at the home? What does it show?"

Brooks cleared her throat. "Unfortunately, the cameras had been switched off. The recording stops about an hour before we think your father left."

"What are you saying?"

"I'm saying it's suspicious, especially given your father's involvement in the chef's death. We also have a witness. We're not taking this person's statement seriously, because of the...nature of it...but we do believe your father is involved in the disappearances. Have you seen him?"

I shook my head, indignant. "No. I haven't. Why do you think the nurses are missing? Maybe they just went home. Or somewhere else."

"Both of their families reported them missing. With the camera footage cutting out, and the recent death, we believe something may have happened to them."

"Look," I said, standing and putting my hands in front of me defensively. "I hope the nurses are okay, but you can't seriously be suggesting my father—a man in his mid-eighties who can't walk, can't see, and can barely hear—has anything to do with it. Maybe you shouldn't be a detective."

Brooks's empty expression didn't change. "The answer is usually the most obvious. No matter how unlikely."

Scoffing, I opened the office door. "We're done here. I need to go look for my dad."

I need to go back to Gary's house.

Storming from the office, leaving Brooks and the uniformed officer to stare after me. I returned to my cubicle, hoping Dad would be there. As I suspected, he wasn't. Still, with the detectives watching me from Trish's office, I started packing my things, and headed to the exit. Brooks tried to catch me—I got the feeling she enjoyed having the last word—but I rushed faster to avoid her.

I pretended to fumble with my keys and headed to my car. Brooks and her partner were heading across to their own car, an unmarked, and waited until they'd left before pulling my keys out and unlocking the door. I didn't want them following me.

"Are they gone?" a whisper came from behind a nearby garbage bin.

"Dad." I sighed. "I didn't know where you'd gone."

He stood from behind the bin, paranoid. "I saw that detective, and decided to get rid of the bones there and then while she was busy." He patted the lid of the bin with a wink. "What did she want?"

"Well, two nurses went missing from the home last night," I said, opening the car door and plonked into the driver's seat. "And you're the main suspect because *they found blood on the fucking ceiling!*"

Dad cursed too, and slammed the door as he got in.

I spun to him, the rage bubbling close to the surface. "What the fuck is wrong with you?"

Dad was taken aback and stared at me.

"You're a total fuck-up, Dad. Rule number one, nobody we know. You've broken that rule four times now. The chef, the nurses, and now Dave."

"Mike, I'm—"

"If you apologise one more fucking time, I will kill you myself."

Dad sat back, swallowing hard, and surveyed out the window. He knew he'd fucked up.

I took a deep breath. "I don't know why," I said, "but I still want to help you. I'm so angry at you right now, for all this mess. For killing Dave. But…we need to find a way to solve this."

He agreed with a slight tilt of his head, still didn't say anything, like a petulant child.

"We have to go back to that house," I said. "The teeth, Sir Brentwood, the guy who convinced me not to buy you real dentures… The answers are all there in that house."

18

PHIL

Mike was right. I was a total fuck-up. He didn't understand what I was going through, how the teeth weren't becoming more and more a part of me, but how *I* was becoming *them*. I hadn't said anything, didn't know how to, but I could feel it. The veins weren't just pumping something into me, they were changing me.

At first, I had liked it, the way they aged me backwards. The way I was able to walk again, how strong and healthy and confident I had become. When I caught my reflection, though, I had to do a double-take. I wasn't me anymore, and the face staring back at me was dangerous. Mike knew it, I knew it.

Yet, he still wanted to help me, even after the incident with Dave. Even after I'd encouraged him to eat his friend.

191

Why did I do that?

I was losing control fast, if I'd ever had control in the first place. In the silence, I nervously tapped the power button on the car radio, and switched the station to 2GB. I needed a laugh. As the male broadcaster started talking about abortion rights like he had a stake in the conversation, I leaned back to let the ridiculousness wash over me. The teeth were sated for the time being; it was okay to rest.

"How can you listen to this shit?" Mike grumbled. "They're homophobic, racist, misogynists."

I swallowed my nerves. "It's so ridiculous it's funny."

Mike choked on a curse word and shook his head. "Funny? Are you serious? This shit is disgusting."

"I agree, it's—"

"Then how is it funny? I know you used to get off on beating up gays at pride parades but for a lot of us, this is our lives. We have a real stake in the outcomes of these conversations. And you think that's funny?" Mike spat, gripping the wheel so tight his knuckles were bone white.

Knuckles were a good part of the body to save, they were like hard candy. Clearing my throat, I pushed the thought aside and went to apologise one more time. Mike's words rung in my head, though: *If you apologise one more time, I will kill you myself.*

He was so angry with me, I believed he might.

Instead, I mumbled, "You're right. It's not funny."

Mike switched the radio off and we sat once more in an awkward, rage-filled silence.

"For the record, I didn't beat up gays. I beat up *one* gay man. And he deserved it."

. . .

1978

Everyone hated gay people. Mostly, they hated gay men. A growing fetish of woman-on-woman action was hitting the shelves and the magazines were found under countless teenage beds. Gay men, though? Something about man-on-man fucking disgusted the masses. I was careful to avoid scenarios where I'd be found out, and committed to Darla in the way Tobias had suggested.

It wasn't a fraudulent marriage, I did love her. I loved our son, too. Mike, only a few months old. He was precious and funny and so intelligent. Darla was a wonderful mother, and I had built a home for them with my career as a policeman.

The lead up to the Gay and Lesbian Mardi Gras had been a difficult time for me, though. I had no doubt that I liked men, I loved Tobias. Even if he had started keeping his distance since the wedding. We hadn't hunted together since Mike was born, but I was hoping to get back into a routine with Tobias now that the boy was a bit older. He was Uncle Toby to Mike for the first few years, but the visits became too difficult for him.

To not be able to touch me.

To not be able to taste me.

Or hunt with me.

I missed it, but I also had my family. The desire, the urge to eat human flesh and guts had diminished a fair bit since Darla had come along. Tobias saw that, too, and I suspected he was searching for someone else to take under his wing.

Then the news hit about the protest. Gays would be running amok in the streets, spreading their agenda, spreading their…whatever. The news media was all over it, running fear campaigns. Even though I wasn't gay—I loved women, too, didn't I?—I felt targeted. Felt the need to hide.

That's why I signed up for the job, to take down the protesters. As long as I was there, I could minimise the damage to those screaming in the streets. Do my bit to protect them.

Rule three: hide in plain sight.

"I can't believe you're doing that," Tobias said.

We were at our spot in the milk bar. He had his hand on my knee under the table, and I didn't move it away. He squeezed at the news, though, and removed it on his own.

"It's to protect people," I whispered. "I don't want anyone to get hurt."

Tobias looked away from me. "You're on the wrong side here," he said. "You know what you are—what *we* are—and you can't ever escape that."

"I know, I'm not trying to," I said, taking his hand in mine. "This protest is going to happen either way. The police will be there to arrest people, and they aren't taking any prisoners, if you know what I mean. My bosses have said as much to me. I *have* to go. I have to help."

"Then come with me. On the *right* side. Not as a cop."

I couldn't and he knew it. I had my family to think about.

He could see the rejection in my eyes, the fear, the complete abandonment of our time together. "You've really changed, you know that?"

"What?"

"You used to be someone I could count on," Tobias said. "We had something special."

"You told me to marry Darla," I reminded him. "You told me to hide in plain sight, which is what I'm doing. Why haven't you?"

He didn't answer, just avoided by gaze. He still held my hand, and I gripped it tight. After a few moments, he licked his lips. "Let's go hunting."

Sighing, I let go of his hand. "I can't. I should get home."

Tobias scoffed, muttered under his breath, and stood to leave.

"What did you say?" I asked.

"I said you're a coward." He grabbed his coat, shoved his arms through the sleeves. "You and I used to have something special. We used to *be* special."

I rested my hands on the table, leaned back in my chair. "Yeah, *used* to be. Things change." I could feel my heart pounding in my ears. I'd never spoken to Tobias like that, never dared defy him, not even on my wedding night when he insisted on a celebratory hunt. Darla had said she understood, and had been asleep when I came in at 3 am.

"I could destroy you, you know," Tobias said, stepping close to the table, towering above me. Techniques like that *used* to work, back when we were "special", which I suddenly realised just meant I had made him feel special. His words sank in as he planted both hands, face down, onto the table. His familiar "I've got you, fucker" smirk spread across his lips.

"What do you mean?" I asked, leaning forward, making sure my eyes met his with a fierce stare.

"The things I could tell that wife of yours. The things I could *do to her*."

I jumped up, grabbed him by the scruff, and pulled him close. People started to notice the scuffle, the milk bar owner heading in our direction. I didn't care. I didn't care who saw, who heard, who recognised my name. I was a respected policeman in this city.

"You need a hand, Phil?" the milk bar owner asked from a few steps away, rolling up his sleeves.

"I'm good, Dan," I said. "My friend and I are just having a chat."

"Well, uh, take it outside, will ya, Phil?" Dan cleared his throat, motioning around the room. "People are kinda uncomfortable with this, mate."

Dragging Tobias by the scruff, I pushed him out the door into the street. He was still smirking, like he had won some secret prize. When I let go with a final, forceful push, he adjusted his necktie and smoothed out his suit.

"That was a bit dramatic," Tobias said.

"Don't you *ever* threaten my family." I stepped to him again, fists ready, my cheeks hot.

"Oh please. We both know I'm your only real family."

"I love my wife and son. It took us a long time of trying before Darla fell pregnant. Mike is a miracle."

Tobias flinched at this, as though I'd punched him in the gut. He stared at me, the smirk fading into a jealous frown. Licking at his teeth, he said, "You best treasure them while you have them."

"What the fuck does that mean?" I grabbed at his collar again, but he pushed my arm away and locked his hand tight around my neck.

"It means," he spat, "that I can *fucking* take them *any time I want.*" He squeezed tighter until the cartilage in my throat started collapsing. "I made you, Phil. I made you what you are today, Mr Policeman. Mr fucking husband and father."

I choked and choked, spluttered a "Let go", though he couldn't hear me. Didn't want to. He was back in control, back in charge, and he wasn't about to let that go.

"I could go to your house right now and your darling wife would let me right in. She'd let me tuck your son into bed. I could snap both their necks in a second and rip out their hearts. I don't do that because I *love* you. Don't ever cross me, Phil, because you don't want to see what I'm capable of."

He threw me to the ground and trudged away, leaving me to cough and choke and gasp for air. He'd squeezed so tight my vision had begun to fail, and as Tobias's blurry form vanished into the night, it was clear where he was going.

Darla, I'm coming.

I got to my feet, unsteady, shaky, and grabbed at the milk bar's brick exterior to help me find my balance. He didn't have much of a head start, I could still make it home in time. I had visions of Tobias entering my home, Darla offering him a cup of tea, and Tobias cradling my baby boy in his arms. Visions of Tobias tearing through their necks and chests, burrowing deep to their ribs, down to their stomachs to let their insides spill to the floor.

My throat was throbbing now, but at least I could breathe. My vision was improving, and I pushed away from the wall, breaking into a run. If I made it home before Tobias, my family would be safe, but as I ran I realised that was impossible. Tobias had driven us here, and he would be halfway at my house by now.

"Fuck!"

The milk bar was a few train stations away from my house, but I didn't have time to wait for the next train. He would have been at my house and in the throes of his next feast by then.

Running through the streets of Sydney, my feet aching, my lungs seizing for air, I finally saw my house. A small two-bedroom thing, with flowerpots out the front and a rusted, metal gate. Tobias's car was there, in the driveway, and my stomach fell.

I'm too late.

Pushing through the gate, I bounded up the four steps leading to the porch, and burst through the door.

"Darla?" I called, gasping and searching the house.

No answer.

"Darla? Honey?" I called louder. "Mike?"

In the living room, I was greeted by Tobias sitting on my couch. Mike on his knee.

"Hi Daddy," Tobias said, that smarmy fucking smirk across his lips. Mike was staring up at him with a toothless grin, making sweet little baby noises.

"Hi," I said. I smiled at my son, trying to stay as calm as I could. "Darla?" I asked Tobias, holding my breath.

He gazed at me but didn't answer.

"Oh, honey, you're home." Darla carried a tray of tea and biscuits into the living room. Setting them down on the coffee table, she continued, "Toby was just saying you wanted to walk home, but it looks like you ran. Are you alright?"

I mumbled that I was, hugged her, and panted into her neck. "I just, uh, wanted some exercise."

"Well, you are sweaty," Darla said, laughing, and pushed me away.

Behind her, Tobias was eyeing Darla with that familiar lust and desire. Hunger. I was ready to jump on him, grab his head and smash it against the floor until his skull cracked open. Until his brains were all over my carpet.

"I was just saying to Darla," Tobias said, "that I'll be leaving town for a while."

"I wish you'd stay," Darla said, passing Tobias a cup of steaming tea. "How long are you going for?"

Mike sat still on Tobias's lap, who blew on the tea as it reached him.

"Hey, let's get Mikey to bed," I said. "It's late and he's tired."

Darla agreed. She lifted the baby from Tobias and left the room.

"Cute kid," Tobias said.

Tobias and I stared at each other in silence, each daring the other to make some kind of move. I didn't know this game, hadn't played it before. But the goal was clear: Tobias wanted my family dead.

"Mike is an angel," Darla said as she returned.

"Phil tells me you had trouble conceiving." Tobias sipped his tea, dropping the comment like it was nothing. Like it hadn't almost destroyed Darla.

Her eyes carried betrayal as she glanced at me, but Darla was so forgiving. She was conscious that I needed someone to talk to about things, and the glance was fleeting. Almost imperceptible.

"When are you leaving town?" I asked, sitting next to Darla.

Tobias blew on his tea and held the cup close to his lips. "Tonight."

I frowned. "Shame."

He smirked. "Don't worry, Phil," he said, lowering the teacup. "Us journalists see everything. People everywhere. I'm never too far from home."

Darla nodded at this, saying how his work was so important and necessary and that it was such an honour to know a man like him. I heard her voice, but didn't follow the words. I was too focused on Tobias. The micro-expressions as he talked—every fraction of a movement from his lips and eyebrows told me something. I'd spent years with this man, knowing him, fucking him, hunting with him. As Darla spoke, Tobias reacted in ways he might not have even consciously been aware of. When she said she was proud of him, his left eyebrow cocked for a split second, and then lowered.

"I read your article the other day on the *gays*," Darla said, sipping once more. "It's just terrible how they want to take over."

A smirk. *I know something you don't know.*

"I don't think they want to take over, honey," I said.

She patted my leg to shush me, to say "the adults are talking".

"She's right," Tobias said, staring at me. "They want to take everything. They want to destroy families."

"I don't think that's true," I said, ignoring Darla's vigorous agreement. "I think they respect the fact that people have families. I think maybe they just want the chance to have their own families, too. And be *left alone*."

Eyebrows lowered. Eyes narrowed. A smirk.

After all that time with him, I had no idea what it meant. He could still surprise me.

And that was terrifying.

"I best be off," Tobias said, setting his teacup on the coffee table. "It's late."

Darla did the same, and stood to show him out. I followed, anxious that he'd make his move at the front door. I stood between them, awkward and nervous, and Darla gently moved me aside so she could hug Tobias one last time.

"You don't be a stranger, you hear?" she said, holding back a tear. "And come back to us soon. Mike needs his Uncle Toby."

"As I said,"—Tobias rested a hand on the nape of her neck, the other on mine—"I'm never too far away. I have people everywhere."

With that, he shook my hand and spun on his heels.

The next few weeks were spent hugging my family for longer than normal, and prepping for the protest. The police were expecting enormous numbers, my bosses spitting about how the gay disease was growing fast and this protest would be our chance to end it once and for all.

It made me sick.

Still, I had spent so long living by Tobias's rules that they seemed second nature. Despite the twisting in my gut that told me to stand up and shout at everyone, tell them that gay people are *people* and that rights shouldn't have to be fought for, I sat still and listened.

Hid in plain sight.

I was on eggshells as it was, from the fear that Tobias was watching me. His bullshit story about leaving town was just his way of gaining more control over me. I knew full well he was still around. The question was, what was he doing? What was he planning? So far, I hadn't noticed anyone hanging around the house or following me at work. I couldn't ask Darla if she'd noticed anything, because I didn't want her and Mike to worry.

His threats that last night rang in my head, though. The more I thought about him threatening my family, the more I wanted his blood. The more I wanted to hunt him. I couldn't help but wonder if that was his plan—feed my addiction through anger. Make me seek him out so we could return to the way we were.

The truth was, I couldn't go back to him. The cannibalism, though, those urges were returning. Every time I arrested a guy, I sniffed at him, feeling the itch in my stomach and groin. Feeling the need to taste every inch of his skin. Somehow, I had managed to resist.

June 24th came around fast, and I was stationed by King's Cross with a couple of other officers—each of us on a street corner. The irony wasn't lost on me as people whistled at us on their way past. The morning march had been okay, so I'd heard, but there were rumours of some night-time activities, and my bosses had dispersed us around Sydney to make sure nothing untoward occurred. Whatever that meant— since the cops were all homophobes, any gay presence at all was seen as untoward.

I waited outside a bar, uncomfortable in the chilly winter night and my blue uniform. I thought it seemed like I was waiting for trouble—*asking* for trouble, tonight of all nights. I really wanted to go inside, have a few drinks, let the marches and the protests just happen. They were needed, and the more I thought about it, the more I realised Tobias was right. I should have been *in* the marches. Fighting for a future for anyone who was different.

A bunch of people had started marching up the street, and I motioned to my colleagues. A nervous younger officer pulled out his baton, gripping it tight. I told him to stow the thing away, it wasn't necessary, but he held it out, ready to swing. The others did the same.

What do I do?

Part of me was done hiding in plain sight, but another part was reminded of Darla and Mike and all that I'd built to have a life with them.

The group kept marching up the hill towards us. In that moment, seeing their faces so full of pride and confidence and just a touch of rage—at their situation, at the world—I folded my arms. I would not be attacking. These people should be free to march, to sing into the night, to be free.

I ignored the evil stares from the younger officer as the crowd grew closer. His chest was puffed out, hands shaking. I motioned for him to lower his weapon, but we had the same rank. He didn't have to listen to me. I wondered if he would have even if I had outranked him.

Chanting and singing and marching, the group neared, their countenances becoming clearer under the streetlights. Men, women, older, younger. It was a wonderful display of solidarity between generations, and I yearned to strip from my uniform and join them.

They came closer still, and I moved to the other corner to calm my colleague down. "It's okay, they're just singing and marching. They aren't a threat."

"I ain't letting any *fags* come near me!" he pushed me away, breathing hard through his nose. The veins pulsed hard in his neck, his rage barely contained.

I snatched his baton out of his hands. It shouldn't have been that easy, he had training, but his anger had gotten the better of him.

"Give that back," he said, his voice threatening.

"I'm not your enemy, mate," I said, "but you need to calm down. They're just walking. Look—they are *peaceful*."

The group was almost on top of me now and I squared up to them. Among the crowd, a face I recognised. A face I had once loved.

Tobias.

He gaped at me, saw the weapon in my hands, and grimaced with an upturned lip. He strayed from the group, heading over to me, and I dropped the baton on the concrete at my feet. To show I meant no harm. The younger officer picked it up and raced to Tobias, the baton held high above his head.

"Stop!" I yelled.

Too late.

Tobias let the officer whack him in the mouth. His teeth shot to the ground in a bloody mess as he stumbled backwards, holding his face. He tried to recover, but the officer whacked him over and over. The group of marchers witnessed what was happening, rushed to Tobias's aid.

"Please, stop," I begged, and grabbed the officer by the waist. I thrust him backwards, smelling his sweat and the sweetness of his musk.

Tobias must have seen the flash of lust on my countenance, because he grinned wide. "You fucking cowards." He spat more blood, staring right at me.

"I'm trying to help you," I told him, as other officers arrived to engage the crowd.

In seconds, I was surrounded by arms and legs and screams, kicking and punching and grabbing. I pulled out my baton to protect myself, used it to defend against the attacks, and begged for the violence to stop. None of us wanted this, not really. We all just wanted to go home, I was sure of it. I lost sight of Tobias in the crowd, didn't know where he was.

A fist flew at me and I stumbled, lashed out in instinct. The baton smacked against a man's chest, and

I whacked him one more time on the back of the knee, sending him to the ground with a low growl. As much as I didn't want to be, I was involved now. I whacked someone else, ordered them to stay down, and grabbed at another's wrist. Yanked them off one of my colleagues, forced them down.

Another fist came, hard. This time in my ribs.

I stumbled, the wind knocked out of me, and fell to the concrete. My leg cracked as someone stomped on me. Another stomp. My knee cracked, I screamed and held the wound, pushed the foot away.

It launched again.

I looked up to beg them to stop.

Tobias.

Smiling down at me, his stare seething with rage.

"What are you doing?" I asked through gritted teeth.

"You're one of *them* now," he said, lifting his leg to stomp as hard as he could. "After this, there's no going back."

"What—"

"Your family is dead."

He motioned to leave, pushing his way out of the crowd. I lunged at him, grabbed his ankle and pulled him down. Struggling in my grip, he kicked at me. Even through my injury, my knee throbbing, my leg a stump from the pain, I moved fast. Baton in the other hand, I whacked him in the spine, and watched him jerk from the impact.

Climbing up his back, I smacked him on the back of the head. He kept struggling. He must have been feasting not long beforehand to have such strength. He squirmed beneath me, and I moved into a sitting position, forcing his hands behind his back and locking them in place with my thighs.

Leaning into his neck, I whispered, "You come near me again, I will end you."

Tobias laughed against the concrete and I pushed his face hard against the cold footpath. "Mr Policeman." He laughed pitifully. "So brave."

His neck pulsed underneath me, the urge coursing through my veins like a bolt of lightning. It took me, and for a moment I was lost. I was alone, not caught in a brawl. It was just me and him, the way it used to be, except this time I wasn't going to fuck him. This time, I was going to eat him.

I bit down, ripped at his neck.

Tobias screamed and laughed that same disgusting sound. "There he is," he said. "There's my boy."

I bit harder, in the shoulder this time, as the fight above us continued. Tobias squirmed and kicked, but we were both aware it was no use. I had him pinned, I could do whatever I wanted to him. I was in control, and I'd end him now before he could make good on his threat and hurt Darla and Mike. I smashed his head against the concrete, twisting it from side to side until I was sure every inch of his forehead and nose had been destroyed.

Flipping him over, he was now dead weight, almost unconscious. Still, the rage bubbling inside me carried my fists to his bloodied mouth and nose and lips. I pounded and pounded and pounded, smashing his jaw and teeth, until his head rolled to one side. Several teeth spewed from his mouth in a gush of blood.

I went to punch him again, to make sure he got the message to leave my family alone.

"What are you doing?" I heard someone ask.

Lifting my head, licking at the red juice on my gullet, I saw one of the other officer's staring at me. The crowd stopped, and I moved off Tobias, wiped my mouth.

"That's a bit much," he said. "We don't want to kill anyone."

The officer helped me to my feet, and I leaned on him. Pointed my baton down at Tobias. "This is what happens," I said to the crowd, "when people threaten us."

I noticed a flash, spun to see a journalist with a camera shaking his head at me between shots.

"Get the fuck out of here," I ordered. People

in the crowd jumped at my voice. "Your march is over."

They began to disperse, a couple of them kneeling to Tobias until I yelled at them to fuck off. To them, I was a crazy, homophobic cop. I would be seen that way in the papers, too, when the journalist published that picture. Nobody else grasped the truth, nobody'd witnessed our history.

Nobody understood how dangerous he was, despite his current appearance.

The journalist was watching me, sizing me up, along with the other officers. My leg was killing me, my knee trembling under my weight, despite the assistance of the other officer, so I made my way to the ground. Sat by Tobias, whose chest gave a steady rise and fall.

"Get an ambulance out here," I said to my colleagues. "For me, and for him." Eyeing the journalist, he took my expression as another "fuck off" and obliged, heading into the nearby bar. I told the other officers to leave, that I'd be okay on my own with him. A few mumbled objections later, I'd convinced them they were needed elsewhere, that these marches were happening all across the city.

When Tobias and I were alone, his breathing slowing, his face a mess, I watched him. We'd been so close, had been through so much together. I didn't understand how it had come to this, why he'd attacked me. He was jealous, angry about my life and the fact I didn't have as much time for him as I used to. He knew I loved him, surely. He had to know that. Yet, here we were, sitting side by side, both injured and waiting for an ambulance. I examined my aching fists as I waited, remembered punching his teeth out of his mouth. I was scratched and bruised and bloodied, couldn't tell where Tobias's blood stopped and mine began.

When the ambulance did arrive, they loaded him up, and helped me inside. It was likely I'd need surgery, they said—the bone was jutting out of the skin on my shin. In my adrenaline and rage, I hadn't really noticed. Just felt the throbbing.

From the inside of the ambulance, staring out into the night before the paramedics sealed us inside, I looked down at Tobias's teeth. Sitting in a pool of blood, glistening red under the moonlight.

For a second, just before the doors were closed, it seemed like the teeth were moving towards each other, and I swore a small figure was hurrying towards them.

. . .

Now

"I only ever saw him once after that," I said.

Mike just listened, but I could tell he had questions. So many questions. There were a lot of things I didn't know how to answer, a lot I couldn't say. It was important that he grasped how much he and his mother were to me, though, and how far I was willing to go to protect them.

"So…" Mike frowned. "You didn't beat him up because he was gay."

"That's what you got from the story?"

"It's not all I got," he said, "but that's an important part of it. The media made you out as the poster child for homophobic cops in the '70s and '80s. It impacted your whole career, led to your drinking."

I didn't have the heart to correct him.

"Led to the divorce and Mum's…passing." Mike choked on the words, had never dealt with Darla's death. Assumed death, anyway, since her body was never found. "Anyway, we're here now," he said as the car pulled up to the house.

"I know this place," I told him. "This was Tobias's house."

We studied each other, exchanged confused glances, and then stared back at the house.

"I'm starting to think maybe there was more to Tobias than you realised," Mike whispered.

"Me too," I said. "Me too."

I didn't want to get out of the car. The last time I'd been in that house, Tobias and I had confessed our love for each other and then devoured a bus driver. At that time, it was the happiest day of my life. The memory now filled me with sadness and regret.

The dentures clamoured—time was running out. Every time they did that, every time I ate a human being, the more I became whatever the teeth were turning me into.

19

MIKE

It occurred to me that I never asked the old lady her name. She'd been so nice to me, invited me in, given me tea and biscuits, and I couldn't even be bothered asking her name. As she invited us in—again—I hung my head a little lower than normal, and mumbled a thank you.

"It's so nice to see you bringing your father out for the day," she said, welcoming us both with an excited hand clap. "Although, he does look like your brother." A jab in Dad's ribs.

He laughed, hearty and throaty and flirty, and it was clear exactly what he wanted. His appetites were insatiable. "I like to stay young," Dad told her with a wink.

"I never got your name," I said, and held my

hand out to her. "I'm so sorry, I feel terribly rude. I'm Mike, and this is my dad, Phil."

The old woman took my hand. Hers was soft and fragile—I could feel the bones just beneath her skin and loosened my grip a little, worried I'd snap her fingers in half. She gazed at me with an expression I couldn't define, and said, "I'm Agnes."

"Thank you for seeing us," I said. "I'm so sorry for another intrusion, we—"

"Pish tosh." She waved my apology into nothingness and began her way to the living room. "You're welcome any time."

Dad and I exchanged glances as we followed her, and I saw him holding his jaw again. *So soon?* He'd not long ago eaten Dave. His stomach growled as we entered the living room, and Dad widened his eyes a bit.

"Someone's hungry," Agnes said with a small laugh.

"You have no idea," I mumbled as Agnes tilted her head at me. "Oh, Dad is *always* hungry these days."

She gestured as if she understood, and left us to sit in the living room, the portrait of Sir Brentwood staring down at us.

"My god," Dad said, breathless. "It looks *just* like him. The spitting image." He'd gotten teary and sucked his lips inward to hold back the coming flow.

"Dad, are you okay?" I asked, squeezing his hand.

"It's like stepping into a memory. I never thought I'd see him again, not even in a painting."

"But look at the date, Dad? 1824." I pointed to the faded, bronze tag. "It can't be him."

Dad stared at the painting, transfixed, taking in the shapes and lines and form of Sir Brentwood. He moved to the painting, caressed Brentwood's cheek with a gentle finger, and inhaled the dust that had settled on the frame. He leaned in close, turning an ear to the canvas.

"Dad?" I asked.

"It's him," he replied. "I don't know how…but it's him. It's my Toby."

I heard the rattle of Agnes's crockery against a metal tray as she returned

. The familiar teacups and a packet of Scotch Fingers shifting left and right as she struggled to keep her hands steady. Racing to help her, I took the tray and set it down on the coffee table. Dad was still enamoured by the portrait, and as Agnes sat in a single high-back chair and straightened her dress, she watched him, considered him, the way he moved.

"Dad's just admiring the portrait," I said, handing out tea. Passing one to Dad, I whispered, "Sit down."

He swallowed hard, full of confusion and shock and love, and took the cup of tea. Moved back to his spot on the lounge, opposite Sir Brentwood.

Sipping, his gaze flicked across to Agnes, who was sizing him up.

"You knew him?" she asked.

I went back to Dad, passed him a biscuit.

"Oh, I don't think that's possible," Dad said, declining my offer of food. We were both uncomfortably aware it wasn't what he needed. "Maybe his great grandson or something."

Agnes shook her head. "My Gary was his sole living heir." She took a Scotch Finger, wiping at crumbs on her dress before taking the smallest bite. "I heard you mention the name Toby… There was only ever one Tobias Brentwood. Him in the picture, that's Tobias."

We all exchanged confused glances for a second, and I motioned to speak. Dad laid a hand on my knee, and I stopped.

"Are you sure, Agnes?" he asked. "I was…friends…with a Tobias Brentwood in the '60s and '70s. Looked just like him." He pointed to the portrait, a slight tremble in his finger.

Agnes pursed her lips. Sipped. Chewed.

"Do you have any of the Brentwood family albums? Any pictures of Gary we can take a peek at?" I asked, breaking the silence.

"Why?"

I cleared my throat. "We're just—"

"Doing research," Dad said, smiling at Agnes.

She softened at the curve of his lips. He had that effect on people, I'd noticed. "You see, I did know a man who *went* by the name Tobias Brentwood. He was a very special friend of mine, and I'm trying to find out what happened to him."

Agnes sighed, rested her teacup on the arm of the high-back chair, and her eyes drifted upwards. "Upstairs." Her voice was less than a whisper. "In the attic."

"The attic?" I asked.

"All the family photo albums are up there." Her face had dropped, her shoulders slumped. "I couldn't… I couldn't look at them anymore."

The air in the room seemed to vanish, the silence sweeping through like a virus, knocking the life out of us. Her husband had died—tragically, violently—and she was all alone in this house with nothing but memories for company.

Dad sensed it, too, the lifelessness of this place. I could tell by the way he fumbled with the teacup, inspecting the pattern, and tracing lines on the surface. He looked back and forth between me, Agnes, and the portrait. His jaw was still motionless, though as I glanced at him, gauging his reaction to Agnes's sadness—her frailty—I noticed the veins in his neck pulsing.

Then in his arms.

They were black.

The sickness from the teeth was working its way deep inside him.

We have to get these fucking things out of him.

"Gary was a nice guy," Agnes said, snapping both Dad and I back to the present. "I don't care what the newspapers say. He wasn't a killer."

"A killer?" Dad asked.

"Gary killed the postman," I said, trying to save her the trouble. "Ate him and then threw himself in front of a bus."

"A truck," Agnes corrected. "Right on the street there. I found him. Well…as much of him that could be found. The truck driver was a mess. It wasn't his fault, though. Gary couldn't live with what he'd done. I mean, can you imagine taking another life?"

Silence.

"Why did he do it?" Dad whispered.

Agnes shrugged, her countenance devoid of emotion.

I had a feeling we all knew the answer. Even Agnes. She knew about the teeth, I was sure of it, knew more than she was saying about Gary's condition, at least. It wasn't the sort of thing you just bring up in conversation, though.

"Agnes," I said gently, "we need to see the photo albums. Is that okay?"

"Sure," she said, and sipped her tea. "Upstairs. The attic entrance is just at the end of the hall. I trust you boys won't steal anything."

Dad and I stood, thanking her for the tea and

biscuits. Dad mumbled his apologies about Gary, and we all but raced up the stairs. Just as she'd said, the entrance to the attic was at the end of the hall, marked by a short string dropping from the ceiling. I pulled it down, stepped back as a set of stairs folded out.

Without a word, Dad and I climbed into the attic, unsure what to expect. What we'd find. Or *who*. Part of me wished Tobias was living up there, feeding on rats and mice, just so Dad could say a proper goodbye to the guy. Maybe even apologise for beating him to within an inch of his life. The other part of me hoped we'd find nothing at all. No albums, no photos. An empty void.

It was a typical attic, though. Australian houses don't normally have attics, but if the house is old enough, built during colonial settlement, it was possible. The attic in this house was huge. Boxes everywhere, piles of junk, old furniture… Some of it was familiar and I assumed it was the stuff that didn't sell from the garage sale.

How did she get it back up here?

"I found something," Dad said, standing by a box labelled "Photos". He had his hand clamped over his mouth. Hungry again. I hoped we'd be done in here by the time he couldn't resist any longer.

We studied the photos together. There were a bunch of albums, sorted by year, and conveniently in chronological order. The first one, right on top, was the earliest—1800-1880.

Flipping through the pages, we saw the black and white photographs—preserved by the album's plastic sheets on every page—were mostly of babies. Each page was a different baby, a name handwritten at the bottom of every photo.

Dad kept flipping, his jaw starting to tremble.

None of the babies grew up. Pages and pages of baby after baby, staring at the camera with blank expressions.

Until the last page.

"What the hell…" I grabbed the album from Dad and stared at the image. He stared on, shaking his head, his teeth chattering away like we'd stumbled on something delicious.

On first glance, the photo was of a regular baby—shiny bald head, chubby cheeks and arms—but the face was all wrong. Older than it should be. The eyes were hollow, angry. And the lips were spread into a wide, thin smirk. Flashing teeth.

"How does it have a full set of teeth?" Dad asked, his mouth stretching a little too wide.

"Look, Dad." I pointed to the name at the bottom of the page. "Tobias."

Behind us, I heard a creaking sound. Turned to it. The stairs were coming back up. I raced over, dodging boxes and junk, and stood on the ladder, hoping my weight would force it back down.

No luck.

Through the decreasing gap between the stairs and the top floor, I saw Agnes's sad air. "Agnes, what are you doing?"

"I'm sorry."

The ladder was all the way up now and I heard a click from the other side. Stamping my feet and calling Dad over, I motioned to the ladder. Jumping on it together, the fucking thing still didn't budge.

"I'm sorry," Agnes repeated. "I can't let the dentures take anyone else."

"Agnes, please!" I shouted.

Dad had ambled off, knowing it was no use, but I tried one more time, slamming my feet hard into the ladder.

"Mike," Dad said, his voice hoarse.

"Come and help me!"

"Mike…"

He was somewhere in the corner, in the shadows, facing the wall. I turned to him, panting. "What?"

No answer.

"Dad?" I started to move to him, but stopped when his body started jerking. "What's happening?"

His entire being trembled, shuddered, and he grabbed at the brick wall.

"Dad, talk to me," I said.

His nails dug into the bricks. His breathing was heavy, fast. Wheezing. Groaning.

"Dad…"

"Mike," he said through gritted teeth, "I can't hold on much longer."

I ran to him, twisted him around so our faces were inches apart. His jaw was stretching again, teeth clamouring and clanging together, searching for their next meal. He pushed me away, teeth bared, hands shaking, and I realised I was it.

I was their next meal.

20

MIKE

"D ad," I said, hands out, reassuring him, "you're not going to hurt me."

It was too late.

He was wild and rabid, he'd lost control. He lunged at me and I stepped back, falling into the box of photo albums. The books toppled, splayed out to random pictures of babies and teeth and little Tobias.

"Dad, stop!" I cried.

He was on top of me now, scratching at my face and chest, his teeth an inch from my nose, biting, biting. Tears flung from him; he didn't want to do this. He wasn't himself, he was the teeth. The teeth.

The teeth.

I kneed him in the groin, watched him spasm a little at the pain, and kneed harder. Specks of spit flew into my mouth and I pushed him off me. He writhed on the floor and I raced back to the ladder. If I could get out, I might be able to find something for him. Anything to just keep that hunger at bay.

Agnes was pacing around down there, I could hear her weak footsteps, her mumbling something about a curse. I called to her, begged her to let me out—just me, for now.

"Dad can stay up here where he can't do any more damage," I said.

He came at me, bit into my ankle, my calf. I screamed and kicked with the other leg. He let out an "oomph" and fell backwards. He'd come for me again, there was no stopping him this time. The teeth were too powerful.

"Agnes, please!"

She'd stopped moving, or I just couldn't hear her over the pounding of my heart.

Dad was back, gnashing and clawing, still on his hands and knees. As I spun to him, I saw he'd taken off his shirt. He was getting ready for another feast, and this time he wasn't worried about plastic sheeting.

I surveyed the scene, searched for something I could use. The attic was full of junk, but it was all cheap and worthless. He was on his feet now, and I braced myself, ready for the attack. The throbbing in my ankle and calf had me worried, but I couldn't think about that.

I dodged Dad's lunge, and raced through the attic as fast as I could on a damaged leg. Checking boxes as I went, I made it to the far side of the attic. Spinning around, I searched for Dad. He was hiding.

Sitting on top of an old chair was exactly what I needed. A steel poker for an old fireplace. The head like an arrow tip, pointy and sharp. And rusted.

I grabbed it, held it in front of me.

"Dad?"

Nothing.

"I don't want to hurt you," I said, "and I know you don't want to hurt me."

Silence.

Just me. Breathing.

I wiped sweat from my brow, my leg shuddered in pain. The bite was deep—deeper than I first thought, and I reminded myself these weren't normal teeth. The bite might not have been normal, either.

Can this curse be transmitted?

Searching the attic, the poker steady in my hand and facing out like a sword, I caught a glimpse of Dad's foot scuttling behind a stack of boxes near the ladder. I went to it, pushed the top box off. It crashed on the floor, sounded like something inside had smashed.

But Dad wasn't there.

He was stalking me, watching me with that fucked up desire coursing through him. Moving around the stack of boxes, his pants and underwear were draped across the floor. He'd stripped. Getting naked to avoid dirtying his clothes during the meal.

Fuck.

It was way too late to save him now. He was in the throes of his addiction, and wouldn't stop until he'd devoured me. I raised the poker higher, determined to find Dad. I didn't know what I'd do when I did find him, but the poker started to shake as I thought about it.

For years I'd thought I wouldn't care if he died, and yet, here in this attic, I wanted him to live. I was terrified at the thought of having to hurt him. Steadying my hand, I breathed out slow, and composed myself. If he came at me, it was too late for him. If he tried to kill me, he wasn't my dad anymore.

And I'd have to kill him.

Making my way through the centre of the attic, keeping my eyes peeled for any movement, I stood just before the ladder. Listened.

Agnes was down there, mumbling again. I strained to hear her.

"He's up there," she said. "And his son."

Who is she talking to?

"I didn't expect him so soon," another voice said.

Who the fuck is that?

As Agnes started to speak once more, I heard movement behind me. I span, Dad jumped at me through the air. I stepped back, and he landed on me hard. I went down, his body weight plunging into my ribs.

My back surged with pain as I smacked into the ladder, the wood snapping under my weight. Dad clutched onto me as we fell through the floor, shards of wood from the ladder landing around me as I hit the carpet on the top floor.

The wind was knocked out of me for a moment. I began to cough and splutter, feeling around for the poker. Dad was next to me, moving slow, but still awake. In the distance, a figure turning a corner, Agnes standing by the wall in shock.

"Please, Dad," I muttered. "Please." I held the poker up, more serious this time. Dad stood above me, towering like a god.

Agnes moved along the wall, hugging it tight, towards the same corner the figure had rounded moments earlier. As she did so, Dad noticed the movement and spun to her.

"You stay away from me!" she yelled at him.

"Someone's gotta be the next meal, lady," Dad growled at her, and grabbed her wrists. Pressed her harder against the wall. "It might as well be you."

Finding my strength, I got to my knees, then my feet, and rushed towards Dad. "Let her go," I ordered. "She doesn't deserve to die."

Dad ignored me, and buried his face in her cheek. Agnes screamed and begged for help—she wasn't asking *me*—but nobody came. I dropped the poker and wrestled at Dad's arms.

"Let her go!"

He elbowed me in the nose, and I stepped back holding the bridge. Felt the blood seeping into my palms. Regaining my balance, I went back, and Dad lunged at me, letting Agnes go. He grabbed my head and smacked it hard against the carpet again and again, until my vision blurred like TV static.

After a few more bangs, my consciousness faded. Dad was up, and the last thing I saw was his naked body throwing Agnes to the ground, and him leaping on top of her, baring those horrible, perfect teeth.

. . .

"Mike, wake up."

Dad was sitting by me. I reached for the poker. Couldn't find it.

"It's okay now, Mike," Dad said. His neck and chest were covered in blood, and his skin was glowing. He appeared around forty years old now— just a touch younger than me. But something else was off. He didn't resemble Dad at all now. His face, his features, everything was different.

He looked like—

"I'm sorry I tried to hurt you." Dad took my hand and helped me sit up. "I had to eat. I *had* to. It was lucky we fell"—he pointed to the hole in the ceiling— "otherwise I don't know what I'd have done."

"I was ready to kill you," I said, holding my head as I sat. "Don't make me do that, Dad."

Dad gazed down at his naked body, stained red, and picked some brain matter from his chest hair. Nibbled at it.

"If the time comes—"

"We have to find a way to get the teeth out of you. I think the answer is up there." We both looked up to the attic again. I didn't want to go back up there. I wanted to go home to Kyle and forget about all this. "I'll go check it out."

Dad grabbed my elbow. "No. You've done enough. I think you should go. Rest."

I shook my head. "Dad, you can't be trusted on your own. You can't even be trusted when I'm here!"

Dad pulled his hand away.

"Look what you did to me!" I shouted, standing and pointing to my wounded leg. "You almost fucking *ate* me!"

"I'm sorry."

"You are always sorry." My voice quivered. "Dad, you've been sorry my whole life. Always fucking something up. Gambling and drinking and abandoning me and Mum. Why am I even here?"

Dad just stared down at himself, drew his knees in tight.

"And now you've eaten someone else, made another mess for me to clean up," I said. A trail of red ran the length of the hallway, disappearing around the corner. "Wait."

Looking up at me, Dad shook his head. "What?"

"I saw someone else. Agnes was *with* someone else."

"I didn't see anybody."

"I did. And he ran off around the corner when we crashed through the attic." I ushered him to his feet, forgetting for a second that Dad was maybe the most dangerous person in the world. Forgetting that he tried to murder me. Right now, we had a bigger problem.

"What did they look like?" Dad asked.

I shrugged and followed Agnes's blood trail around the corner. Her hollowed-out carcass had been shoved against a door, lying across the threshold. Eyeing Dad, he apologised once more—*Always fucking sorry, never changing*—and I opened the door.

It was an empty bathroom.

"Are you sure?" Dad asked. "You're sure you saw someone else?"

"They were talking. About you."

Turning from the bathroom, I headed to the next door, near the landing at the top of the stairs. Empty. We searched every room on the second floor, to no avail. I stopped at Agnes's bedroom, held back a rush of sadness as I examined the lifetime of objects she'd collected. Now a bunch of useless junk.

Her room, like the others, was empty.

Whoever it had been was long gone.

To tell our secret.

"I'm going to search the attic," Dad said, throwing his hands in the air. "And get my clothes back on."

"How? The stairs are gone."

Dad shrugged. "I'll figure something out."

"Sure," I said. "I'll go wait in the car."

Making my way downstairs, I didn't bother searching for the mystery figure. If it had been me, I'd have ran away and never stopped. Whoever it was, they weren't hanging around to say hello. As I hobbled through the house towards the front door, I stopped at the threshold, peered out a nearby window to the street.

My car was in the driveway, and along the road, there was a police car.

Fuck.

Opening the door, I bumped into Brooks and her uniformed helper striding up the steps. "Oh, hello there, Mr Benson." Brooks smiled. "Fancy seeing you here."

"Uh, hi?" I said. "What, uh, what's going on?"

"We need a word," Brooks said. The uniform had a notepad at the ready.

"Are you here for me?" I asked.

Brooks nodded coyly.

"How did you know I was here?"

"We have a warrant to trace your phone." Stepping closer, Brooks noticed my leg, the blood seeping through the fabric of my pants. "What happened there?"

Her gaze lifted from my leg to see beyond me into the house, searching for signs of a struggle. "Dog bite," I said, thinking fast. *A warrant? What the hell?* "I was just on the way to the hospital, so if you'll excuse me."

"Sure thing," Brooks said, standing aside. "I'll just meet you there."

I walked past her. She stood with her hands on her hips, watching my struggle and not offering any assistance. Just those eyes on me, searching for something. The truth, probably. She suspected something was up, she'd be a fool not to realise Dad had killed all those people.

"Mike, I found something—" Dad came down the stairs, stopped halfway when he saw Brooks.

I swivelled round fast, but I was too far outside to see him. Couldn't tell if he'd cleaned up, or just thrown the clothes over his bloodstained body. When the uniformed officer didn't react to seeing Dad on the stairs, I gathered he must have at least wiped the blood away.

"Who've we got here?" Brooks asked, studying me and then Dad with that cold, piercing cop stare. She stepped into the house, hand still at her hips, but lingering at her holster.

"That's, uh," I scrambled to think.

"Robert," Dad said.

Neither Brooks nor the uniformed officer recognised him, despite seeing him at the nursing home, and then at the office. He was changing so fast now, was essentially a different person.

"He looks like the guy in the painting," the uniform mumbled to Brooks.

She agreed and introduced herself. My thoughts were racing, though, and I couldn't hear their words. It was true. He did bear quite a strong resemblance to Sir Brentwood. From the 1800s.

How is that possible?

I moved back up the steps and stood in the doorway. Studying Sir Brentwood and then studying Dad, he was now the spitting image, was just missing the top hat.

"Mike," Brooks said, calling me back to reality. "Hospital?"

"Right," I said, and headed back to the car without giving Dad another glance. I just hoped Brooks would meet me at the hospital, and not meet another fate while I left Dad alone.

Part of me—a sick, twisted part—knew it would be easier if Dad did kill her. If he just ate her up like the others and shoved her bones in a drawer somewhere. I hated myself for even thinking that, for even *wanting* it.

As I drove to the hospital, ignoring a call from Kyle, I organised my questions in a row. In a nice little order, so I could work through them.

How did Agnes get all that stuff into the attic?

Who were all those babies, and why did baby Tobias have a full set of adult teeth?

Who is the mystery man I saw in the house?

How do I get those teeth out of Dad?

There was another question, but I didn't want to ask it. Didn't even want to think it. Yet, it came to me, just as another call came in from Kyle.

If worst comes to worst, can I kill my own father?

21

PHIL

"You're the second Robert we've met today," Brooks said.

I cursed myself for not thinking faster. Mike had all but told me to get fucked after I'd spat that name out. My body might have been getting younger, might have been changing, but my mind wasn't any sharper.

"I am?" I asked, moving to the ground-floor landing.

Brooks flashed a knowing glare and ignored the question. Instead, she introduced herself with a flash of a badge. "Is the homeowner in?"

I swallowed hard and shook my head. "She's out. Not sure when she'll be back."

"And you are?" Brooks asked.

Her uniformed assistant got his pen ready.

"Robert…Jones. I'm Agnes's nephew." My hand had a slight tremble as I lifted it to shake hers.

The detective took it, gave it one shake, and dropped it. Wiped her hand on her pants. She began inspecting the house, plodding slowly from the kitchen to the dining area, back to the living room, scanning each room with that suspicious glare.

"What do you need to see Agnes for?" I asked.

Brooks stopped by the painting of Sir Brentwood—Tobias, as impossible as that was—and studied him. "A relative of yours?"

I gestured with a half-shrug. "Great-grandfather or something." *What is she doing here?*

My teeth were itching now, which hadn't happened before. It was almost like hay fever, when the roof of my mouth would tingle and itch and beg for attention. The teeth were doing the same. Despite my full stomach and Agnes's fresh corpse stinking up the hallway a few metres above us. Despite the immediate danger of Brooks's suspicions, they were hungry, and the hunger always came first. The ends of each tooth itched and itched and no matter how hard I grated and grinded them, it wasn't going away. Part of me wondered if it was my own hunger now, if I was too far gone, or if the teeth were getting stronger.

"You must be devastated about Gary," Brooks said, stuffing her hands into her pants pockets, and leaning back on one foot.

"Oh yeah." I hung my head a little. "He was always so nice."

"Uh huh." Brooks gave a slight nod to the uniformed officer and he wrote something on the notepad. "Where's the dog?"

"It ran away," I said fast. Too fast. *Shit.* "I mean, it wasn't even our dog. A stray, I think. Mike scared it off, but, uh… Well, you saw the bite."

The bite… I want more.

The teeth hadn't spoken to me in a while, but here it was now, at the worst possible time.

Mmmmmm…

"Uh huh." Brooks frowned, traipsed past me, her attention shifting upstairs. "What you got there?"

I had forgotten about the book in my hands, what I'd rushed downstairs to show Mike. Among the photo albums, another book. A ledger. The Brentwoods had run an adoption agency in London, bringing the business to Sydney in the early 1900s. The albums were of babies they'd housed. All but the last one. Tobias. The Brentwoods had adopted him themselves, moved him to Sydney when he was just a boy.

The book I held was evidence that Tobias was born in 1880.

Evidence that he'd always had the dentures.

I hadn't had time to read it all, just glances here and there, but every photo of the kid with the teeth—my teeth—gave me shivers.

"It's just some family history I've been looking for," I said, and offered Brooks the book.

She declined.

Thank god.

She walked past me one more time, circled around, the scent of her perfume lingering. A detective wearing frangipani perfume seemed odd, but as I sniffed it, I wanted more. My stomach grumbled and the teeth clamoured again.

And again.

"Are you good?" Brooks asked, noticing me shaking and holding my jaw.

"Yeah," I said. "Just a sore tooth."

"Uh huh."

The uniformed officer wrote something else down, and I swallowed, trying to think of some story I could tell them. Some half-truth that might be believed as a whole truth. Brooks was about to head upstairs, her hand on the railing. The thin blue veins were just beneath the skin, *ba-bum ba-bumming* the blood up towards her slender fingers.

Bony…

Her arms were strong, muscly. I tried to shake the voice away.

Frangipani…

Breathed hard through my nose. Her abdomen had a slight paunch.

She'll be a quick meal…

"Brooks, was it?" I asked, licking my lips.

She stopped on the first step. "That's right."

"You can't go up there. Not without the owner's permission." I knew police procedures like the back of my hand. They hadn't changed much since I was on the job, and I liked to keep up-to-date on these things in general.

Brooks acknowledged the sentiment by flashing a hollow smile. She understood she was doing the wrong thing, just hadn't realised I'd know it, too. Stepping back down to the ground floor, Brooks asked me when Agnes would be back. I heard the words, but the teeth were speaking to me now. It was so loud, chanting and echoing inside me.

My blood started pumping faster, my mouth ached as Brooks walked past me a third time. The uniformed officer's pen was scratching at his fucking pad again and I could feel my fingers curling into fists. I tried to calm myself, tried to ignore the voice in my head, but the words were fast and loud and hungry and desperate and angry—

"Robert?"

Quick meal…

The uterus is tasty…

Raw ovum…

Eat her…

Eat her…

EAT HER

"Are you okay?"

I snapped my head to Brooks, breathing, breathing, breathing. She recognised something in my stare, in the absence of a reply. Her hand reached for her weapon, but I was fast. I threw my book at her, lunged at her, tackled her to the ground. The uniformed officer dropped his pen and pad, but I grabbed at Brooks's holster, slipped the gun free, and aimed it at the poor guy.

The blast was louder than I remembered it ever being, and he dropped to the floor with a surprised countenance. A line of blood trailed down his forehead.

For a moment, I was frozen, shocked by my own actions, knowing it was me—*me*—who had shot the officer. The teeth were hungry, they would eat and maim and devour, but I had shot him. I had murdered him.

Brooks seized the opportunity and smacked the weapon from my hands. It flew over the dead officer, went sprawling across the floor and we both went for it. We leaped over the uniformed officer, his body limp and fleshy beneath mine. Brooks's fingertips snatched at it. Mine too. The teeth began to take over, pulsing, my jaw stretching. As Brooks continued to reach, sliding herself forward, her fingers slipping against the gun's handle, I crouched over her back.

Slid up her body into a sitting position, wedged her arms under my legs.

You've got her...

EAT

EAT

"NO!" I screamed.

Brooks had the gun firm now, but her arms were useless under my weight. She squirmed and kicked, but the teeth were right. I had her.

"I don't want to hurt you," I said, grinding my teeth hard to stop them from chattering in her ear.

"You just murdered my partner." Brooks was close to tears, but the anger seethed through.

EAT HER

"I can't," I said. "I don't want to."

The teeth itched, the veins moving through my body. My neck tightened, my arms too. The veins were all through me, all the way to the edges of my toes. As the teeth shouted and screamed and ordered me to eat the detective, who writhed underneath me, it was all too clear that I couldn't be saved. It was too. I was lost.

Mike's efforts were useless.

"I won't do it," I said, fighting the urge to lean down and rip off the detective's face. I'd done it before, to countless people. And that was *before* the dentures had taken me. I was a fucking monster, and I deserved a bullet in the head.

Straining as hard as I could, I latched onto whatever remnants of control I had left of my body, and forced myself off Brooks's back. I crawled away from her, over the uniformed officer, across the room to the staircase, and pushed my back against the wood. Drew my knees to my chest.

Brooks was up, on her feet, didn't pay any attention to her injured partner. Her eyes were laser-focused on me, the gun aimed right at my head.

"Shoot me," I begged. "I can't be stopped."

"What the fuck is happening here?"

My jaw stretched and Brooks's dropped. She saw the black veins running from the teeth. Growing down my throat and inside my skin. The sharpness of the teeth, like a piranha's, waited to shred her apart.

EAT HER

"Kill me!"

EAT HER

"Before it's too late!"

EAT HER

Brooks reached around her belt for handcuffs, and threw them at me. "Put them on. Tight."

EAT

EAT

EAT EAT EAT EAT

I tried, I really tried. I wanted to slap them around my wrists, tighten them as much as they'd go. I wanted nothing more than to comply. I began to reach for them, but the black veins in my arms and hands took control.

"Please…" I begged as my mouth stretched wider still.

"What *are* you?"

My head shook, but it wasn't me doing it now.

I was a passenger, pleading with the teeth not to stand. Not to ignore the gun trained on me. Not to step towards Brooks.

But I did.

"You have to…" I managed. "You…*HAVE TO!*"

The gun was still on me, but she wasn't pulling the trigger. Even after I'd executed her partner, whose corpse was sending an itch to my stomach and groin. Despite the situation, the teeth wanted to eat his entire body.

No leftovers.

"Step away," Brooks ordered, "and put on the cuffs."

We both realised I wasn't going to, and she stepped forward, gun trained on me.

"Just shoot," I said. "Please."

The veins in my neck were popping and pulsing in anticipation, and Brooks could see it. I stepped closer towards her and she aimed the gun at my leg. The bullet zipped straight through. She shot again, and I buckled at the knee.

"Stay down!" Her voice boomed through the house.

EATHEREATHEREATHER

On my knees now, blood seeping from my leg, I still went for her. It was the teeth, enduring and focused on their next meal. I was just a vessel, I fathomed that with absolute certainty. As I crawled towards her, the bullet wounds throbbed. Not in pain, though.

Something was different about my blood. I hadn't considered what the teeth and the veins were doing to me on that level before. I'd only thought of the veins as puppet strings, forcing me to do their bidding. They were changing me, though.

"Get back!" Brooks screamed.

I was at her feet now, my fingers scratching at her ankles and shoes.

"I will shoot you," she warned me.

Good. Do it.

EAT…

I glanced up at her and smiled, my teeth bared and hungry.

It must have been the hunger in my eyes, or the shiny perfection of my teeth. She must have seen something in me.

Because then the gun pressed hard against my skull, and—

BANG.

22

PHIL

1985

D arla was dressed up and ready to go. I raised my head from the bed, groggy, and wiped my mouth against the pillow. A trail of thick saliva was left on the fabric and I laid my head back down. I didn't care that my cheek was on the wet patch, and ignored the chill it sent down my body.

"Are you coming or not?" Darla didn't even look at me, she just stood by the bed with a hand on her hip, already knowing the answer.

"Ugh," I groaned. "Babe, I don't feel so good."

She sighed. "You went out drinking again."

I had been to all the bars the night before, at least twice. Prowling. Hunting. Fucking. Darla was aware of some of it, but she didn't know about my meat-eating habits. I'd managed to keep that from her, even if she did know about what she suspected were affairs. She'd smelled cologne and perfume and discovered lipstick on my collar, on my underwear. Had seen the winks between me and whoever I was planning to eat.

It wasn't fair. I knew it wasn't fair. She deserved better.

After Tobias and I fought in the street that night, like savages, something in me changed. A switch had been flipped, and I couldn't turn it off. Senses heightened, the urge to devour anyone who walked by became so strong. Without his help, his guidance, I was powerless against it.

The only thing that dulled the urge was copious amounts of alcohol. Sometimes drugs, too. I was lucky my bosses hadn't clued on yet, though it was just a matter of time. Either Darla would say something or I'd just be found out, stinking of beer and tequila and whatever else I could get my hands on.

"Well, I'm taking Mike with me. I don't want him to see you like this"—she glanced at me with an upturned lip—"again."

Mike.

My son.

My pride and joy.

He stood by the door, behind Darla, and waved at me. I lifted my hand, just a little, and waved back, before the weight of gravity got too much. My hand collapsed back to the bed, and I rolled away from him. From both of them.

"Where are you going?" I asked, pulling the covers over my head. The sun was too bright.

"Church," Darla spat. "Where you should be going."

I ignored her and listened as they shuffled about the house, preparing to leave. The front door slammed and I pushed the covers back down to get some oxygen. The urge to sleep was overpowering, but I wanted to stay awake. Darla's words were still ringing in my alcohol-riddled brain. The hatred emanating from her still burning against my retinas.

The car engine rattled outside and disappeared down the street.

Lying there, alone, the house was silent. Yet it seemed so loud, deafening, and the walls caving in around me. Crushing me with their nothingness. Until—

From the kitchen, I heard the kettle boiling.

Darla and Mike are gone, though.

Alert, I jumped from the bed.

Someone was in the house, fumbling with knives and forks and God knew what else. We kept a cricket bat in our wardrobe, and I grabbed it, closing the door as softly as I could. Stepping into the hall, my head throbbing, vision blurry from the hangover, I squinted for a clearer image.

A man.

Dressed in black.

Creeping up the hall, cricket bat ready to swing, the man approached me.

Smiled.

"Long time, Phil," he said.

Lowering the bat, I stared until the shapes formed a familiar body. I raised the bat again and swung hard. The wood clanged against the wall as the man ducked. "What are you doing here?" I spat.

The man sighed, picked up the kettle, and poured steaming water into a mug. "Here, drink this. You need it after last night."

His appearance was different—older.

"Tobias, what are you doing here?"

"You're getting careless." He pushed the coffee towards me, the aroma calming me, despite his presence. "I know, I know, you're surprised to see me."

I nodded.

"I'm not here to hurt you, I promise," Tobias said, holding his hands up defensively. "Drink your coffee."

I sipped from the mug. He always knew how to make it perfect. He made so many things perfect, back in the day. Until it wasn't perfect anymore. Until it was dangerous and violent.

"I've been watching you," he said.

I put the mug down and gripped the cricket bat anew.

"You don't need that," he said, smirking. "I came to talk, that's all."

"We have nothing to say to each other," I said. *Except that I'm sorry and I miss you and I love you. I love you so much.*

Tobias sighed. "Well, then can you just listen?"

I moved to the kitchen table, an old wooden thing with burn marks and whitish rings from not using coasters. Tobias sat opposite me.

"I'm getting older. Ageing," he said, gesturing to his body. Touching his hairline, he traced a finger down one cheek. He was still gorgeous, but he was older than he should have been. "I need your help to stop it."

"You can't stop ageing."

"I can," he said. "I have been. But I'm not as good at hunting without you anymore."

"How is that my problem?"

"I have a proposition for you." Tobias leaned close to me. "Can we forget about the past, and go back to the old days? We go hunting together, keep each other safe. I... I miss you."

The cricket bat was looser in my grasp now. Something about the way he was staring at me made me want to throw it away. Made me want to climb over the table and forget about the horrible things we did to each other, and just remember the good times. The feasts, the sex, sharing our dreams under the stars while covered in blood.

"I miss you too," I whispered. My head was getting heavier.

"Good," Tobias replied, taking my hand in his. The cricket bat fell to the tiled floor with a slap. "Because I need a favour."

I blinked. Looked at him. Those eyes. His smirk. Those teeth. His teeth… They appeared to be perfectly fine, like nothing had ever happened. *Dentures, probably.*

"I need a fresh body."

"We can go hunting," I told him. "Just as soon as I feel a bit better. This hangover is—"

"No," he said. "You don't understand. I need to make sure you stay with me. I need to know you're committed."

"I am. I'm sorry about everything, Toby, I am. I'm glad you fixed your teeth. Your smile is so beautiful."

"The teeth were never really injured. Just a setback." Tobias waved away my comment. "Are you committed to *us*?"

I said I was, made it sound as impassioned as I could.

"Good. And you can prove that to me?" Tobias asked, squeezing my hand.

"I'll do anything you want to prove my commitment."

"Good. When your wife and kid get home"—Tobias could embody such sweetness, such innocence when he wanted to, as he did now—"you need to kill them."

I snapped out of the hold he had me in. Kill Darla? Kill Mike? Tobias was gazing at me with such love and care, but I saw it now. Behind that, behind the sparkle, hidden deep in his pupils, the raw hatred for my family.

"You know I won't do that," I said, and pulled away from his grip. Standing, the chair slid back against the tiles with a high-pitched squeak, until it hit the back wall.

Tobias just stared at me, blank.

"You know…" My vision went blurry once more, my head heavier and heavier. As I stepped away from the table, my legs buckled underneath me. "I… What's happening?" I fell face-first onto the tiles, my cheek banging hard. A sliver of blood pooled at my lips. It tasted like heaven.

"Insurance," Tobias said. "In case you fought me on this."

I tried to stand, tried to move, but my body was dead weight.

"Just a little something in the coffee, no permanent damage." Tobias kneeled before me, caressed my hair and smelled me. "Fuck I have missed your scent. You smell like home."

"Why…" I couldn't form proper words.

"It's not revenge, Phil," he said. "In case you're thinking that. No, I've spent the last few years watching you. I've seen you become this empty void.

Hiding your desires from your family, staying out late to eat and drink and fuck. You're a drunk, Phil. A pathetic drunk. You've lost your way."

He was right, I knew he was right. Darla knew it, even Mike probably knew it.

Mike. I could only think his name, couldn't speak it. Couldn't move, couldn't do anything. My eyes started to close again. I held them open with every bit of energy I had left.

"And I've realised that the problem isn't your urges. Your problem isn't the cannibalism." Tobias stroked my hair with such gentle care, and ran a finger down to the pool of blood near my lips. Tasted some and moaned. "Your problem is your family. They're in the way of you being *you.*"

I tried to shake my head. I loved my family, I loved my son. They wouldn't understand the urges, wouldn't know how to love me back if they truly understood what I was. I had to hide. Hide in plain sight, isn't that what he taught me?

"So what we're going to do is just wait," Tobias said, his voice lowering to a whisper. "When Darla and Mike get home, we're going to play a game."

...

My hands and feet were bound to one of the dining table chairs. My head hung low on my chest, and I breathed hard as I tried to lift it. My vision had cleared, but I was tired. Mike was sitting with Darla across from me. Their lips were twisted in confusion and fear, especially little Mike, who had no idea what was happening.

Darla didn't, either, but she at least had suspicions. She'd asked a few years earlier if Tobias and I had ever been together, had asked if I had sexual urges for men. When I'd denied it, she went quiet, as though she understood I was lying and didn't know how to coax the truth from me.

"Ah, you're awake," he said, and stopped pacing. "We've been waiting for quite some time."

The light streaming through the living room curtains was dull, faded. I must have been unconscious for hours.

"Phil, what's going on?" Darla asked, staring at me.

I shrugged, unable to speak just yet. I had nothing to say, anyway.

"Cat got your tongue, Phil?" Tobias asked, leaning down to speak into my ear. His tongue lapped at my earlobe and he moaned in pleasure.

All I could do was regard my family, my loved ones—Darla and Mike. My son, only seven years old, terrified at the sight of his father tied to a chair and some man he didn't remember waving a knife around. I struggled at my bonds, the rope grinding into my skin as I did so.

"Remember I said I wanted to play a game?" Tobias asked me.

Shooting him a spiteful glare, I muttered, "Everything is a game to you."

Tobias laughed. "On the contrary. This game is quite serious."

"Phil, what's happening? Why is he back here?" Darla asked, squeezing Mike tight in her arms. He had started crying, unable to process the situation. The sense of danger grew each moment the knife pointed at his loved ones.

"It's okay, honey," I said, but we all knew I didn't mean it. My voice was scratchy and weak, and I didn't yet have the energy to fake it. "It's all going to be okay."

"What Phil isn't saying," Tobias said, moving around the chair to stand behind me, "is that he has to make a decision tonight." He placed the knife at my neck, pressed the edge of the blade against my skin.

"What decision?" Darla asked.

"You or your son," Tobias said with a shrug, like it was nothing.

"What do you mean?" Darla kept her stare trained on me, avoiding Tobias. "What does he mean, Phil?"

I swallowed hard against the blade, and choked on my words before managing to speak. "He wants me to choose who dies."

Darla opened her mouth to speak, but all that came was a horrible, terrified panting sound as her worst fears were confirmed. She pulled Mike closer as the word "dies" sank into my seven-year-old son's brain.

"We're not playing your game, Tobias," I said.

He laughed. "It doesn't seem like you have a choice."

The blade pressed harder against my neck and I wished he'd just slice me open and be done with it. Tobias was never that generous, though, and I thought fast for a way out of this mess.

"Why…are you…doing this, Tobias? You two are…friends…" Darla cried through deep breaths. She pushed her body back against the lounge, instinctively trying to get away from danger. There was nowhere to go.

"Friends, is it? That's what I'm reduced to." Tobias let the knife drop a little and stepped around the chair towards my wife and son. "Phil and I were lovers. More than that, we were… We were special together."

Darla upturned her mouth at the word "lovers" and flashed me an *I knew it* glare. Intertwined was the knowledge that this was all my fault. Whatever I'd been up to, whatever she'd suspected me of doing, it had brought Tobias here tonight.

"Shall I tell her?" Tobias asked, his gaze fixed

on her. The knife was trained on my family, steady and firm. The blade held intentionally at Darla's eye level.

"Don't," I said. I was still coming off whatever drug he'd used on me, but I was conscious enough to realise what he meant.

"Don't tell me what?" Darla asked. Even now, with the fear and the uncertainty, she was angry. I didn't want things to end like this, didn't know if I could handle it. "Tell me what, Phil?"

Tobias moved to her once more, the blade a whisper from her eye. "Tell her, Phil, or I'll cut her eyes out."

"Tobias, please—"

"FUCKING TELL HER WHAT WE DO!"

I couldn't see his face, but I imagined he was smiling, even as he screamed at my wife. Straining against the knots around my wrists, I could feel the rope loosening. Not enough to slip free, but it gave me hope. I just had to keep him busy for a bit longer. Keep him talking, keep his attention away from me.

He turned around.

Fuck.

"You tell her or I will," he said. "And she will have no choice but to listen as I chew on her eyeballs."

His eyes held nothing but the truth in that moment. No deception, no exaggeration. He would do it, right in front of my son. There was no doubt in my mind.

"We're…cannibals," I whispered. Darla

laughed, despite herself. I glanced at her, then dropped my head down of pure shame, and shook in apology. "We hunt people. We take them somewhere secluded, and…"

"Yes, yes, go on," Tobias said, taunting me. "And what?"

"We eat them."

"Tell her the rest," Tobias said.

Darla covered her hands over Mike's ears. "This is some kind of… Well, this is a joke." Darla stared at Tobias. "You're joking. I suspected there was something between you two. I sensed it went deeper than friendship, that it was… an affair. I… It's the way he looks at you. So full of lust and desire and need. But the rest, it's…"

"The night you two met," Tobias said, licking his lips, "we were going to kill you and eat you. But this one"—he gestured towards me—"liked your perfume. Decided to marry you instead."

Shooting me another glare, Darla's eyes were filled with tears. I stared back at her, mouth trembling to hold back my own emotion, and begged for her forgiveness.

"So," Tobias said, clapping a hand against the knife handle, "the game."

"Kill me," I said. "Please."

Tobias yawned. "Boring. That's so passé. Everyone says that. No, you have to choose. Darla, or Mike. Darla, Mike, Mike, Darla, who's it going to be?"

"I can't." I hung my head, I couldn't look at Darla, didn't want to look at Tobias. He couldn't be serious, he couldn't do this to me. "Why *now*? After all this time, why are you here *now*?"

"Choose."

"I can't."

"CHOOSE."

"I won't."

"CHOOSE!" Tobias rushed back to me and stabbed the knife into my thigh. "CHOOSE!"

Screaming, I shook my head and gritted my teeth. "I WON'T!"

With Tobias distracted, Darla leaped from the lounge, shouted for Mike to run, and lunged at Tobias. Mike did as he was ordered and ran from the room. He didn't even glance back. The back door slammed shut as Mike made it outside. Darla was on top of Tobias, but he was strong—so strong—and she was no match. I wouldn't have been, either, even with my police training.

"Darla, get out of here!" I yelled at her.

Tobias whacked her across the side of the head, knocking her off him. She held her bruised head for a second, but came back at him. She scratched at his eyes and neck, and Tobias laughed as he grabbed her wrists, threw her to the ground.

Reaching for the knife in my thigh while I struggled at the rope—almost untied—Tobias pulled it free with a slimy squelching sound, and lunged down at Darla.

"Darla, run!" I screamed.

Tobias grabbed her by the hair, and swung the knife into her cheek and Darla screamed.

"You should have played the game," Tobias said to me as he stabbed my wife through the heart. "Now see this? See what you made me do?"

I screamed and screamed until there was nothing left. Darla fell back to the floor with a thud, still staring at me with hatred and terror.

"FUCK YOU!" I managed, but Tobias was already on his feet. Bending over Darla, picking her up. "Get your fucking hands off her!"

Without another word, he lifted her over his shoulder, and headed to the door while I screamed at him to put her down. Stopping at the exit, he said, "This isn't over, Phil. You will play my game. One day."

23

PHIL

I felt it go in. The sensation of bone cracking and splintering as the bullet dug into my brain. My vision went dark for a few moments, everything ended. Somewhere inside me, despite my heart stopping, the teeth chattered. I could feel it, even through the absence of consciousness.

The light came hurtling back, and my eyes sprung open.

Gasping and spluttering, my head ached and throbbed, but I was awake. Scanning the room, gripping Brooks's ankle.

"What the FUCK!" she screamed.

I heard her finger against the trigger.

I was up, fast. The pain in my leg was gone. My vision was red, blood and brains and gunk obscuring the world. But I was up, grabbing Brooks by the throat.

261

I took the gun, threw it away. It landed with a thump on the stairs.

The teeth were angry. They'd been attacked, harmed. It wasn't about me, the vessel. It was about them. They cared for their own wellbeing, nothing more. As I squeezed Brooks's neck tighter, feeling the cartilage bend and crack under the pressure, I knew the same was true for me. I had only ever truly cared for myself.

Darla was gone because of me.

Tobias was gone because of me.

Mike stayed away from me because I was selfish.

"Kill me," I said, knowing the gun was out of reach and her oxygen was running out fast. "Please."

She choked and wheezed, struggled against my grip. I tried to loosen it, tried to let her go, but my hands were too strong. The teeth were pumping their poison through me and I couldn't control them. I truly was a vessel now, a puppet. Walking in a body that wanted nothing to do with me.

"Kick me in the groin," I told her.

Brooks considered me, confused, but I begged her to do it, and she obliged. The pain seared through me, but I didn't let go. Squeezed tighter instead.

"Again!"

She kicked harder. My balls shot up inside my body, and I doubled over in pain. The teeth weren't impervious to pain, you just had to get the intensity right. With my body doubled over, the grip around Brooks's neck loosened enough for her to slip free.

"Run," I managed through the pain.

"You're under arrest," Brooks spluttered. She reached once more for the handcuffs, but saw me recovering.

"I can't hold back for long. Please, get the fuck out of here… Get Mike. He'll know what to do."

Brooks stared at me for a second before nodding. Glancing down at her dead colleague, she left him on the floor, grabbed her gun from the stairs, and raced to the door. I watched her go to her car, yelling into her phone for backup. I'd won. I'd beaten the teeth, just this once. Brooks stood by her car, threw open a door and positioned herself behind it with the gun trained on the house.

"Come out with your hands up," she yelled at me.

I sat on the bottom step of the stairway. The bullet wound in my head was already healing, the black veins coalescing at the injury, repairing brain matter and bone.

I picked up the book with Tobias's baby photo in it, and clutched it to my chest. For now, I was me, but the teeth were planning something. While they healed the vessel, they plotted. I could sense it through the itching at the end of each tooth.

Looking at the book, I opened to the page of Tobias.

How could he have had the teeth his whole life?

It did explain a few things about his behaviour, but I was sure there was more to it than that. I remembered how I had knocked his teeth right out of him, pummelled him almost to death. Is that what it would take to get them out of me?

Staring out the front door to Brooks, I wondered if I could ask her to beat the living shit out of me. The teeth began to stir at the thought, at the knowledge that their vessel was intending them harm.

Mike would do it. He'd do it to save me.

A crack in my neck came hard and fast, and I groaned. Feeling the spot—bone jutting from the skin—I drew my hand back to see blood. That was new.

Another crack.

More bone, coming from the side of my neck now. It wasn't as hard as bone should be, and it was wet, gooey. More like a growth. As another crack came—from my back this time—something pressed against my spine. It was painful, but also warm and inviting.

Without even realising it, I stood up, the book clutched tight in my hand.

The portrait of Sir Brentwood seemed to stare right at me as I headed for the front door. Some part of me grasped what was happening—what I needed to do. As I headed outside, towards Brooks and her car, it all became clear.

Mike. I need Mike.

24

MIKE

Leaving Dad alone with Brooks and her partner was the worst possible outcome I could imagine. Not only had he killed and eaten Agnes, but Brooks had managed to get a warrant to track my phone, to follow me around. Dad wasn't going to like that. Not one bit.

She was suspicious, but there was no way she *couldn't* have put the actual pieces together. She was probably figuring Dad was a serial killer coming out of hiding after years of inactivity. It happened all the time, if the true crime podcasts Kyle was always telling me about were anything to go by.

The only solace I had as I arrived at the hospital was that Dad was ageing backward, so Brooks wouldn't recognise him. Hell, I didn't recognise him. Well, that wasn't exactly true. He was the spitting image of Sir Brentwood now, which made my head spin. It was clear that the teeth were changing him, but they seemed to be turning him *into* Tobias. However that was possible, I had no idea.

I hobbled past a few people in the emergency waiting area, some with blood oozing from their bodies, others just holding a broken arm or another comparatively minor injury. A shirtless guy pressing a towel against his abdomen stared at me. I headed to triage; the nurse sitting behind a thick plexiglass window asked my details and the nature of my injury. I pointed to the wound on my leg and said, "I was bitten."

She raised a curious eyebrow, but said nothing. Just typed away into a computer making a medical record for me. She motioned behind me to indicate I take a seat, so I sat there and waited. Every minute that passed increased my anxiety—Dad was back at that house, doing any number of unimaginable things to Brooks and her partner, and anyone else in the vicinity of the dentures. With Brooks on my back, though, I needed to do the right thing, leave a trail of evidence behind to show that I wasn't not part of Dad's scheme.

Except I very much am part of it.

Now that I was alone and able to think about the last few days, the craziness of it all, I realised just how awful my actions had been. I hadn't killed anyone, but I was protecting a monster. That's what Dad was now—maybe what he'd always been.

A monster.

I wanted to believe it was all down to the teeth, but that wasn't true. He'd been a cannibal back in the 1960s, all the way through to… When? When exactly did he stop? Was it when he stopped seeing Tobias?

A memory pulled at me again, and I shook it away.

No, don't.

Pushing memories away was something I was very good at, though I didn't really know why. Sitting in the emergency ward, ignoring the wails and cries of the other patients, I embraced the memory. It started with Sir Brentwood, that much I already gathered. How, I wasn't sure, since the portrait was from the 1800s.

Still, he was familiar.

How did I recognise Sir Brentwood when he'd been dead for a century before I was even born? Why did I remember his voice, and—

A flash.

Mum screaming at me to run.

Dad tied to a chair.

A man—Tobias?—attacking us.

"Fuck," I said, and a guy holding a bloody rag to his abdomen surveyed me, figuring me out.

The memory was clear now. I had run, I had gone to the neighbour and they'd phoned the police. By the time they got there, Mum and the man were gone. Dad had freed himself from the chair and was weeping over a pool of blood on the floor.

That was the last time I'd seen my mum.

How could I not remember that?

Dad always told me it wasn't real, just a silly nightmare. He'd insisted for years that Mum had died in a car wreck, that I had dreamed another scenario. After a while, I started to believe it, until the memory faded and I stopped having "bad dreams".

Why would Tobias do that, and what does all this have to do with Sir Brentwood?

Tobias's surname was Brentwood, Dad had confirmed that. In my head, though, he was the same person as the one in the portrait. None of what was happening was possible. Maybe in some made-up world, but here in the real world, those things didn't happen—the dentures, eating Dave from the office, growing younger, none of it—yet, it was real. I'd been there for a lot of it, had helped cover it up.

Was it any less ridiculous to think Tobias was the same Sir Brentwood? His picture had been in the photo album, too.

My head was reeling with all the possibilities, all the information I'd learned over the last few days. The memory of my mum telling me to run, the last thing she ever said to me. My stomach lurched at the knowledge that it was real, that my mother had tried to save me and my dad, and had only saved me.

There was something else, too. The guy at the coffee shop. The one who told me not to spend any more money on Dad.

Why had I listened to him?

It hit me hard.

"Fuck." *He* was Sir Brentwood. He was Tobias. "He's been following me."

The guy holding his bloodied abdomen was staring at me now, nodding like he understood my plight. "Fuck that guy," he said.

"What?"

He sneered, his countenance twisting into a deep anger. "Some dude's following you, you fuck him up."

I mumbled a general agreement, my focus drifting to the gang tattoo on his bicep. Despite his violent lifestyle, in that moment I realised I wasn't so different from him. We were both here with injuries related to intense violence. His was probably a gunshot or a stab wound, mine a bite. By my cannibalistic father.

Bloody Abdomen guy was right, though. Whoever Tobias was, whatever he wanted, he was setting me up. Dad, too. Some kind of game he was playing—I remembered Tobias saying those words that night, and I searched my memory harder for more answers.

Nothing came.

"You gotta protect what's yours, bro," the guy said. He couldn't have been any older than Kyle, and I couldn't help but feel sorry for him. He must have seen the flash of pity in my eyes, because he turned away with a *pfft*.

"You're right," I said. "I have to protect my family."

And I would do it a hell of a lot better than Dad did.

The clock had shifted to the next hour, and I still hadn't been seen, which was not unusual for public hospitals. The gang member had been in and out already, and I waved a little to the triage nurse hoping she'd notice me. Hoping she'd tell me how much longer I would be waiting. Not that she'd know, really. It wasn't up to her.

I pulled out my phone, admired the wallpaper of me and Kyle mid-kiss for a moment, then unlocked with Face ID. I navigated to Kyle's contact, and hit "Call". The phone rang a few times, and with each second he didn't answer, my stomach dropped.

"Hey babe," he answered.

I beamed at the sound of his voice. At the word "babe", which I genuinely hated. In that moment, it was everything to me. "Hey," I said. "I was just calling to say I love you."

Kyle hesitated. "Are you okay?"

"I'm fine," I said. The worry in his voice sent

shockwaves through me, and I almost burst into tears. That was one thing about Kyle—he could always tell when I wasn't myself. "I just wanted to hear your voice."

"Oh, babe, that is so sweet. I love you, too."

My heart pulled at the words, tugged at them and wrapped them around my body. I didn't realise how much I needed to hear it back until he'd said it. How important it was that he was there, that he felt something for me, even though I'd been assisting a serial killing cannibal.

"I'm in hospital," I told him, changing the subject before I succumbed to my emotions. "It's nothing to worry about. Just a dog bite. Long story."

"Oh my god!"

"No, it's okay. I just wanted to let you know what's happened, but I'm alright."

Kyle gulped on the other end. "Okay. Is it serious?"

"Just a flesh wound, but I need a shot, that's all. I'll be home for dinner."

"Oh, that reminds me. Your dad phoned, too. He said he'll also be here for dinner tonight."

My dad? But Dad had introduced himself to Kyle as my cousin. Why would he change that now?

"Babe?" Kyle asked.

"Did he say when?"

"Yeah, he said he'd be over in the next half

hour. That was about a half hour ago, so I'm expecting him any minute."

"Kyle, get out of the house!"

"What? Why?" Kyle asked, panicked.

I leaped from the chair and raced as fast as I could to the exit. They slid open and I rushed to my car. "Just go!" I hung up, thrust the phone into my pocket, and opened the car door.

With the way Dad had sniffed at Kyle, wanting to taste him… If Dad was on his way to Kyle, it only meant one thing.

My body shook as I engaged the ignition and headed home, speeding past red lights and weaving through traffic. I wasn't going to fail Kyle the way Dad had failed me and Mum.

The house seemed quiet as I approached. Empty. It was too early for the lights to be on, though, so I couldn't be sure. I pulled into the driveway, left the car in park, and crashed through the front door. I heard movement somewhere—towards the back of the house. I raced through the living room, ignoring the thrashing, pulsing, pounding pain in my leg. Through the dining area and the kitchen, and saw Kyle outside, in the backyard. Next to him stood—

Tobias?

I opened the sliding door to the backyard, and Kyle spun to me. He was laughing.

So was Tobias. He was older, a lot older. He

appeared frail, but not as bad as Dad had been before the teeth took over.

"Ah, there he is," Tobias said, his voice gravelly.

"Who, uh, who are you?" I asked, pretending I didn't recognise him. "Kyle said my dad was coming over."

"I'm sure he'll be here soon," Tobias said. "He's just wrapping some things up with Brooks."

I nodded, glancing between Kyle and Tobias. The sight was unseemly, and it hurt to breathe.

"I'm an old friend of your father's," Tobias continued. "But I think you know that already, don't you?"

I frowned. "What are you doing here?" I asked.

Tobias wrapped an arm around Kyle and pulled him close. "I came to meet the family. It's been a long time since your father and I saw each other, I've been *dying* to see you again, Mike. Do you remember the last time I saw you? I sure do." His lips curled into a wicked grin.

"I remember," I told him.

Kyle was frowning, sensing my unease.

"Kyle, can I talk to you in the kitchen for a moment?" I asked.

He went to move and Tobias stepped with him, not letting go. "What a wonderful idea," Tobias said. "Let's all have a drink."

It was going to be challenging to get Tobias

away from Kyle. In the house, though, there would be more options. Especially in the kitchen, with all the knives.

Tobias dragged Kyle towards the house. Kyle tried fighting back a little, but not much. He was scared—who wouldn't be?—and unsure what this strange man was capable of, even if he appeared old and frail. I assumed Kyle read the fear in my expression, and decided the best course of action was to follow my lead.

Except I didn't have a lead.

Just the knives in the kitchen.

My phone vibrated in my pocket, and it occurred to me that perhaps I could call the police. Detective Brooks. She was tracking me, anyway, she'd be over in a few minutes.

"Don't even think about calling the police," Tobias said. I shot him a scowl; he just exhaled sharp through his nose. "I'm old, not deaf. And I'm certainly not stupid."

We were at the back door now, stepping inside the house. "Shall I put the kettle on?" I asked. "I hear you like a good cup of coffee."

"Ah," Tobias said with a smirk. "So your dad *has* been telling tall tales about me."

I sniffed in a weak show of superiority. "I know everything."

Kyle glanced at me, begging for help him. To

tell him what the hell was going on. I avoided his gaze, knowing there was no way I could be honest with him about any of this. Not if I wanted him to stick around.

Pushing Kyle to the kitchen bench, Tobias forced him into a stool. "Stay."

He did as he was instructed, though I could tell he was sizing the old man up, determining weak spots and deciding if he should take the chance to attack while he could.

"Leave Kyle alone." My voice was harsher than I'd intended it to be, and I placed a hand on Kyle's shoulder to keep him down. A message—*Stay out of this, please.*

He seemed to understand, and continued staring down Tobias like he wanted to kill the old man. Me and him both.

"Do you know why I'm here?" Tobias asked.

"I'm assuming it's about the teeth," I said.

Nodding, Tobias flicked on the kettle, then spun to me, arms folded across his chest. "I'm tired and old, and I don't like it." He paused, seeming wistful, regretful. "I need the teeth back."

"You need them…"

"Back, yes." Tobias smirked. "You didn't know that, did you? I don't think your father ever knew, either."

He is the same Tobias from that baby book. With the weird teeth. He had them his whole life?

While I tried to wrap my head around the fact that Tobias had either been born with the dentures, or gifted them as a baby, he removed three mugs from a cupboard, and rifled through the pantry for the coffee grounds. Just instant, that's all I kept. Coffee machines were too much trouble.

"I would gladly give them to you," I said, "but they don't come out on their own. You should know that."

"Oh, I do." The kettle boiled, sending wisps of steam into the air. "They only come out if the vessel is dead. I would do it, but…" Tobias shrugged.

"But what?"

"Your father and I started a game a long time ago. We never finished it."

CHOOSE.

The memories rushed back, though I didn't want to believe they were real. Tobias tied Dad to a chair, made him choose who to kill—me or Mum. When I ran out, went to the neighbours, Mum was gone. I couldn't believe Dad had agreed to let Tobias kill her. The fact that the game never ended meant Dad never chose. Which also meant—

"You killed my mum?" My voice was a whisper, bubbling with rage.

Tobias poured hot water into three mugs, ever the civilised gentleman. "I did." He was so casual about it, shrugging as he twisted his back to me.

In that moment, I didn't care if Tobias was old or weak or fragile. I didn't care if he held a secret strength, on loan from his time with the teeth. I raced towards him, grabbed the kettle from his hands, and whacked him in the face with it. Boiling water streamed through the air, burned at my skin.

Tobias recovered fast, lunging at my waist in a tackle. He was stronger than I anticipated, and forced me back against the fridge with a crash. I brought the kettle down hard on his back, barely noticed Kyle storming over to help.

"Kyle, get out of here!"

He wasn't listening. He pulled the old man off me and threw him to the ground. Tobias collapsed in a heap on the tiled floor, cackling, despite me jumping on top of him and slamming the kettle into his face. Harder and harder.

He kept laughing, like my efforts were the funniest thing in the world. Kyle had his phone in his hands, shaking from the adrenaline, dialling someone. The police, I was sure. On the one hand, it was a good idea, because this guy was an intruder. On the other, I didn't trust the police to think of me as a victim anymore.

Not that I ever was, really.

I glanced at Kyle to tell him not to call, and that's all it took.

A moment of distraction.

Tobias slammed his bony fist into my stomach, then into my nose, and I was down. The kettle rattled across the tiles, boiling water pooling as it went. He was up before I realised what had happened. Up, and across the kitchen to Kyle, who had tried to run, tried to punch at the old man. A swift kick to the groin had Kyle doubled over, decommissioned long enough for a second blow to the back of his head with a sharp elbow.

He was on the floor, his phone nowhere to be seen. I got to my hands and knees, tried to stand but my head was woozy from smashing into the fridge. Crawling to my partner, my hands burning as I moved through the puddle of boiling water, Tobias grabbed Kyle's head and force it into the corner of the kitchen bench.

Kyle fell to the floor, a wet red spot on his head where he'd been struck. Eyes closed.

"Fuck you!" I screamed, getting to my feet.

Tobias, swift and controlled, raced to a knife block just past Kyle, and swooped back to me with a butcher knife at the ready.

"Say that one more time," Tobias said, breathing hard.

I opened my mouth, but the words didn't come. Just a sense of pain and surprise as Tobias slashed at my chest with the knife.

The trail of red seeping through my clothes

confused me. I met Tobias's eyes again, and that smarmy smirk spread from ear to ear. His head came at mine, the dull clap of skin against skin, and I was down, this time being dragged across the room and thrown with ease onto the lounge.

"What are you—"

"Shh," Tobias said, frustrated. "Just relax."

"You're not going to eat me, are you?" I tried to stand, but my body was weak.

Tobias held up a syringe. I hadn't even seen it before. Hadn't felt it, either.

"Leave…Kyle…" I fought to focus on my words. They were jumbled, my thoughts drifting in and out as whatever drug he'd given me worked its way through my body.

"Hush now," Tobias said. "It'll all be over soon."

25

PHIL

"Don't come any closer." Brooks held her weapon firm, and as much as I wanted to raise my hands up and get to my knees to let her take me, the teeth had other ideas. She screamed at me again, then into a radio calling for backup. From my time on the force I understood how it worked, that backup always took forever—it wasn't like the movies, where the police cars all piled into the street at once. Not even close.

"I can't stop," I said. "I have to get to my son."

"Your son?"

"Mike Benson."

Her cheeks flushed—confusion, doubt—and then she shook her head.

"I can't explain, but it's true."

Brooks took the safety off her weapon and

281

moved around the car door as I approached. "All I know for sure is that you're a fucking killer."

As the words were spat at my face, the truth of it all came crashing down on me. I couldn't live like this. I couldn't ask Mike to live like this, covering for me and my fucking cravings. I'd gotten away with this shit for too long. In my heart, I knew of only one way to stop me for good.

I have to die.

Except the bullets didn't work. I had just regrown my skull and now I had jagged pieces of bone sticking from my neck and back. Something had changed when Brooks shot me. Something had activated, I could feel it. Even as I kept trudging to her and she pulled the trigger again.

It should have hurt, the bullet landing somewhere in my gut, but I sensed the veins rushing to the site of the injury. The bullet fell to the concrete, and Brooks fired again.

"Stay down!" she cried, even though I wasn't down at all. "Stay the fuck down!"

My teeth chattered faster, faster, and my hand tightened into a fist.

"Get away from me, please," I begged her through gritted teeth. "Before it's too late."

My jaw expanded, showing the teeth in all their glory, the edges jagged and sharp, waiting for something to tear into.

"What the fuck are you?" Brooks cowered behind the car on the other side, gun still trained on me, though we both shared an unspoken, tacit knowledge that it wouldn't work.

I shook my head, as much as the teeth would let me. "I don't know."

Throwing the book at her, I moved around the car fast, grabbed at her. She dodged, ran, but I grabbed her hair. Fucking ponytails. Yanked her back hard, and pulled her into my arms. Wrapped her in a hug from behind, and sniffed at her.

Still not as tasty as a man, but the teeth weren't in it for taste this time. They wanted to kill her just because they could. A message to me that I was powerless. A message to her for trying to harm them. I fought as much as I could, but as Brooks struggled and fought against my grip, my teeth sank into the back of her head.

The bone of her skull cracked under the force of the teeth, and she screamed in defiance as the first portion came away. I chewed on the flesh and hair and bone, swallowed loudly as Brooks begged for mercy, begged for help.

The street was quiet, and even if it hadn't been, the teeth didn't give a shit. As the crushed bone went down like gravel, I bit harder, my tongue squeezing into the hole I'd created, tasting her brain. It was soft and gooey. Goddamn, I'd missed this stuff.

My jaw clamped down, and despite myself, I relished in the sound of cracking bone and the squelching of brain matter between my teeth. Her body started to go limp in my arms, and part of me was disappointed. I missed the chase, the *teeth* missed the chase. The days when they could stalk people through dark alleys like Jack the Ripper and feast with the rats.

"Please…" Brooks groaned as I brought her to the driveway and tore at the hole in her head. She was too weak to move now, and I'd taken enough chunks of her brain that she her sense of reality, of her body, of her own existence, was crumbling.

The teeth were excited now; the rumbling in my stomach. The jagged edges protruding from my neck were tingling. But I'd already eaten, I was full. My belly was heavy and as I wolfed down more brain matter, licking it from my fingers as the juices trailed down my wrists, my throat seized.

The urge to vomit rose with that heat in my cheeks and neck; that heat when stomach contents wanted out. Buckling over Brooks, who was squirming underneath me—still begging for help, but in nonsensical groans—I unleashed the chewed-up, stringy, wet, gelatinous brain chunks onto her chest.

She tried to move, but the nerves in her brain were all fucked up now, and she just jerked against the concrete.

Wiping at my mouth, the teeth clamouring with excitement again, I picked up the book and stood. Walked to the car, leaving Brooks to writhe and squirm, a mindless sack. Inside the car, keys dangled from the ignition, and I smiled. The teeth *made* me smile.

They wanted me to go to Mike. No, not Mike. *Kyle.*

They liked how he smelled, wanted to taste him.

Go there, old man…

I was already on the way.

. . .

History had a funny way of repeating itself, and I feared it was happening now as I rushed to the house. That night I'd ran home to Darla and Mike, I knew something terrible was about to happen. The same feeling coursed through my veins now, as I rushed to Mike and Kyle. Tobias was gone, though, and this time I was the enemy.

Yet as the photo album sat on the front passenger seat, opened to the page of Tobias, I wondered if he was somehow still with me. Guiding me, guiding the dentures. It was stupid, I understood that, but pieces of the puzzle were starting to fall into place. I'd seen the image of baby Tobias with a full set of adult teeth. That was from 1880, though. He must have been a relative of the Sir Brentwood from the portrait. That would have made him Tobias the Second or something. Which meant *my* Tobias would have been the sixth or seventh.

Were they all cannibals? Did they all have the teeth?

It was a waste of time thinking about it now. I needed a plan. The teeth wanted Kyle, his delicious body, but I wanted Mike. I needed his help, again. It wasn't supposed to be that way. Parents weren't supposed to rely on their kids for help. It was the other way round. Yet Mike had always been there supporting me, ever since Darla…left.

No wonder he hates me.

Except he had been helping, even when I'd eaten Dave, his friend. And he still wanted to help. Mike was at the hospital, though, the other direction from his house, and the teeth made me press harder on the accelerator to get to Kyle faster. The poor kid had no idea what was coming—the teeth had very specific plans for him.

His house was just around the corner now, and my hunger started afresh, despite the ache in my guts and more and more bones jutting out from my skin. Mostly around my abdomen now—like something was grabbing at my stomach, wrapping around it; the veins were pushing deeper inside me, if that was even possible.

I left the police car parked diagonally across the lawn, and raced into the house.

Inside it was dark, all the curtains closed. A strip of light penetrated the room as the front door creaked wider. Standing in the glow of the afternoon sun, I peered through the house, calling for Kyle. My voice was low and smooth, endearing. Charming.

I'd had a lot of practice at this. No man could resist.

"Ah, there he is," came a voice from another room. "We're in here."

It was familiar, but gravelly and older. Surprised, I followed the voice into the living room, stopping at the entrance. A man stood facing me, his back to Mike and Kyle, both tied up on the lounge, unconscious. A butcher knife sat on the coffee table in front of them.

"Surprise, Phil."

"Tobias?" The teeth stopped chattering, shocked into stillness. "Is it really you?"

He opened his arms wide. "I had to come see you."

"What have you done to them?"

Tobias glanced behind him and sighed. "Oh, them. I needed to give you some motivation. To finish our game."

The teeth started anew, clamouring. My guts trembled and shook and fought to stay upright. Something was happening to me and I had no idea what. My jaw stretched in hunger and rage, and Tobias smirked. It wasn't filled with sadness this time. It was pure joy.

"There they are," he said, clasping a hand to his chest. "My babies."

"You want the teeth?" I asked.

Tobias stepped to me, nodding. "I miss them." He got closer, unafraid of the threat I posed. "There's a lot you don't know about me. About the teeth."

I was frozen. With all my intention to come and eat Kyle—who was laid out on the lounge like a fucking turkey, waiting for my hungry lips—I couldn't move. Despite what Tobias had done to Darla, his eyes still mesmerised me. His touch, as he caressed the nape of my neck, still calmed me. After everything. All the hatred and anger and spite.

I still loved him.

"The Sir Brentwood in the portrait is me. Well,"—Tobias cocked his head in thought—"it's a version of me. You see, the teeth have been in my family for centuries. I don't know where they came from, I don't know why they exist. I just know they are part of me. No, that's not right. They *are* me."

"What the hell are you talking about?" I asked, the urge to run to Kyle starting to overtake me again. The more I gazed between Kyle and Mike and Tobias, the more I wanted to eat all of them. Their scents— sweat, fear, anxiety, muscle, sexuality—mixing together in a broiling pot of desire that festered in my groin.

Even though my guts were thrashing, the veins tangling and pushing at my organs.

"The teeth choose a descendant. Anyone, really. And they turn the wearer into the original owner of the teeth." He motioned towards me. "Like they're doing to you."

"You had the teeth when we met?"

He sighed. "I've had them since birth. I was born with the knowledge of who I am, though as a baby it was an implicit, tacit knowledge. I grew into it."

Mike was starting to move, stirring awake with a heavy groan.

"I had them until you beat me half to death," Tobias said with that wry smirk. "Remember that? Well, here's another thing about me you didn't know. I had a family, too."

"Bullshit," I spat. "After the way you went on about me having one, there's—"

"Agnes was my wife. Well before you even met Darla. Gary was my son." His expression was cold, hollow. "Unlike you, I never kept my life a secret from them. They knew all about it, and they loved me, anyway. Gary collected the teeth that night after we were taken to hospital."

"But…"

"I wanted to spare Gary the life I'd had. Eating people isn't for everyone. I would eventually become like you, anyway, and the cycle would start anew. Agnes and Gary needn't have suffered. But you killed my darling Agnes, didn't you?"

"I suppose that makes us even."

Tobias scoffed, but didn't argue. Sized me up once more, as Mike blinked a few times and his brain fog began to lift. He strained at the bonds around his wrists, but he was still weak. I could smell Tobias's skin, old and rotting and somehow still something I wanted to eat.

I leaned into Tobias's hand, my cheek caressing his skin. He let me bask in the glory of his touch for a moment, closing my eyes and calming the teeth. The pain in my stomach calmed for a moment, too.

He ripped his hand away, and my guts retched.

"Why didn't you…" Mike asked from behind him, "put the teeth back in?"

Tobias turned to him. "What?"

"When your son collected the teeth that night," Mike said. "Why didn't you put them back in? Agnes said Gary found the teeth in the attic, so you haven't been wearing them for years. That's why you're so old."

"It's true," he admitted. "I didn't put them back in." He faced me then. "You freed me that night. I hadn't ever had the chance to live *without* their influence. You gave me that. Gary hid the teeth from me at my request, but the teeth had been inside me so long that they left me…changed. I still have the urge, as you found out…that night."

I didn't need to clarify what night he was talking about. I didn't even need to ask him why he did what he did to Darla. She wasn't really part of the equation. Neither was Mike. We all understood that by now.

"But lately," he continued, "I've been facing my own mortality. Cancer… It's everywhere." Tobias frowned. "So I begged Gary to give me the teeth, it was the only way to survive."

"Except he put them in…" Mike said, still tugging at the bonds on his wrists.

"I don't know why he did that," Tobias said. "But after he… After the accident, everything became clear."

"What—"

"It's your fault," Tobias said, staring deep into me. "All of this is because of you."

There were no words. I had nothing. His son putting the teeth in had nothing to do with me, yet Tobias was huffing and breathing hard, staring at me with daggers.

"If you hadn't done what you did," he said, "my son—and my wife—would still be alive." He took a second to compose himself. "So, I concocted a plan. One final game. And this time, you *will* finish it."

The veins in my stomach pushed against me harder, and I doubled over, retching. They were snaking up my neck this time, instead of down.

Wanting out. The teeth chattered, clamoured, and ached for food, but by stomach and the veins didn't want anything now. I needed to hurl, the veins climbing closer to the back of my mouth.

Tobias eyed me cautiously. "It's happening. We're running out of time."

"Time for what?" Mike asked.

"The cycle is starting again."

26

MIKE

As Dad doubled over, trying to spill his guts, I nudged at Kyle. His head injury was pretty bad, the blood was still seeping from him. I shifted across the lounge to him, wincing at the pain in the open wound on my chest. I jabbed him in the ribs, and whispered his name. He responded with a weak groan. I just needed him conscious enough to untie me so I could call the cops out here and get him some help.

"Come on, Kyle." My voice was hoarse and forceful.

One eye opened a little, just enough that I could see the white. His pupil started to roll back to the front and I breathed a little easier.

"Kyle. Bub. Wake up, please."

The other eye opened and I jabbed him once

more as I glimpsed Dad and Tobias. Dad was standing upright now, but holding his stomach. He seemed to be really ill, and the bones jutting from his body were a new development—the black veins were starting to inch their way up from his bottom eyelids.

"Kyle!" I hissed.

He was more alert now, tried to reach to his head wound, and blinked in confusion as he realised he was restrained. I raised a finger to my lips to shush him, and he replied by way of a slow bob of the head.

"Untie me," I said.

Kyle fumbled at the knots around my wrists, still groggy from the head wound and spiked coffee.

"You have to choose," Tobias said. He and Dad looked back over at us, saw Kyle removing the rope from my wrists, and sprang into action. Tobias raced to the butcher knife, Dad on his heels, and leaped onto the lounge.

I lunged forward at the same time, and we crashed onto the floor in a heap. The blade slashed at me again and I cried out as the skin on my arm tore open. Above me, Tobias flashed his disgusting fucking smirk, and swiped the blade.

Dad was on his back, and Kyle came at him—still sleepy—to shoulder him with his full body weight. Tobias rolled off me to the floor, brought the knife down to my stomach.

The blade chopped into me, buried in the fatty

flesh of my belly. Kyle dove over me, his hands still tied, and tackled Tobias once more.

"Leave him alone!" Kyle cried.

I sat up, my back resting against the lounge, and stared down at the knife jutting from my belly. Dad kneeled beside me, suddenly unaware of the struggle between Kyle and Tobias. His teeth started their dreadful sound, wanting the meat in my belly and whatever else it could take.

"Dad," I managed, "help Kyle. If you're hungry…eat Tobias."

He wasn't listening, enamoured by the sight before him.

"Dad! Fucking listen for once!"

He snapped his eyes to mine, then followed my finger as I pointed to Kyle and Tobias rolling around on the floor.

"I'm sorry, Mike," he whispered.

I imagined his teeth coming down on me, but it was his hand. He tore the butcher knife from my belly and screamed as he pushed Kyle out of the way and grabbed Tobias by the scruff.

"You don't hurt them," Dad said through gritted teeth. He spasmed a little as he forced Tobias flat on the floor. He was still unwell, but fighting whatever was happening to him. Fighting the hunger.

Tobias laughed, despite Dad's weight on him, despite him drawing the knife to his neck.

"Why are you laughing?" he asked.

Tobias didn't respond. Just laughed that horrible, smarmy laugh. Like the whole thing was some sick fucking joke.

I couldn't see Dad's face, but his voice told me everything I needed to know. The pained whispered that came.

"Mike," he said, holding back another spasm. "Get Kyle out of here. I don't want him to see this."

Kyle came to me, still in shock and terrified. He helped me stand, and I ushered him to the bedroom. Told him to call the police. I closed the door behind him, leaving me on the other side.

With Dad.

I stood there, holding my belly, and watched as Dad gripped the knife handle with one hand, and pressed down on the top of Tobias's head with the other.

The laughter stopped, followed by a faint whisper: "The cycle is starting again."

"Don't make me do this," Dad whispered back.

"You have to. I always loved you, Phil."

Dad didn't respond. Instead, he brought the butcher knife up and thrust it down fast.

The blood spatter rained through the room, covered my furniture, the walls, everything. Dad repeated the action, chopping, chopping, and I stepped closer to confirm what I thought was happening.

Tobias's head was half-severed, the bones and cartilage snapping under the force of the blade. Dad kept chopping until Tobias's head rolled a few inches from his body. Throwing the knife away, Dad lifted the severed head like a trophy.

"Fuck you!" he screamed.

I took another step forward, intent on going to Dad's side, but stopped when he screamed again, letting a deep, painful roar fill the house. I almost cried at the sound, the wailing in his voice, the years of torment and torture and guilt finally coming loose as he held the head of his old friend. His old lover. His old enemy.

Cradling the head in his arms now, Dad brought his own head down to meet it, their foreheads touching, and wept.

"Dad?" I asked. "Are you…" There was no sensible way to end that sentence. He wasn't okay, there was no way he could be. None of us were okay, and I thought about Kyle, alone in the bedroom with a head injury, wondering what the hell was happening.

Dad fell silent, staring down at Tobias's head, blood seeping from the jagged neck hole, and bits of spine dangling out. I couldn't fathom what he was thinking, and then realised what would come next. In order to satisfy the teeth, he'd have to eat. I'd told him to do it, too. Told him to eat his old lover.

Leaning over the corpse, Dad began to nibble

at the bloodied flesh on Tobias's still corpse. I moved back to the bedroom door, my hand on the handle, when I heard the groan.

This wasn't the groan of pleasure I'd heard from Dad before. Not the same as when he ate Dave. This was something different—something painful.

"Dad?" I asked, turning back to him. The stab wound in my belly was almost unbearable, but my concern for Dad was more profound. Even after everything, in spite of all he'd done. He was still my dad. He'd saved me and Kyle from Tobias. I couldn't let him down now.

"Mike…"

"Dad, what's happening?"

He stood from the corpse, still holding the head in one hand. His cheeks were streaked with tears and blood and the teeth were clamouring hard now. Vigorous and excited. Setting the head on the lounge, it rolled back into the cushion.

"Dad? What are you doing?"

Moving towards me, Dad's jaw kept stretching until I could see the back of his mouth and the veins protruding up his throat.

"Mike…" he managed. "Run."

"Tobias is right there!" I yelled. "Eat him, for fuck's sake!"

Dad shook his head. "The teeth don't want him. I don't know why."

As he raced towards me, I threw the bedroom door open, slammed it behind me. Kyle was in the ensuite attending to his head wound. I had to get him out of there, to the hospital, away from Dad. My only options now, as I forced my full weight against the door to keep Dad out—banging and screaming to be let in—were the windows. Above the bed, a thin horizontal window that ran almost the length of the wall. I might not make it through the space, but Kyle sure would.

"Kyle! Get out the window!"

He stumbled into the main bedroom, hands soaked with blood, and stared at me with half-open eyes.

"Please. You have to get help!"

"Babe, I don't feel right."

"Just do it!"

He finally did as he was told, climbing onto the bed and reaching for the window. He was unsteady, his feet kicking at the pillows and the blankets, until he had stretched far enough to push the window open.

"I can't…"

"DO IT!" I pushed hard against the door with my back, my feet digging into the carpet. Dad was pounding at the other side, and the wood shook and bounced on its hinges so hard I thought it would come right off.

There wasn't much time and Kyle was scratching weakly at the glass, unable to get himself up.

Fuck.

Without thinking it through, I ran to the bed, jumped up next to Kyle and grabbed him by the waist. I hoisted him up and he slid through the window to safety with a thud on the grass outside.

"Get help!" I cried.

It was too late.

The pounding had stopped, the door was open.

Dad was staring at me.

Ravenous.

All I had was my body weight. I hoped it would be enough. Dad came towards me, his teeth chattering and begging for my fatty flesh. I was going to give it to him. Running across the bed, I dove at him, and we crashed to the carpet, smashing into the door and a low entertainment cabinet.

Dad's face changed as he hit the ground, blood dripping from the corner of the cabinet. The veins protruded from his body now, snaking down the bones jutting out of his neck.

"Stop, Dad, please!" I begged as I grabbed at his hands.

He was too strong, and slipped free of my grip. His fist came at my nose. I didn't have time to dodge. The cartilage in my nose cracked and broke as I fell back to the carpet.

"I told you to run, Mike," Dad said, getting to his feet.

I glared at him, about to beg for my life, when he stopped. Put a hand to his belly and retched again. His eyes grew wide and I recognised the uncertainty, the fear within them. He didn't know what was happening. I hoped the teeth didn't know, either, though Tobias's words rang in my ears: *The cycle is starting again.*

I started to get up, holding my nose and wiping blood so I could see, when Dad came at me with more fervour than last time. Even through his pain, he wanted to destroy me. To eat me until he was picking flecks of fatty tissue from his teeth with my own bones.

He took me by the ankle and dragged me backwards through the house. I grabbed the entertainment cabinet, the spot dripping with his blood, but he yanked hard and I slipped. I tried to grab at walls and corners and the kitchen bar stools, but each time Dad just yanked harder and tightened his grip on my ankle.

"Where are you taking me?" I asked.

"You'll see."

27

MIKE

The boot space wasn't as bad as I imagined—it always seemed so claustrophobic in films and television, but in reality, I could roll over and shift my body around to change positions. I'd seen documentaries where people kicked out the back taillight, or had found a way to unlock the boot from the inside, push the centre back seat down.

It was worth a shot.

After kicking and elbowing the taillights, all I had to show for it were bruises on my toes and elbows. Those fuckers weren't going anywhere. So, I'd shifted a third time to try and push against the centre back seat.

I could feel it moving, jiggling against the clamps keeping it in place. We were in a stolen police car, though, so I wasn't sure what extra layers of security—if there were any—had been installed. Still, the seat was jiggling, and the adrenaline coursing through me had given way to hope.

Managing to shift around, my head and neck pushed together against the back and roof of the boot at an awkward angle, I kicked hard against the seat and it shot down. Moving fast, before Dad had a chance to react, I shifted around and crawled through the gap, my belly and thick body straining against the tight space.

"What the fuck, Mike?" Dad yelled.

Glancing at our surroundings, I recognised the area. We were heading towards the new housing development of Crest Falls. Where there were blocks of land ripe for the burying of my inedible bones. If we got there, it would spell my end.

I kept forcing my way through and grabbed at Dad's hands and arms. He was vulnerable now, while he was driving—without a seat belt, no less. His teeth snapped at me, but he had to keep his eyes on the road.

His eyes.

I covered my hands across his eyes and held them there as tight as I could. He scratched at me, shook his head around to loosen my grip, but I couldn't. Wouldn't. This had to end now, whether I made it out alive or not.

The car started to swerve into oncoming traffic. The blaring horns of other cars, meant to deter me, made me smile. We were going to crash into something sooner or later, and then I could end this once and for all.

Dad wanted my help. This is how I could help him. *Truly* help him.

"Mike, stop!" Dad seethed through gritted teeth.

He let go of the wheel. Grabbed my hands, pulling at my fingers until they snapped.

Screaming, I recoiled; three fingers on my left hand were bent in the wrong direction, the bones jutting out their sides. The car veered back to the correct lane, and for a second I lost the hope that had been building inside me. The twisted, sick hope that I could kill my father.

Despite the incredible pain in my hand, stomach, chest, and now my nose, I climbed around to the driver's seat and shouldered Dad hard. He struggled against me, his teeth dug into my upper arm, and I screamed over and over. With the two working fingers on my left hand, I gripped the door handle, and pulled.

It flew open, the motion unsettling Dad a little as he retched and gagged. He reached for the door, but I had forced my way between him and the steering wheel, and was punching his smarmy, disgusting Tobias-inspired face.

Dodging my punch, he struck me hard, the

broken bones in my nose cracking further. He pressed harder on the accelerator, and I jerked back against the steering wheel. We started veering again, and despite wanting my dad back—despite wanting to find a way to end this peacefully—it was clear what had to be done.

Smacking him hard in the mouth, enough to break his concentration for just a moment, I took him by the torso, wrapped in a bear hug, and leaped from the car.

The road came at us hard and fast. My shoulder bone was forced from its socket as I crashed against it and rolled. Dad cried out as flecks of his skin were ripped from his face and arms as we tumbled across the tarmac.

I heard the stolen police car crash, saw the flames, and a blur of tyres, cars, potholes, and then dirt as we rolled off the side of the road and down a short but steep hill.

Somehow, I was still conscious. Somehow, I was still breathing.

Despite the shoulder throbbing and limp, despite my other injuries now exacerbated by the impact of my body against the road, I was still breathing. My lungs burned, my head pounded, my whole body felt so heavy. Coughing in the dirt as it scratched the back of my throat, I dreamed of getting to my feet. It was all I could do—every time I tried to move, I failed.

So I watched the sky, the clouds swirling and drifting, aimless. Like Dad and I had been doing so many years. I tried to move, ordered my body to *do something*, but my limbs and torso were heavy and bruised, and the knife wound in my belly went so deep I could smell my insides.

Dad could move, though. It wasn't him anymore, anyway. At least, I hoped with everything I was that it wasn't him. It had to be the teeth. Those *fucking* teeth that I'd brought into this family. Lying there in the dirt, I laughed. Just a small chortle.

Family.

I hadn't thought of us as a family since Mum… Since what happened to her. I hadn't thought of us as anything but two people who were stuck together until one of us died. Yet as he stood, stretching and cracking and retching, that was all I could think about.

Dad was my family.

It didn't change anything, though, which was the sad thing. I still had to end this, and the only way I could figure was to kill him. If that were even possible in my condition.

He stood over me now, sick and broken and determined to fucking destroy me. The black veins were jutting from his fingertips now, they'd outgrown his body. They'd outgrown *him*.

The cycle is starting again.

Taking me by the arms as I screamed at the

throbbing in my dislocated shoulder, Dad began to drag me. Just as he had at the house. Except this time, there was no question as to where we were headed. I knew his intention.

He was doing what Tobias had taught him, and as he dragged me, I managed to turn my head to the left. Saw the wooden frames, the concrete slabs, the empty blocks of land. We'd made it to the housing development, the prime spot for a dumping ground. It was the middle of the day, but the site was empty—typical.

"I'm sorry, Mike," Dad said, his mouth hanging loose, his words distorted from the veins snaking from his jaw.

"Stop…saying…that," I managed. Every word felt like the last I'd say. My energy was draining fast, and the closer he dragged me to my final resting place, the harder it became to let go, to give up.

I thought about Kyle, hoped he had gotten to a neighbour, received some medical help. The police were probably at my house right now, searching for us. I wanted to live, wanted to see him again. Wanted to sort our shit out so our relationship would last. Holding back regretful tears, I didn't want Dad to see me like that. Didn't want to give the teeth the satisfaction.

Dad stopped dragging me, hands on his hips, and twisted in a circle to scan the area, to make sure we were alone.

"This is it, Mike," he said.

His words were hollow. He was still fighting, still retching and trying to stay upright. The bones sticking from his body had gotten worse, too. It was like the veins were pushing him out of his own body.

This was it. Unless I could crawl away on one arm.

He kneeled and rested a hand on my belly wound. Letting the blood seep through the gaps between his fingers. I watched him sniff at me, was repulsed by the sight of my father getting ready to eat me alive. He grimaced himself, tried to keep his mouth closed.

We were way past that now, though.

The veins were all through him, the teeth owned him now.

And they were about to make him eat me.

"Dad," I said, swallowing hard. "I don't blame you."

He stopped sniffing for a second, and considered me. The teeth had changed his eyes so much that I couldn't recognise Dad in them anymore. Yet somewhere, a tiny glimmer, he was in there. Just enough that if I searched hard enough, I could see him. In that moment, though, I understood I was talking to the teeth.

Telling them I didn't blame *them*.

Which couldn't have been further from the truth.

His pause, his staring down at me, gave me enough time to throw the hardest punch I could with whatever strength remained. I'd gotten lucky, caught him by surprise. He fell backward, and I leveraged my body weight against my working arm to flip myself over. I suspected it was futile, this last ditch effort.

But I couldn't give up.

I had to get back to Kyle, back to my life.

Just ahead, a pile of concrete fragments, discarded after some drilling or whatever. Metal pipes jutted from the sides. I dragged myself along the dirt, Dad just behind me.

Dragged harder.

Screamed as I dug my fingernails into the dirt, pulled as much as my muscles could, burdened by the weight of myself as I struggled to get closer to the concrete.

Dad was up once more, recovered, and laughing. The same laugh Tobias gave before his head had been decapitated. It seemed like so long ago, but it must have been less than an hour earlier. His laughter carried on as he ambled past me, heading for the concrete pile.

"Looking for a weapon?" he taunted. Inspecting the pile, he made a show of choosing just the right one. "Hmmmm. This one? No, not big enough." Picked up a small chunk with jagged edges. "This one?"

I pulled myself along, sure he would bring the concrete fragment down on the back of my head. Split my skull to make his job easier.

He returned it to the pile, and found a stray metal rod. "Ah," he said, holding it up to the sky. "This. This is perfect."

Rolling me onto my back, Dad pressed his foot into the wound in my belly. I gritted my teeth, determined not to let the dentures get excited at my weakness. I would not be screaming anymore, no matter what happened.

"Where do you want it?" he asked.

I swallowed, my voice failing me. I wanted to tell him to fuck off, tell him I loved him, tell him I forgave him for what he was about to do.

"Dealer's choice, then."

Holding the rod like a sword, he raised it high, the veins from his fingertips snaking around the metal as though it wanted to absorb it. Lick it, taste it.

He brought it down.

I grabbed it.

Hadn't even meant to, it was instinct. That fight or flight that wouldn't let me go without doing everything I could.

Dad was surprised, pushed hard on the rod to force it down. Inches from my already-bleeding chest, I had gripped it. He pushed harder, and I steered the direction away from me. It hit the dirt, and I yanked the rod as hard as I could. Dad's grip loosened, the veins around it stretching like wet glue. I yanked again as Dad stomped on my belly to distract me.

The pain rippled through my body, but I used it. It gave me purpose. I could feel pain. I could feel everything, and I wanted to feel Kyle's arms around me, enveloping me. Dad, the teeth, nobody would stop that from happening.

I yanked once more, the rod came free. In one swift motion, I stabbed it through his thigh, and Dad recoiled. The rod was still tight in my grip, a wet squelch music to my ears as Dad fell back and the rod slid from his leg.

Still weak, I found my own legs had recovered enough to help. I used them to pivot toward Dad. Stabbed again, bringing the rod into his stomach. Blood splashed into my open mouth, and Dad wrapped his hands around the rod, pulling at it.

The veins were in overdrive now, growing longer out of his fingers, out his sides, his neck, his mouth. Reacting to the violence, the injury.

Dad studied me, and that tiny semblance of his true self was brighter now. It was in there, rising to the surface as the veins wrapped around the rod, pooling at the site of the wound. His hands let go, though, and a flash across his face—a second of control against the teeth—told me what to do.

Again. Stab me again.

And I did.

The veins were thick and viscous, but I managed to pull the rod free. Stabbed, just as Dad— my *real* dad—wanted.

A high-pitched sound came from his mouth. It wasn't a scream, not a yelp. I'd never heard such a noise, not from a human being.

The teeth are dying.

Except Dad's bones were now almost pushed completely from his body. His skin was deflating as the veins pulled at his insides, Dad screeching, screeching, screeching.

I pulled the rod free, pushed myself up, and watched, repeating to him, "I'm sorry, I'm sorry, I'm sorry…"

He was too far gone. The veins pooled at his mouth. A giant lump formed in his chest, pulling up to his heart.

"What the…"

Nothing should have surprised me, but as the lump kept moving, up his throat, the teeth started to come free.

They plopped to the dirt with a dull, wet sound, covered in saliva and veins, and the lump kept rising, forcing Dad's mouth wide. The jaw cracked and split. His body convulsed until his eyes closed.

For the final time.

Dad was dead, and the knowledge both

devastated and satisfied me. I never got to hug him one last time, but at least the teeth were out of him now. He was no longer being controlled. He could rest.

As I wiped away my tears, I saw a lump was still there, in his throat. I'd thought it was the teeth, but they were sitting on the dirt now. This was something else.

And whatever the lump was, it was rising.

The job wasn't over yet. Dad would have wanted me to end this. The only way I could think was to bury the teeth, deep in the earth, where nobody could ever, ever find them.

I was in no condition to dig, and I was all too aware that something else was happening now.

The teeth were sitting in the dirt, but the veins were still connected, retracting somehow into the dentures as they pulled the lump from Dad's mouth. Something pink and fleshy was tangled among the veins as it hit the dirt.

"Fuck," I whispered.

It was a heart.

Dad's heart.

Still beating.

I moved back a little, gripping the rod tight, not sure what to expect.

The veins began to build a protective case around the organ. Began to build themselves into something new. I dropped the rod, terrified. Twisting and tangling, knotting themselves into something fresh, the veins changed colour. Changed *texture*.

The veins had become skin, and were now growing arms and legs around the heart.

I recognised the soft outline of a face, the hollow spaces for eyeballs that had somehow, impossibly, begun to form.

The eyes were green. Just like Dad's.

Just like mine.

As the veins coalesced into a tiny shape, I remembered the photo album—the babies. All those children, but only one had the teeth. Tobias. I thought he'd been given them *after* his birth, had never stopped to consider that the teeth might have been responsible for his very existence.

That the teeth, like they were doing now, had birthed him.

The dentures kept retracting the remaining veins, sucking themselves into the new body lying naked in the dirt. Settling into place inside the new baby's mouth, I understood the process was complete.

The new cycle had started.

I raised the rod at the baby. Had only one choice. It could end here, right now. One whack over the head and I could fracture the skull, toss the baby in a hole, and forget any of this ever happened.

But it is just a baby.

The face had finished now, the baby sitting up

and staring at me with those innocent green eyes. They weren't just green *like* Dad's, I saw that now. I recognised the glint in them, the one I'd been staring at for so many years.

They were Dad's eyes.

Somehow, he was in there. Inside that baby.

I lowered the rod. Looked between the baby and Dad's dead body. Just stared at the husk left behind by the veins' decimation of him. They'd taken his heart, his eyes. Maybe other organs were wrapped up in there, in the new shell.

Maybe it is *Dad.*

The baby flashed me a smile, the dentures clamouring inside the chubby cheeks. It seemed innocent, somehow.

"Hey!" a voice called from the distance.

A man ran towards me, holding a white hard hat as he did. He was tearing through the construction site, radio in hand, his orange hi-vis flapping in the wind.

"Are you okay?" He stopped just a few feet from me. Just clear enough to see what was going on, but not to get involved.

I muttered an, "Fine.".

His gaze fell to the baby, then to Dad's body. Then back to me, filled with uncertainty.

"He attacked me," I said, indicating to Dad. "He…attacked…my baby."

It was happening again, the weakening. The adrenaline was fading, the shock and guilt and hurt taking its place. It became hard to stay awake, but I held on, needing to know what the baby was doing. He was just sitting there, staring at me with that toothy grin.

"You look pretty banged up, man," the guy said. "I've called for help, someone is coming soon."

"Thank you," I replied, and lay back on the dirt.

"That kid yours?"

"Yes. He's mine."

It was true. Whether or not he was biologically mine, or even a fucked up, biological reincarnation of Dad, that baby was mine. Everyone else who knew anything about the dentures was dead. Agnes, Gary, Tobias, Dad. As far as I was concerned, I had the only records left, except the book burning in the police car up the road somewhere.

Yes, he was mine.

He was my family. And you don't give up on family.

No matter what.

28

MIKE

Three Months Later

Dad was officially a missing person. He hadn't been seen since he left with those two nurses a few months earlier. They hadn't been seen, either. I wanted so bad to go to their families and give them closure. To confirm they were dead and that they would never be coming back. I couldn't say a word, and only Kyle and I could appreciate why that part of my life would remain in perpetual silence.

I had closure, though, and I hated myself for it. I hated that I got to know the truth while those other families had to suffer for the rest of their lives. I'd thought about anonymous letters, but Kyle suggested leaving it alone. Those sorts of things could be traced, and it would just lead to trouble. We had already undergone enough police inquiries to last a lifetime. Neither of us wanted to re-open that door.

317

It was strange being a parent. Kyle often said the same thing. He didn't quite believe me about all that I'd told him, but after the decapitation, the attacks, the near-deaths, and the strange new baby, he deserved the truth.

All of it.

He'd taken a few days to wrap his head around it, which surprised me. I was still wrapping my head around everything that'd happened, and it had been *months*. He seemed to adapt a little faster, which came in handy for feeding time.

Phil, his name was. At the time, I'd chosen to name him after Dad, but really it was like naming a cat. You could call it whatever you wanted, but the cat was the only one who truly knew its own name. I had a feeling my son—the new shell for the teeth—would be the same.

Despite all that had happened, the fact that the teeth were in there and what that meant for our future, I couldn't get rid of him. It was nurture, in the end. I was sure of it. Nature had very little to do with who we became. It was nurture.

Some things, though, were nature. Our tastes, for instance. Baby Phil's tastes were very much based on blood. And bone. We hadn't tried him on humans, would wait as long as we could to do that. The one time he'd bitten my finger during a blood feeding, he'd clapped his hands in glee, so I appreciated there was a developing need for it.

"Maybe we look for diseased people," Kyle said.

We were sitting at the breakfast table, Baby Phil's bib loose around his neck as the teeth chattered. He sipped blood from a straw, and burped. Kyle and I rubbed at his back. I was impressed with Kyle's parenting—he was gentle, caring, patient. It made me love him even more.

"What do you mean, 'diseased people?'" I asked.

"Well,"—Kyle sipped his coffee—"we both know he's going to want to eat humans at some point. But maybe we can train him to choose people that will make the least impact. Like…diseased people. The incurable ones."

I scoffed and snorted a little, winced. "Don't make me laugh," I said, and held my belly. The injuries were healing, but the butcher knife had gone quite deep, and it was taking time.

"Sorry," Kyle said. He sometimes, out of reflex, scratched at his own scar when he gazed over at me. Reminded himself of the damage Tobias had done to him that day. I thought the scar was cute, but he was trying to regrow his hair to cover it. Scratching at it now, he chewed on some toast. "I just mean," he said, swallowing the Vegemite, "we want to make sure Phil is a good person. We don't want him to be Jack the Ripper."

"I know what you mean. I guess I was hoping we could train him as a baby that eating people is bad, and that he can just have live animals."

The way we spoke about this as though it was the most ordinary breakfast conversation in the world still stunned me. Like we were discussing the weather.

"What time are you leaving today?" I asked.

"In about ten minutes."

I gave a quick, "Uh huh",, wiping stray drops of blood from Baby Phil's lips with my napkin. He hadn't ever tried to bite me again, just the once. He'd *never* tried to bite Kyle. I wondered if that was Dad's way of showing respect, telling me he approved or whatever. Really, I was just glad to keep all my fingers, which were still healing from when Dad snapped them. It would be a few more months of physio to get them fully working, but at least I didn't need any more surgeries.

"Well, I'll be home early," Kyle continued. "I don't want to be away too long today."

He was always a sweetheart these days. No more weird jealousy that I used to put down to youth. And no more *Home and A-fucking-way*, thank god.

"I'll be okay, I promise. You take your time," I said. He got up and kissed me on the lips, soft and slow, the way he always did now. Like he was savouring me. It was the trauma of almost dying. He was still riding the wave of being alive, taking pleasure in the everydayness of our lives.

I loved it.

He kissed me once more, then went to Baby Phil and lifted him from the highchair. "Who's a good boy?" he asked, making funny baby noise. "Gooooo goooo gaaaaa… Ahhhh I wuv you soooo muuuch!"

This, I did not love.

It wouldn't always be that way, though, and I found a way to cherish the moment. Kyle being a dad, me being a dad. These things sometime came later in life, but I was no less proud to be raising a kid.

Kyle laid Baby Phil back down and collected his things. One more kiss later, and he was out the door.

"Well," I said, one hand under my chin as I peered at my baby, "we ought to get ready to go. Whaddya say, kid?"

Julie, the nursing home manager, had called the day before to let me know they couldn't hold Dad's room any longer. Special circumstances being what they were, they'd been nice enough to let me keep paying for the room, in case Dad was found. Even though he'd be facing some serious questions about the missing nurses and the blood on the ceiling, and who knew what else.

Three months was a long time for them to hold it, considering there were new inquiries every day. Or so the head nurse had told me. It was a long time to keep paying for his room, too, especially when he was never coming back. The money situation was always nagging at me, as it had months earlier. I reminded myself that was how Tobias had infected me with his comments in the first place, and pushed the concerns away. I had money, I could spare a little. It didn't matter. Besides, the police were still asking us questions, filling details and blanks, asking who the men who attacked us were. If we'd ever seen them before, if we could even guess as to why one of them might have wanted to hurt Detective Brooks.

That was one thing I couldn't forgive Dad for. I could even get past Dave from the office, but Brooks had been a real stand-up sort of person, seeking truth and justice. To be left for dead like that and then not even die… She'd been a vegetable since that day, her family reportedly unwilling to pull the plug. Miracles happened all the time, so they told the media.

So did evils.

I picked up Baby Phil, determined not to let him end up doing that to someone, and tucked him into the baby seat in the car.

More than anything, it astounded me that The Wiggles were still so popular, and that my baby wanted to listen to them, of all things. I imagined maybe chainsaw sounds, or screaming, or something. No. He wanted classic Wiggles, "Hot Potato" blaring through the speakers as we drove to the home.

It was an odd feeling listening to that music while what I believed to be the reincarnation of my father bopped along in the back seat, flashing those perfect teeth. Even stranger was the fact that I was on the way to collect Dad's possessions, which I'd already decided to keep in case Baby Phil wanted to see them when he got older.

In case he remembered his past life.

I was still getting used to the stroller. It wasn't like the ones that were around when I was a kid. It was some crazy, expensive thing with cup holders and a fucking built-in Bluetooth system. The kid at the store told me I could link my phone to it and measure the wheel health or something. Kyle had nodded along at the time, like it was totally normal. It had four wheels and it held a baby. What else did it need?

I waved at Julie as I came in, and she swooned at the baby. Her mouth formed an "O" and I was sure she was about to start the whole goo-goo gah-gah shit that Kyle loved so much, so I got in quick with a, "Hi, Julie. Thanks so much for holding the room this long."

She snapped her lips to a straight line, back to business. She ran a cool hand through her dyed red hair, revealing a streak of grey she'd missed. "Oh, think nothing of it. We're happy to help. I'm sorry we can't hold it longer, it's just… You know how it is. People are getting old and decrepit every day."

The way she said that, like it was a burden, changed my perception of her.

"But this widdle guuuy," she said, coming

around the desk to greet Baby Phil, her pointer finger extended in a slight curve. I winced, hoping he wouldn't bite it off. "He's sooooo cuuuuute!"

"Thanks," I said.

"But, uh, if you don't mind me asking…" I guessed what she was about to say. "I thought you were gay."

"Are. Present tense. It's not 'was gay', because that would mean I'm not anymore. Which, I very much am. My *much* younger partner can provide details if you need them." My friendly tone was as fake as her dye job, and we both understood it.

"Oh," she replied. "I just meant… I didn't think adoption agencies…"

"All good, Jules. Just here to get my dad's things."

She gave a small wave before digging herself too much of a hole, and let me pass. I knew the way to the room, and she was too embarrassed to escort me.

As I wheeled the stroller to Dad's old room, I stood at the door. Baby Phil didn't react in any way, didn't show he recognised the place. I hadn't expected him to, but was disappointed, nonetheless. I avoided Mrs Denton's piercing stare coming through a small gap in the door behind me—nothing has changed, then.

His room was just as we'd left it, just a bit dustier. I was paying for maintenance, which hadn't happened, but I wasn't about to make a big deal of it. I just wanted to clear his stuff and move on. I had a new life now, with Baby Phil and Kyle, and I wanted to get back to it. All the guilt and regret about years wasted hating Dad, it was too much. He wouldn't have wanted that, and neither did I.

I just wanted to get started with—

"Phil?" I asked, peeking down into the stroller.

He was gone.

29

PHIL

Mike was good to me. He didn't have to be, he should have killed me that day in the construction site. I like to think I wouldn't have killed him, but the teeth were so far into me that I wouldn't have had a choice. I was a puppet. I didn't deserve a kid like Mike, didn't deserve to be alive.

My memories of that day are pretty basic, and I can't articulate anything. In a way, I was still a puppet, but it was more…symbiotic. It was me and the teeth now, and despite what they'd done to me, what they'd done to Mike and all the others I'd eaten, I was connected to them.

I was connected to Mike, too. He fed me, cleaned me, and loved me. Him and Kyle both. It was beyond me why they would choose to do that. To take in a strange baby made of ancient, cursed teeth was incomprehensible. Especially when it held the heart and misshapen soul of an old, serial killer cannibal.

Yet, they had. I wasn't complaining, quite the opposite really.

Except the teeth still had a hold, and I wasn't sure if it was feeding on my cannibalistic nature, or I was feeding on theirs. It was dangerous, but for now, as a baby, I couldn't do anything about it.

It was the sight of the room that did it to me. Not the room, exactly, but the sense of where I was. Back in that death hole where Mike had stuffed me away from the world. The nursing home, where I'd reacquainted myself with human flesh.

The chef, she was a decent start.

The nurses, they were good, too.

Mike paced around the room, wearing his contemplation expression, and I remembered about the bitch across the hall. Always fucking watching me.

Then it sort of just…happened.

I was out of the stroller, crawling out of the room.

Mike hadn't noticed. I checked behind me to make sure. He was still surveying the room, deciding what to keep and what to throw away.

The familiar chattering started in my jaw, and I didn't hate it. I *welcomed* it. Tooth against tooth, clamping away and making that dead, biting sound drew an excited "Ooga!" from my baby lips.

There she was. That old bitch, Mrs Denton,

just staring at me. Looking down at me as I made my away across the hall.

"Hello, little one," she said, and opened her arms out to me.

I stopped crawling, reached up with a soft groan—still charming, even as a fucking baby—and she stepped out of her room.

Picked me up.

Hugging me close to her chest, my face poking out of the crook in her neck, the world spun as she swivelled around to take me inside her room. Closing the door behind her, she sat me on the bed and gave me a "coo-chee-coo" under the chin.

Flashing my teeth, I licked her finger.

She tasted old and rotten.

Good enough. For now.

30

MIKE

Mrs Denton closed the door, holding Baby Phil. The old woman probably thought it was her baby. I knocked on the door, but she didn't answer. Her glare was always glued to people like a hawk, but now that someone needed her, she wasn't available.

Typical.

I knocked a few more times, and when she didn't answer, I pried the handle down. It was rusted and hard to move with my still-healing fingers, but I opened the door.

"Fuck."

She was on the ground, surrounded by a pool of blood, hair matted to her cheeks and clothing. Based on her position, I guessed she'd tried to reach for the phone—a landline—but the phone was still in its cradle. Her arms were extended towards it, though, and I couldn't help but notice the baby-sized bite marks on her neck and arms.

Baby Phil was on her back, gorging himself on the flesh of her arse. His little mouth and clothes were caked in fresh blood, and he made these weird sounds I couldn't describe. Something told me he was *very* happy.

I rushed inside the room, closed the door as quietly as I could to avoid detection, and just stood there, back pressed hard against the wood.

Baby Phil gazed up at me, a bit of Mrs Denton's butt hanging from his lips. "Ooooh," he moaned, but it seemed like he wanted to say something else.

"What the fuck?" I hissed. "You can't just do this!"

He just stared at me. What else had I expected?

"I wasn't ready!" I knew it was wrong of me to be upset about my lack of preparedness, rather than the fact that my infant son—who was really my father—had killed a person and was eating her in front of me.

Wrong, for sure, but it was my new reality. It was the choice I'd made when I let him live.

The flesh fell from his mouth and Baby Phil squealed with glee. For a moment I was full of anger and rage and regret, sure I should have killed him when

I had the chance. I hadn't, though, and now I was stuck in this situation. Again.

That's what you did for family, wasn't it? Look after them, feed them, make sure they're happy. Clean up their messes. That's what this was, just a mess. It could be cleaned, and Dad had shown me how. I reminded myself I would have to check the ceiling for blood, and was already planning what furniture to stand on if the need arose.

"Wait there, little man," I said, and went back to the stroller.

Kyle and I had agreed to keep supplies in it, in the many, many pockets it had. One thing I had insisted on was plastic sheeting. When it's rolled out, it seems like a lot, but the way it's packaged, it was just a roll that fit into the side pocket of the stroller.

We also had a scrubbing brush and some cleaning equipment in there. It all fit perfectly. It was almost like that's what it was designed for.

Taking the stroller, I headed back to Mrs Denton's room.

"I'm not happy about this," I said to Baby Phil, who had moved to the thighs now. Fleshy and meaty, I could see the appeal. The fact that I *could* see the appeal worried me to no end. "But let's keep this just between us, hey? Your other daddy doesn't need to know, does he?"

Baby Phil burped and I took that as the only answer I'd get.

Sighing, I let him finish his meal while I rested against the wall. I hoped it wouldn't be too long, because the clean-up would take a while and I didn't want to get stuck in traffic.

The things we do for family, I thought, while Baby Phil's surprisingly strong hands tore into Mrs Denton's back and pulled out sections of spine.

Just as Baby Phil dug deeper into Mrs Denton, almost burrowing his tiny body right inside her like a tunnel, my phone rang.

"Hush, Phil," I said, holding a finger to my lips. "Hey, Kyle."

"Just checking in," he said, his voice heavy with concern.

"I'm fine," I said. "We're both enjoying the day."

He sighed, relieved. "Good. I'm almost done here at the office. Do you want me to pick up some lunch on my way home?"

Looking down at my son, covered in blood and pulling at Mrs Denton's intestines, I said, "That would be great. Thanks, Kyle. I'm starving."

THE END

About the Author

David-Jack Fletcher is an award-winning, bestselling Australian horror author, specialising in LGBTQI+ horror and comedy fiction. His work has appeared in several anthologies across the US, the UK, and Canada.

He is also the founder of Slashic Horror Press, an emerging queer horror indie press focused on promoting under-represented voices and stories.

When not writing and editing, David-Jack can be found on the couch with a book, cuddling his dogs and his husband.

www.fletcherhorror.com
www.slashichorrorpress.com
linktr.ee/djfletcher

A Note from the Publisher

We want to thank our readers for their support and enthusiasm. Your passion for stories fuels our commitment to bring you the horror that is strange and horrifying in the best of ways.

We appreciate any and all reviews, so help us out by leaving your thoughts online.

Thank you again for spending your time with us and remember to…

Follow us everywhere: @trubornpress
Subscribe to our newsletter today!
www.trubornpress.com

Content Notes

Cannibalism
Graphic Violence
Death
Mental Deterioration
Strong Language
Sexual Content
Substance Abuse
Hate Speech
Psychological Horror

www.ingramcontent.com/pod-product-compliance
Lightning Source LLC
Chambersburg PA
CBHW020243010826
48973CB00006B/1630